THE
UNSAVORY
CRITIC

THE UNSAVORY CRITIC

Ken Dalton

Different Drummer Press

For further information concerning *The Unsavory Critic*, email the author at ken@kendalton.com

ISBN 978-0-692-79673-3
• Humorous—Mystery—Fiction. 2. Pinky—Delmont (Fictional character)—Fiction. 3. Bear—Zabarte (Fictional character)—Fiction. 4. San Francisco, California—Fiction. 5. Copenhagen, Denmark—Fiction. 6. Stockholm, Sweden—7. Skellefteå, Sweden—8. Camden, New Jersey —Fiction. I. Title.

ACKNOWLEDGEMENTS

This novel came together with the help and assistance of the following;

From our Swedish daughters, Eve Reimers and Susanne Lundmark—to Ulla and Janne Petersson who graciously invited us into their home outside of Skellefteå, to Susanne's family who welcomed us to Sweden, on the fourth of July, with a gigantic family party and B-B-Q, and finally to Joe Gellura for his informative and colorful memories of Camden, New Jersey.

To my artistic son, Hugh, who reads the first draft of the novel and then creates the provocative covers that make each Pinky and Bear Mystery a work of art.

To Wendy Maxham, and the other mystery members of my editing staff for another exceptional picky, picky job of editing.

To Dr. Ye, and all the staff, nurses and Pharmacists, that dwell in the magical land of room 170, also known as the Kaiser Infusion Center, for giving me my fifth year of remission.

To the long suffering members of my writer's group:

Omar Eljumaily

Dr. Pat Winters

And the divine Sarah Andrews

Finally, to my wife Arlene, for remaining my lover and best friend as we enjoy the fifth year of my remission.

This book is dedicated to my younger brother, Richard Dalton. As I fight through my tears to write these words, Richard is working through the last pages of his creative, and interesting life.

I credit my brother with the initial encouragement to write and for that alone I will be forever grateful. But there was much more to our relationship than his support. It is only at this moment in time, when I am about to lose him, that I realized the heartbreaking loss of a brother's love.

Richard, I will miss our wonderful email discussions concerning anything and everything—the struggles we had growing from boys to men—but most of all, I will miss you!

CHAPTER ONE

J. Pincus Delmont-Carson City, Nevada

I stood by the door of my brand new Tesla S with upgraded interior, upgraded suspension system, and upgraded sound system as bitter memories of my lunch with Willow Stone, my beautiful ex-wife, would not go away, as if my mind was locked in an endless loop.

Infamy, thy name is Willow!

I made my way toward the front door of my building and with each step, my rage decreased as I placed her affront toward me into a proper perspective. Over the course of my exceptional legal career I had often tasted the sweetness of success mingled with the occasional—and entirely unjustified—bitterness of failure, but never had I been left with a total absence of hope. I supposed there is a first time for everything.

Bent, but ultimately not broken, I marched through the front door of my legal establishment and headed past my secretary's desk, seeking the security of my private office.

As I moved past Lu, she exclaimed, "Pinky, you have a phone call and you're nearly late for an appointment with a client. He'll be here in less than thirty minutes."

Ignoring her comment, I dragged myself into my office. "Hold all my calls."

She shot back, "I can't hold your calls! There's a man named Charles Godwin on your line and he's been waiting for you. He said you've worked together on a murder case. And before you close your door, I have a personal problem to discuss with you once your meeting with the client is completed."

Lu's voice eventually broke through my malaise of misery. "What did you just tell me?"

Lu said, "I have a personal matter to discuss with—"

"Later!" I slammed the door and poured myself a healthy portion of my finest single malt, and dropped into my chair.

As I sipped the golden nectar, my disastrous lunch with my now formerly favorite ex-wife played through my mind, forcing me to relive a bad dream:

I hand Willow the ring, a token of my eternal fidelity, but she has the effrontery to place my offer of perpetual love onto the ring finger of her right— not left—hand. Momentarily confused, I question if I should point out that she has placed the ring on the wrong finger. She admires the four-carat diamond as the gem refracts the ambient light off the expertly-cut facets. She lowers her hand to the table. "Pinky, judging —"

A buzz from my intercom snapped me back to

the present. I poured a second shot of whisky into my glass and snapped, "Damn it, Lu, I told you to hold my calls!"

"And I told you, Charles Godwin is waiting for you to pick up your phone. He needs to talk to you at once."

I knew I had to pick up the call, but Willow's remarks, as if her words were an inexorable glacier grinding toward the sea:

"Pinky, judging by the size of the rock, this ring is worth a small fortune, and as such, I cannot accept your unconditional gift due to the obvious conflict of interest concerning our professional work. However, I can, and will, contribute this ring, in your name of course, to the YWCA Shelter for Battered Women in Carson City."

Seldom during my legal career had I ever been rendered speechless, but Willow's retort, and her callous disregard for my feelings had turned me momentarily mute. My God, didn't that woman know the ring had set me back more than $53,000!

Lu's voice broke through my reverie. "Pinky? What's going on with you? You haven't picked up your call."

Willow's cutting remarks moved onward, carving a chasm through my mind:

"I'm positive that the shelter will come up with a unique way to make good use of your generous contribution and—"

Lu screamed, "Pinky, answer me or I'm going to

call an ambulance."

"Lu, I am fine. Tell Mr. Godwin I will be with him in a moment."

I knew I had to return to the present but the conclusion of my disastrous lunch returned:

Willow lifted her wine glass and took a sip.

"Now that I've decided what to do with this ostentatious bit of jewelry, your proposal to marry me a second time requires a response. Pinky, I accept your proposal, but with one caveat. The wedding will take place twenty-four hours after I watch a herd of elephants fly over the Golden Nugget Casino." She glanced at her watch and jumped up. "Now, if you'll excuse me, I have an important meeting that requires my immediate attention."

For her to have spurned my heartfelt offer of matrimonial bliss over a gourmet lunch of perfectly poached sea scallops in a white wine caper sauce caused me to reevaluate my future with her. In my darkest scenario I had not anticipated that my ex-wife could toy with my fragile emotional state in such a dismissive way.

The flashing light on my phone forced me back to reality, and I considered the man who was waiting for me on the phone. Charles Godwin was more than a co-worker on that murder case. He and I had been the top-of-our-class as we matriculated at the UC Hastings College of Law in San Francisco many years ago. Perhaps this phone call would be an excellent opportunity to remind Charles that by

4

the time graduation rolled around, I had scaled the mountain to the top of the class while he had plummeted to second place.

But Hastings was not my last encounter with Charles. A few years ago, as the Sonoma County District Attorney, he had referred me to a San Francisco corporate attorney who graced me with a $500,000 retainer, no strings attached.

I reasoned that his call might take my mind off Willow. I took a sip of whiskey, hit the intercom button and barked, "Lu, put him through."

Lu said, "Put him through? He's waiting on hold. And don't snap at me that way. Show some courtesy, as we have discussed in the past, or you'll have to find another whipping girl to run your office."

I downed the rest of the whiskey. "Lu, I apologize, but I received some devastating news during lunch."

"Oh . . . and don't forget, we still need to discuss my personal situation."

"What personal situation?"

"The one I told you about when you walked by me not three minutes ago."

"Right." What did that woman have up her sleeve? "Lu, if we are good for the moment, I am going to pick up the call from Charles."

"We're good."

Each day she became more and more difficult to deal with. I made a mental note to contact Louis

Loomer, the owner of Rapid Replacement, to explain my delicate situation, and see if he could come up with a potential solution.

I poured a little more whisky into my glass and pushed the flashing button. "Charles?"

"Pinky, we haven't talked—"

"True. If my memory serves me well, two years ago you sent me a photo of a man who had drowned in a tank of cabernet sauvignon. Please do not inform me that you have another purple body on your hands?"

He laughed. "No, nothing like that. By the way, I was reelected as the county's District Attorney due to your help on the Hellman case. To show my appreciation I'm shipping you a case of my favorite Dry Creek zinfandel."

Interesting. He had sufficient appreciation to send me a case of zinfandel, but not quite enough to ship me a decent Alexander Valley cabernet.

"Thank you, Charles. Now if you will excuse me, I am going to be late for a—"

"Hold on, that's not why I called. Are you familiar with the Restaurant Critics Award Dinner that's held every other year in one of the major cities of the country?"

"Is that the award given to identify the best, and the worst restaurant critics in America?"

"It is. A few days ago I attended the award dinner in San Francisco with my lovely wife."

"Good for you. Now, I am—"

"Obviously, you haven't read what happened during the culinary feast."

I took a sip of the whiskey. "And obviously you have. Charles, I am a very busy man, and—"

"One of the critics died, and I need you to come to San Fran—"

"Hold on for a moment, I have an emergency call from an important client." Aha! So Charles' request might turn into an all-expense paid vacation in San Francisco. That would alleviate some of the pain of Willow's cold-hearted expropriation of my $53,000 diamond ring. I buzzed Lu. "What does my court schedule look like during the next two weeks?"

"You have half-a-dozen court appearances, the first one tomorrow morning at ten."

"Reschedule all of them due to personal reasons. I must go to San Francisco to say a tearful adieu to my favorite aunt who appears to be on her death bed."

Lu said, "I'm very sorry to hear that. What's wrong with her?"

"My good woman, I am an attorney, not a doctor. Just tell the court clerk a disease that sounds plausible."

I hit the flashing button. "Charles, client crisis averted, and I have cleared a few more moments for you in my busy day. Please continue."

"Pinky, as a true gourmand, I'm surprised you missed the Critics Award Dinner. America's culinary elite came to San Francisco and prepared a memorable feast."

My heart palpitated at the thought. An *amuse-bouche*, followed by heavenly hors d'oeuvres, exceptional entrees, and delicious desserts, all expertly paired with the proper wines.

"My good man, I have to admit you have my mouth watering, but as you stated, the dinner happened a few days ago and I remain unaware why you have wasted this much of my valuable day telling me about it."

Charles said, "After the much anticipated pasta course, Strozzapreti, an extremely rich dish that can be translated into English as 'choke the priest', a pallet-cleansing salad was served."

"Charles, as I stated earlier, I am a very busy man so cut to the chase, as my investigator Bear would say."

"After the salad, and before the main course was served, Simon Rand, generally regarded as the most untrustworthy restaurant critic in America, keeled over and died. At the time, it looked as if he had suffered a fatal heart attack."

"My good man, I am painfully familiar with the man's writings. Rand would carry on and on to make sure the reader knew just how intelligent and brilliant he was, generally to the detriment of his primary raison d'être, reviewing the food, ambiance, and service of a restaurant. Frankly, to this connoisseur of fine dining and reader of reviews, good riddance. Now, this conversation has gone on for an excessive period and I remain in the dark as to why you continue to steal time from my busy law practice."

"I am coming to that. Yesterday, after an autopsy, the coroner determined that Rand did not die of a heart attack as was originally assumed—and this is confidential—I have been told that, while the authorities await the results of toxicology tests, the police investigation is moving forward on the probability that Rand was poisoned."

"Poisoned? I'm sure most gourmands felt that Simon Rand was a pathetic restaurant critic, but not enough to murder the man. Has your confidential informant told you that the police are looking at a specific person of interest?"

My intercom buzzed.

"Just a moment, Charles, I have to pick up another call."

"I'll wait."

"Lu, you know I am on a very important call. Why—"

"Pinky, your appointment is waiting and he told me to tell you he's not in the habit of waiting for anyone."

"Who is it?"

She whispered, "Mr. Dudek."

Oh my God, Jake Dudek! The man with a stainless steel right arm and a hook in place of his hand. What else could happen to me today? "Lu, inform Mr. Dudek I will be with him momentarily."

"Pinky. I understand the man has a disability but that hook at the end of his arm scares—"

I cut off the intercom and returned to my phone call. "Charles, I have an office emergency so I have to rapidly conclude this conversation. What is it you want me to do?"

"Come to San Francisco. I have a man with deep pockets, similar to the attorney I set you up with during the Paul Hellman murder investigation. I am positive he will retain you to investigate Simon Rand's death."

"My good man, as you well know, I am not an investigator and as such I do not feel—"

"Pinky, I guarantee you and your whole team will be handsomely paid."

"Tell me, have the police any leads?"

My intercom buzzed.

"Hold on Charles." I hit the intercom button. "Lu, this is the last straw. I am still on the call from—"

"I know that, but Mr. Dudek told me to tell you that he's kicking down—his words not mine—your office door in five minutes whether you're off the phone or not."

"Thank you, Lu."

I hit the flashing button. "Charles, cut to the chase."

"The police have identified numerous suspects, but I'm only interested in the one who goes by the name of Erik Rundstrom. Have you heard of him?"

"Strangely enough I have. The April issue of *Bon Appétit* anointed Erik as the culinary boy-wonder of the west coast after they visited his new restaurant that goes by the inscrutable name of Mission-1803."

"That's the same man."

"And why do the police show an interest in this man?"

"Eric's new restaurant closed a few months after Rand's scathing review, and he was the chef responsible of the food course that Simon Rand consumed prior to his death."

"And what is this man to you?"

"I roomed with his father, Gregor Rundstrom, at UC Berkeley, during my undergrad years. Gregor is one of the wealthiest men in Sweden."

The wealthiest man in Sweden? I glanced at my watch. Four and a half minutes before Dudek bursts in. "Charles, do not say another word. Just answer my next question with a simple yes or no. As of this moment, do you retain me as your attorney?"

"J. Pincus Delmont, you are my attorney of record. As we speak I am sending to you, via PayPal, one dollar to meet the retainer requirements."

"Excellent. Now that we have established our attorney/client privilege you know me well enough to understand that handsomely paid is not much of an inducement. Contact Mr. Rundstrom and inform

11

him that I will require a retainer of $750,000; no, make that $1,000,000. Make sure that Rundstrom understands that I make no guarantees concerning the eventual freedom of his son, Erik."

"Pinky, the situation can't wait for Rundstrom to wire you the money. I need you here now!"

Charles' tone was close to panic. "Fine, I will come to San Francisco and check into the Hotel Drisco. If Erik is charged with the murder of Simon Rand, I will work with you on his defense team, but I will remain in the background as I am not licensed in California. Tomorrow evening at six, we will meet at Gary Danko's charming establishment in North Point where you can buy me dinner while you explain the details of the case."

"I'm afraid that Gary Danko's restaurant is a touch expensive for your old school chum who's forced to scrape by on a District Attorney's salary. How about meeting at Barney's in Cow Hollow? They have the best hamburgers in—"

"Charles, Gregor Rundstrom will pick up the Danko tab. Goodbye!"

I sat back and poured myself a final splash of whiskey to celebrate. Three sips later, a smile crept across my lips. I raised my glass in a mock toast. "To Grandfather Delmont, your sound advice to be resilient remains my life's credo. And to Willow, my former favorite ex-wife, a new client just expressed an affection for me to the tune of $1,000,000 and an all-expenses paid vacation in San Francisco. Life does not get much better than that!"

After I tossed down the last of the whiskey, I dialed Bear's number.

"Hey, Boss, what's up?"

"A brief call to inform you to be ready to travel at a moment's notice."

"Where to?"

"San Francisco for a week to ten days."

"Boss, me and Flo are pooped. Just got back yesterday afternoon. We had to go all the way to Vegas to track down that bail jumping dude. What's going down in Frisco?"

"More later. Just be ready at a moment's notice."

I hung up and hit the intercom buzzer. "Lu, open a new client file. The name is Erik Rundstrom. Within twenty-four hours, his father, Gregor Rundstrom, will wire $1,000,000 to my bank. Inform me the moment that transaction has been completed. And first thing tomorrow I leave for a week or two in San Francisco."

"To care for your aunt?"

"Of course to care for my aunt. Now, inform Mr. Dudek I will see him after I spend a penny, to quote the British."

"Pinky, we still haven't talked about my personal problem."

"I don't have time for than now. Lu, the moment Dudek closes the door to my office, call the police."

Before I could push my chair away from my desk and make way into my private toilet, the office door flew open and there loomed the volatile Mr. Dudek.

CHAPTER TWO

Bear Zabarte-Carson City, Nevada

My afternoon started out slicker than snot.
Everything was set. I was sitting in my special
chair. The built-in beer cooler was filled. The Red
Sox were down four runs in the bottom of the ninth
inning, but the bases were loaded. There were two
outs, but that new kid, Yoas Cesspool, or something
like that, was coming to bat and he was a hell of a
clutch hitter.

That was when Flo yelled from the kitchen.
"Hey, I know it's my week to clean the apartment,
but I need your help to move the table so I can mop
the floor. You're not still watching that same stupid
baseball game are you?"

I grabbed the remote and killed the sound.
"Nope. Just sitting here downing my last brew. I'll
be there in a second."

The pitcher wound up and fired to home plate.
The blind ump called a pitch a good six inches below
Yo's knees a strike.

"Damn."

Flo called from the other room, "I'm still
waiting for you by the table, and why did you just

say damn?"

"The beer was too cold."

She said, "That's your bad tooth acting up again. Did you make an appointment with the dentist like I told you?"

"Yah, sure."

The next pitch was even lower and the dude-in-blue called strike two.

"Jesus, what an idiot."

Flo said, "Did you just call me an idiot?"

"No! Not you, Babe."

Then the Yo Dude swung and hit a frozen rope to left field. Three runs crossed home plate, but Yo Something tried to stretch the single into a double and he was tagged out. My Sox lost by one run, and shit, Flo walked in before I could kill the TV.

There were times when Flo could be a giant pain in the butt, and this looked like it was gonna be one of them. But that was okay 'cause I didn't give a shit how much she yelled as long as I could watch her boobs bounce around under her sweat shirt like a couple of rabbits in heat.

She stood in front of the TV, waved the mop at me, and flashed her nastiest stare. "I thought you told me that—"

"The game was over, Babe. That was just a replay. Just wanted to be sure that idiot ump at second base made the right call."

"Well?"

"Well what?"

16

"Did the ump make the right call?"

"What call?"

"Bear, are you shining me on?"

"Babe, I'd never—"

The phone rang, and for a second I thought I'd dodged Flo's next bullet, but with the Red Sox losing, and Flo biting at my butt, I shoulda known better.

Flo grabbed the phone. After she listened for a second, she handed me the mop, and her pissed-off look went away. "It's Fergus Murray."

Jesus! Fergus Murray calling all the way from Scotland. I hadn't seen, or even thought about Willow's cousin for a long time. A couple of years ago we all had to hustle over to Scotland to solve a cold-case murder that Fergus, and all the other dimwit Scottish cops couldn't figure out on their own.

Flo said, "How's Ettamae doing? Oh, wait, I'll put your call on the speaker so Bear can join the conversation."

I yelled, "Hey, dude, how's it hanging?"

Fergus said, "Bear, unless you can further explain what 'it' is I have no idea how to respond to your salutation. Now, assuming I may continue, I have some bad news concerning Ettamae's grandfather, Ollie. Whilst performing his duties as the DJ for the senior dance at the town center, he put a record on the turntable, laid his head down, and, to quote the Bard of Avon, 'For in that sleep of death, what dreams may come, when we have shuffled off this mortal coil.'"

I said, "Shuffled off what?"

Flo said, "Ollie died. Fergus, is there more to the story?"

"Aye. The folks dancing didn't know anything had happened until the music stopped. Needless to say, the news of her grandfather's death has devastated Ettamae."

I glanced at Flo. Tears were starting to dribble off her chin.

I said, "Fergus, sorry to hear about Ollie. He was a nice old dude. By the way, how's Frank Bramble doing?"

"Very well. The last time I saw him he was sporting a red bow tie and squiring the widow MacGregor around town in his venerable London cab."

"That's Frank, all right. He's not gonna let that wonky eye of his stop him from trying to make time with the girls."

Flo's phone burped up a beep that meant somebody else was trying to get us. She said, "Fergus, I have to pick up another call. Bear and I'll call you back soon."

Fergus said, "I hope so. I have more important news to pass your way."

After I heard Fergus click off, I said, "What'd ya think he meant by more important news?"

"Who knows. We'll call him back after I finish

this call." Flo pushed a button, and shit, the next voice in the room was Pinky's.

"Hey, Boss, what's up?"

"A brief call to inform you to be ready to travel at a moment's notice."

"Where to?"

"San Francisco for a week to ten days."

"Boss, me and Flo are pooped. Just got back yesterday afternoon. We had to track that bail jumping dude all the way to Vegas. What's going down in Frisco?"

"More later. Just be ready."

I growled, "Hold on. You can't just call up and tell me and Flo to go to Frisco 'cause . . . "

It took me a couple of seconds to figure out that Pinky wasn't there. "Babe, the shrimp just hung up on me!"

CHAPTER THREE

Pinky-Carson City, Nevada

I forced my facial expression into a calm, confident smile. "Good afternoon, Mr. Dudek. Please come in and sit down."

"Hey, can the mister crap. It's Hook." His eyes darted left and right.

I gestured to the chair sitting in front of my desk. "Please sit down."

He lurched forward, hooked the arm of the chair with his prosthesis, and slid the heavy leather seat against the left exterior wall. "Shyster, I don't sit anywhere unless my back's against a solid wall."

I wanted to respond but my mouth felt as if I had just ingested a small box of cotton balls. Finally, I said, "Can my secretary get you a coffee?"

"No coffee, but I wouldn't turn down a glass of that fancy-ass Scotch you keep hidden inside the credenza behind you."

The hair on the back of my neck stood up. "How did you know I—"

"Shyster, shut up and pour me three fingers so I can get out of here.

"Right. Three fingers of my finest single malt."

As I pulled out the bottle of whiskey, I pondered how he could know . . . then it hit me. Some years back, Dudek knew the exact location of my floor safe, and then he had opened the safe in record time, without the combination! I guess I should feel gratified he had left me some whiskey during one of his clandestine visits.

Dudek took the glass and tossed the nectar down his throat, the same way a dog inhales its dinner.

He said, "Okay, now let's get to the reason I'm here."

I looked attentive and said, "Mr. Dudek, I am all ears."

He waved his sharp, stainless steel appendage in the air. "How many times do I have to tell you? It's Hook."

"Right. Mr. Hook, why do you need to see me?"

Why is Lu taking so long to summon the police?

Hook said, "I don't need anything. I'm representing a certain, unnamed judge who wants to offer a little quid pro quo."

Quid pro quo? My interest in this cretin's proposition jumped tenfold. "Tell me, Mr. Hook, what does the unnamed judge want from me?"

"It seems that the judge has been stuck in an unhappy marriage for a bunch of years. He wants out."

My mind raced through a mental list of local judges to see which one fit the criteria. "I am not sure what I can do to achieve the judge's expressed desire, but regardless of my concerns, what do I receive from the quid pro quo?"

"The ability to adjust the time and dates of your appearances, no questions asked, in the unnamed judge's court for ten years."

I maintained my stoic mask while inwardly I was dancing the jig. Unlimited rearrangements for ten years! This judge must really want out of his marital obligation.

"Mr. Hook, for the moment, let us say that I am interested. But first, exactly what is it the judge wants me to do?"

"There's this doll, Adelaide Carlucci, who resides in Camden, New Jersey, and the aforementioned judge wants you to fly to Camden, check the babe out, and if everything looks on the up and up, come back and report to me."

"That seems easy enough. I'll tell Lu to make a reservation for me on the . . . oh, I am sorry. First thing tomorrow afternoon I am committed to defend a man falsely accused of murder in San Francisco. The case will take me a week, perhaps two, but—"

Dudek leapt out of his chair and his right arm flailed the air. The sharp hook flashed by my face and missed my nose by no more than a millimeter. "No buts, Shyster. Perhaps I didn't make myself clear. The unnamed judge wants you to fly to Camden tomorrow morning. If you know what's good for you and you want to stay on the right side of the grass, you'll be eating dinner in New Jersey tomorrow night."

The intercom buzzed "Yes?"

Lu said, "The police tell me that most of the force is working a five car accident on Highway Fifty. They will send a squad car by as soon as possible, perhaps as soon as twenty minutes."

"Yes, Lu. You may take an hour off to go shopping."

My mind raced. Is this delay law enforcement's way of getting back at the attorney who gets his accused clients released as fast as they can arrest them? I would have to settle my dilemma with Hook by using my verbal skill and cunning.

"Shyster? An extra hour to go shop?"

"You know females."

Hook rapped his steel device on my desk. "I'm getting tired of waiting"

"Please allow me a moment to consider all my alternatives."

I could give up a million dollar retainer along with a week or two of vacation in San Francisco with all expenses picked up by my client. No way that would ever happen. Hold on, the solution was a phone call away. "Mr. Hook, I could send Bear and Flo to Camden in my stead."

He nodded. "That's true. In fact those two would do twice the job you could do in half the time. I'll check with the judge and get back inside an hour." Dudek moved his hook toward my face and

23

maneuvered it's sharp point inside my left nostril. Then he lifted his right arm, ever so slightly. "Shyster, while I'm gone, don't leave this office, don't talk to your secretary, and don't call anyone. Got it?"

Careful to not nod my head, I said, "Loud and clear, Mr. Hook."

Dudek stormed out of my office and rushed past Lu. The instant I heard him slam the front door to my building, my heart, which had been about to pump its way out of my chest, began to slow down. I jumped up, rushed to my bathroom mirror and checked to be sure the tip of that hook had not damaged my left nostril. The instant that I determined that my elegant proboscis remained unscathed, I grabbed the phone and called Bear.

CHAPTER FOUR

Bear-Carson City, Nevada

After the shrimp hung up, Flo called Fergus back and now she was blowing her nose on a hanky that she always carried with her. That hanky thing was weird. Flo, my mom, and Grandma Zabarte, always had a hankie stuffed somewhere. Like those babes all knew that any second something bad was going to happen and they'd need a hanky to mop up the tears.

Flo's hanky thing sorta reminded me of the old baseball bat that I kept near the cash register at The Old Globe Saloon. Damn near every time I tended bar I was glad that bat was handy 'cause sooner or later one of the drunks would go bonkers and I'd need to tap 'em up side of their head to slow them down. Kinda the same way Flo, Mom, or Grandma Zabarte used their hankies to swipe away their tears.

All of a sudden the stuff dripping off Flo's chin stopped and she said, "Fergus, it's four in the afternoon here. What time is it in Scotland?"

"Midnight."

She pushed the speaker button and said, "I

have a funny feeling there's more to this call than informing us that Grandpa Ollie died."

Me and Flo listened to nothing for a long time 'cause Fergus didn't say anything. He was really good at that 'cause I think, as a cop for all those years, he wanted to be sure his mouth wasn't running faster than his brain.

"Aye, Flo. As usual, you are a step ahead of me. Over the past few months Fiona has not been well. She has numbness in her feet and hands along with general chronic fatigue. Her doctor is perplexed. She told Fiona the numbness might be a symptom of MS while the chronic fatigue could be a symptom of Fibromyalgia. Regardless, most of the household duties, and all the daily responsibilities for disciplining the children have become mine."

Flo said, "Fergus, I'm sorry to hear about Fiona, but what I really hear you saying is that controlling a family of boys and a teenage girl is not a piece of cake."

After another long stretch where Fergus didn't spit out any words, he finally said, "I will agree that I am more comfortable disciplining the boys. Believe me, Fiona and I have loved that girl from the first day she joined our family. But she's older now, growing up, and she's beginning to attract many of the young lads in Pitlochry."

Flo said, "Cut to the chase. What are you trying to say?"

"Now that her grandfather has passed, Fiona

and I wonder if it wouldn't be better for Ettamae if she returned to America? We both feel the move to her homeland would prove beneficial for the lass, and for my sanity."

Flo glanced in my direction, but I didn't say anything 'cause I was still thinking about poor old Ollie. The dude was as blind as a bat and played records at the senior dances in Pitlochry. I know that sounds looney. I mean he couldn't see what the next record was going to be. But it turned out that the old farts who were dancing liked to be surprised and the last I heard, the dancing at the senior center became the hottest show in town once Ollie took over as DJ.

Flo said, "Fergus, I hesitated to answer because I was waiting for Bear to nod his head, or say something, but he's not responding. But don't worry. I'll fly over and pick up Ettamae."

Flo's going to do what? I jumped out of my chair. "What did you just say?"

"I am going to Scotland, pick up Ettamae, and bring her back home to Carson City."

"Babe, I don't mind you going to Scotland and shoot the shit with the kid but she can't come back here!"

"Why not? She lived with us once, remember?"

It looked like me and Flo were about to jump into a swamp filled with nasty water, snakes, and those big bumpy things with all those teeth. I had to do something to slow this Ettamae thing down. I

27

opened the door on my beer refrigerator, pulled out a cool one, popped the cap and grabbed a couple of seconds to think back to those days when the kid lived with us.

Don't get me wrong, Ettamae wasn't a bad kid or anything, but it was like she was sitting on my shoulder every time I popped the top on a brew, or when I checked out the teenaged babes laying around in their bikinis by our pool, or when I'd say shit, or damn, or something worse. Shit, except for the hours I'm sleeping, or working for Pinky, that's mostly all I do everyday!

Back when I was a kid growing up in Elko, my mom worked long hours as the head cook at the Star Hotel. My dad chased down sheep in the desert. So once I hit fourteen, mom and pop asked Grandma Zabarte to move in with us. We all knew that Grandma's job was to keep an eye on me—to make sure I didn't do something stupid, hurt myself, or end up in jail.

So once Grandma Zabarte moved in, every time I was about to do anything dumb, I'd look over my shoulder, just to make sure she wasn't there. And it looked like Ettamae was going to be my new Grandma Zabarte. Grandma had white hair and wrinkles on her face, Ettamae had red hair and freckles, but both of them knew how to stick to me closer than a politician in a lobbyist's back pocket.

If I told Flo that Ettamae could move in, I was sure I'd freak out inside a week. But if I told Flo that the kid couldn't come back, me and her would be over and if that happened, I might as well hand her my pistol and tell her to pump a couple between my eyes.

"Yup. I remember when she lived with us."

I was waiting for the shit to hit the fan when Flo's cell burped. "Excuse me, Fergus, but Pinky's bugging me again. I'll get back to you in a few minutes."

Pinky said, "Bear, there has been a change in plans. Have—"

Flo said, "Pinky, it's Flo, not Bear. First, don't ever hang up on us again. Second, we're not a couple of gladiators, sitting on the bench, waiting to be called to the coliseum floor for a fight to the death. If you want our full attention, and expect our total cooperation, you'll have to treat us like human beings. Now, what is the change in plans?"

Like I said before, Flo can be a giant pain in the butt, but when she shifts her sights onto Pinky, it's time for me to sit back, relax, and enjoy the show.

I yelled in the direction of the phone, "Yeah, just like Flo said. What's the scoop?"

We listened to the boss snort for a couple of seconds. Like he does when he's pissed off.

Finally, Pinky said, "First, I will remind you both that each month you receive an extremely generous salary, along with an outstanding benefits package. According to Nevada law, as your employer, I have the right to expect your industrious efforts in return for my compensation. As we all know, the two of you just returned from your last investigative assignment in Las Vegas, an all-expense paid trip most grateful employees would call a vacation. However, in the spirit of quid-pro-quo—Flo, please explain the Latin term to Bear after I hang up—I am sure you will look forward to completing your new assignment. That said, you are about to embark on trip to Camden, New Jersey."

I snorted, "Camden, New Jersey? That's a hell hole. What's there for us?"

Flo said, "Pinky, for the first time today I agree with Bear. I'm sure you are aware that Camden had the highest violent crime rate in the United States in 2012 with 2,566 violent crimes per 100,000 people. That's 6.6 times higher than the national average of violent crimes.

"Florence, I was aware that the violent crime rate was above average but that is not the reason why I am sending you there. You and Bear are to look into the personal background of a young woman named Adelaide Carlucci."

I said, "Who wants to know?"

Pinky said, "I am sorry, but that information must remain confidential."

Flo said, "Let me guess. You have a client who's looking to marry her."

I said, "And me and Flo are going to check her out to make sure she's not a gold miner. Right?"

Flo said, "I think you meant a gold-digger.

Pinky, are we close to the mark?"

Pinky said, "As I previously stated, the reasons must remain confidential. However, if you proceed along the lines Bear suggested, your assignment will be completed. The client has agreed to pay all the expenses for your economy airfare and one hundred and fifty dollars per day for your expenses. However, the client will require a detailed accounting of your daily expenditures. Flo, I will depend on you to maintain a comprehensive record of each legitimate expense item."

Flo yelled, "Pinky, even in a dump like Camden two people can't find a decent motel, and three meals for a hundred and fifty. Get your cheapskate client to bump that up to two hundred bucks a day or we're not going."

Now it was Pinky's turn to scream. "Florence, you will go to Camden and get by on your expense allowance or—"

After a quick swig of my brew, I said, "Boss, the expense money's not bugging me. Why don't you go?"

"I have another assignment."

Flo jumped. "And where's your assignment?

"San Francisco."

I growled, "Hold on. The last time we talked, me and Flo were going to Frisco, but now Camden? Boss, that's chicken-shit. You always get the good places. Remember last year? You went to Hawaii while me and Flo ended up in hushpuppy heaven."

"Bear, Florence, as your employer, I have given you this assignment and—"

I glanced at Flo and she flashed a thumbs down. I said, "Boss, we ain't going to Camden."

Now it was our turn to hang up on the little shit so Flo did!

CHAPTER FIVE

Pinky-Carson City, Nevada

My God, those ingrates hung up on me! Not many years ago Bear was as malleable as a lump of fresh clay. He was a barely adequate bar-tender who had killed a man and I had saved him from the needle, or twenty-to-life.

And then he attempted to stiff me, J Pinkus Delmont, the attorney who had saved him from a murder conviction. But being the generous person that I am I allowed him to work off his bill as my investigator.

But the ideal work relationship between Bear and myself vanished the day that woman returned with him from Los Angeles. Florence Sunderlund has been a thorn in my side from the first moment we met.

Now Bear, with her encouragement, refused my latest work assignment. They both have a lot of nerve. I will drag him, and that woman, before the State Employment Commission and they will soon discover that I, as their employer, have the power to . . . the door to my inner sanctum opened and interrupted my thoughts. Lu stood there. Her classic Asian beauty was marred by a surly stare.

I said, "Yes?"

"Pinky, when you walked by my desk this afternoon I told you that we needed to talk. Multiple phone calls have passed, plus a visit from Mr. Dudek. If you want me to continue to answer your phones, lie to the court clerks so they will rearrange your scheduled court room appearances, and each day provide you with a minute by minute schedule of your events, you will stop everything and listen to me now."

I could see that she was a touch upset, but I had no idea as to the reason. "Lu, please come in and sit down." She ignored my offer of a chair. "Can I pour you a glass of white wine, a soft drink, a shot of—"

Tears trickled down her sculptured cheekbones. "Pinky, I can't drink wine. I'm pregnant."

I must admit that my normal stoic expression vanished. "Lu, I . . . ah . . . when did this happen?"

"Not that the duration of my condition is any of your business, but over eight months ago."

"Eight months? How could I—"

Lu turned and presented me a side view of her figure. My God, there was a noticeable bump underneath her clothing.

I said, "I can't believe I missed that."

She said, "Neither could I. Day after day, week after week, month after month you waltzed by my desk without a glance. Pinky, you are the most egocentric person I've ever known. Now, listen to what I have to say for a change. I have an appointment in thirty minutes with my OB/GYN. She seems to feel that the baby could be born early. It's time for you to find a temporary replacement. I think four weeks will allow me the time I need to have the baby and organize my life so I will be ready to come back to work."

And after all I have done for Lu. Now the woman brands me as egocentric? I might have been a touch self-absorbed concerning her condition, but when it came to my employees I consider myself to be benevolent, if not altruistic. But there are some who questioned the motives of Mother Tressa. I sighed. "After the birth, what do you plan on doing with the baby?"

"I'll have to bring her here with me each day. That way I can keep your ship running a straight course, feed and nurture my child as needed, and continue to earn the money I require to maintain my accustomed lifestyle."

Hold on, she plans on supporting herself and the baby? There had to be a father in this affair. I said, "Who is the child's father?"

"That's none of your business. Now, should I contact Louis Loomer at Rapid Replacement, or do you want to make that call yourself?"

I hesitated. I could see no reason why Lu should carry the burden of her child by herself. "Lu, I will agree to have you bring the child to this place of business each day, but first, you must give me some background on the father."

Now it was her turn to ponder. After a moment she said, "His name is Dennis Choi. He's an oceanographer and has a position on Cape Cod with the Woods Hole Oceanographic Institution in their Climate Change department."

As Lu told me the unprincipled man's name, she wavered and her knees started to buckle. I jumped up, ran around my desk, and slid a chair under her. "Please sit down." As she sat, I decided to comfort her with a slight stretch of the truth. "As an attorney I have dealt with this sort of situation before. There are legal issues to be settled. Have you informed Mr. Choi about the baby and his long-term responsibilities?"

Lu considered my statement and shook her head. "Pinky, in the time I have worked here nearly all your legal work has been involved with criminals. Mostly murderers. I didn't realize you had any experience with family law."

"Don't you recall that young man last year, Gotthold Zweibel, who felt he was being cheated out of his inheritance?"

"Pinky, in case you've forgotten, that man kidnapped us and forced you to drive your car to your condo at Lake Tahoe where we both nearly died. That's as far from a family law case as you can get."

"True, but you must admit it began as a family

36

law matter."

Lu threw up her hands. "I give up! Dennis relocated from Wuhan, China, to America three years ago. He was born and raised in the city with more than ten million people and premarital sex was traditionally frowned on and unmarried mothers are shunned."

"Where did you meet him?"

"He attended an Oceanographic conference in Reno about eight months ago."

I said, "And."

"We met, he returned to the east coast, and that's all I am going to say."

A loud crash startled us both as Dudek slammed through the street door of the building and bellowed, "Shyster, Hook's here! We need to talk."

He stormed into my office and noticed Lu sitting in a chair. "In private."

I said, "Lu, we will continue this conversation after Mr. Hook leaves."

As she turned to leave my office I realized just how pregnant Lu actually was.

Dudek poised his hook over my mahogany desk and growled, "The judge in question says that you go to Camden or . . ."

"Or what?"

The tip of his hook nailed the sleeve of my imported Emporio Armani single-breasted suit. Then, as if his stainless steel implement were a tiny farm plow, the tip ripped an inch-long furrow in the one-hundred-percent-virgin worsted wool. Not a large gash, but big enough for me to realize what that hook could do to my body. "Mr. Hook, please assure the judge in question that I will be on the first plane tomorrow morning to the east coast."

Dudek smiled, and as his lips parted, a dark gap appeared where three upper front teeth should have been. He tapped the woolen furrow on my sleeve with the tip of his hook. "A professional reweaver can fix that little tear in your jacket sleeve. I recommend Johnson's tailor shop on South Virginia in Reno. They do excellent work."

The pronged assassin, using his hand, reached into his shirt pocket and pulled out a card. "Here's my private number. Call me after you get back from New Jersey. And Pinky, don't screw this up or the judge in question could . . . na, you don't want to know what he could do."

Dudek spun around and thundered out of my office.

CHAPTER SIX

Bear-Carson City, Nevada

The phone rang. Flo said, "That'll be Pinky. He's going to fire us, or send us to San Francisco, and I'd bet on San Francisco."

"Babe, one of these day you're going to push him too far."

"True, but until we reach that point, I'll never know how far I can go." She hit the button and said real sweet, "Hello, Pinky." Flo smiled and nodded. "Hold on. I'll put you on the speaker."

We both heard Pinky say, "I have considered what Bear said concerning a fairer distribution of the locations of investigative assignments, and have changed my plans. I will be going to Camden and the two of you will take over the San Francisco assignment."

Flo gave me a 'that was too easy' look, then she said, "Did you just present the San Francisco assignment in the form of a question? Such as, Flo, Bear, would you care to go to San Francisco to conduct an investigation?"

Pinky snorted, "Florence, do not push me any—"

Flo interrupted. "Whatever. Pinky, By the way, do you recall Ettamae? The young girl from that case in Northern California where the winemaker drowned in a ten-thousand-gallon tank of cabernet?

"Skinny child? Red hair? Freckles? Mouth ran like Niagara Falls?"

I said, "That's Ettamae to a T."

Pinky said, "The last I heard the child was living in Scotland with her grandfather. I fail to understand why that girl could have anything to do with your San Francisco assignment."

I said, "Boss, Grandpa Ollie just bought the farm."

Pinky's voice sounded real tight. "I am sorry to hear that, but what does his demise have to do—"

Flo interrupted again. "Put a sock in it and listen to me. Before we step one foot closer to San Francisco, talk to your client and explain to him that you are sending a three-person investigative team to Bagdad-by-the-Bay. Tell him that one of your top investigators has just completed a job in Scotland and your client will have to cover the cost of airfare from Glasgow to SFO. We'll pick up Ettamae at the airport. She'll be an integral part of our team and her expenses will be included with ours."

Pinky cried, "But she is nothing but a child!"

Flo said, "Her grandfather just passed away and she needs our help. If you have a problem with that, then you can find someone else to do your San

Francisco investigating."

"Florence, I am fed up with your incessant ultimatums. First, you make outlandish demands to increase your salary, followed by paid health insurance, and then vacations! Now you are talking about adding a red-headed orphan to—"

I wasn't sure where Flo was going with this whole Ettamae thing, but I wasn't going to let the boss throw my Babe under the bus. "Hey, lay off Flo! She was real close with Ettamae and wants to help out the kid now that Grandpa Ollie's gone. Like Flo said, we all go to Frisco, or nobody goes. Discussion's over. Got me?"

The Shrimp shouted, "I can understand you wanting to bring her back to Reno, but—"

Flo said, "Pinky, like Bear said, the time for discussion is over."

"Damn you, and . . . I'm the . . . but . . . " The boss sputtered like that for a few more seconds. The he calmed down. "All right. I will call the client and inform him that my team in San Francisco will consist of three investigators and he will be responsible for a one-way coach ticket from Scotland to San Francisco. God help us all if the man ever discovers that one of the investigators is a mere child. That settled, be in my office in an hour. Now, I have one more item to discuss. Florence, were you aware that Lu is pregnant?"

"Yes, and not just pregnant. More like about to give birth to a little girl."

"And how long have you known?"

"I noticed she radiated a special glow that seems to go with pregnancy. I'd say that was about six, maybe seven months ago. Why?"

"Nothing. Just checking. I will see you two in—"

Flo said, "Pinky, didn't you realize Lu was pregnant?"

"As I stated, I will see you both in my office inside an hour."

Pinky clicked off, and I said, "What was all that Lu stuff about?"

"I'm not sure. I'll check with Lu when we get to the office."

"Babe, me and you got to talk about this Ettamae thing. We both live in this apartment and I have some say in what goes on here."

"I agree," said Flo. "By the way, I think I pushed Pinky about as far as I should go."

She did have the way of knowing just how to change the subject when she wanted to. I growled, "Hey, we were talking about Ettamae, remember?"

She said, "Don't worry, we'll have plenty of time to discuss Ettamae." Flo winked. "But right now we have forty-five minutes and Pinky asked me to explain quid pro quo to you."

I wasn't exactly sure what Flo's wink meant so I said, "Okay, explain away."

"Quid pro quo means something for something, or a favor for a favor." She pulled her sweatshirt over her head. "Now, there are talking favors, and then there are special kinds of favors. We could talk about Ettamae living with us right now, or I could explain quid pro quo in the bedroom. It's your choice. Ettamae or the bedroom?"

The sight of Flo's bodacious ta-ta's turned my knees to applesauce. I think I'm going to like this poco poco stuff. "Gotcha. I vote for the bedroom!"

CHAPTER SEVEN

Pinky-Carson City, Nevada

I sat back and considered what could only be called a calamitous afternoon. For a moment I could not decide what had been most devastating— my ruined one-hundred-percent-virgin worsted wool Armani suit, Willow's callous disregard for my heartfelt affection, or my pending trip to the undesirable Camden, New Jersey. After a moment of reflection I decided that my afternoon had not been my best, but with the knowledge that I had risen to the challenge in times of adversity, I picked up my phone and dialed Willow's private line.

She answered on the second ring and just hearing her voice validated to me that I was on the road to recovery.

"Pinky, I told you at lunch I had an important meeting."

"My sweet. Please bear with me for a moment. Lu is pregnant and as soon as I hang up from this call I am going to contact Louis Loomer at Rapid Replacement for a *locum tenens*. But the real reason for my call is that tomorrow morning I fly to the east coast on a very confidential legal matter."

Willow said, "Everyone in Carson City knew that Lu was pregnant and frankly I don't care where you are going tomorrow, or why! Tell me why you called or I'm hanging up."

"My love, I could be absent from my practice for a week or two, and my girl Friday could also be gone. I am seeking your assistance to find a paralegal, or even an intern, who could keep a hand on the tiller of my legal ship, so to speak. Can you suggest a candidate who is presently in your employ? A person that you feel would gain valuable knowledge while working with me, the most successful defense attorney in the state of Nevada?"

"Pinky, you are a human dichotomy. Two hours ago I refused your proposal of marriage, yet here you are, back again, asking for favors as if nothing happened at lunch. You are like the desperate vacuum salesman who keeps ringing the doorbell after you tell him no."

"Willow, it was not easy to call you and ask you for help. Believe me, if I—"

"Okay. Answer me one question, honestly, and I will see if I can find some help for you. Are you ready for the question?"

"Yes."

"When did you discover that Lu was pregnant? And be honest with me or my assistance is off the table."

I did not want to admit my ignorance concerning Lu's condition, but I could see no other way to solve my dilemma. "Today, about an hour ago."

"You've just won the first prize of one of my paralegal interns, but as nothing in this world is free, your new paralegal will cost you. Somewhere in the neighborhood of twenty-five percent more than the county's present paralegal salary. Agreed?"

At the moment I had trouble following the gist of Willow's conversation because the sweet lilt of her voice had mesmerized me. "I am sorry, my love. Would you repeat that last part?"

"Pinky, if you don't stop addressing me as my love, or my sweet, I will require you to call me District Attorney Stone. Now, you have to agree to pay the paralegal more than their existing county salary."

"I agree."

"We have a deal. Bye."

I sat in silence and replayed the tone of Willow's side of our conversation. As I ran through her lyrical vocal inflections a second time, I concluded that there was a definitive softening of her voice at the conclusion of our phone conversation. I smiled and poured myself two fingers of single malt. Today's lunch was just a temporary set back. Sooner or later, she would recognize the error of her ways and come back to me.

And thanks to the woman I must now reinstate as my favorite ex-wife, I will have a paralegal to look after the legal aspects of my practice during my absence.

I swirled the golden liquid in my glass. Now to the easy part. It was time to take care of the secretarial, clerical, and organizational aspect of my office. I took a sip and dialed Louis Loomer.

He answered between the first and second ring. "Rapid Replacement. We fill your staffing needs rapidly." Loomer's voice was so loaded with sugar that I feared a potential type B diabetic attack.

"Louis, Pinky Delmont here. Starting immediately, I will require a short term replacement for Lu."

"Good afternoon, Mr. Delmont. To be sure I understand your request, you stated you will need to cover the present position held by Lu, your legal secretary. Trust me, for Rapid Replacement, that's no problem, but could you define short-term in a more precise way? Are you talking weeks, or months, or perhaps a year? Just how long do you anticipate Lu will be gone?"

The man's question caught me off guard. Lu had told me four weeks, but even to this uninformed bachelor, four weeks did not seem long enough. "Eight weeks should be sufficient."

"Mr. Delmont, if you are considering covering Lu's time off the job, I believe twelve weeks is considered the gold standard for maternity leave. It's interesting to note that if we lived in Sweden, Lu would be entitled to 480 days' leave, and if she

47

produced twins she would be entitled to an additional 180 days."

"Louis, we do not live in Sweden and I am a very busy man. Now, I have—"

"And during those 660 days Lu would earn 80% of her salary. Of course you would not be obligated to pay her salary: the Swedish government is committed to cover that expense, so—"

"Loomer, cease your drivel. Eight weeks is long enough. Goodbye!"

Lu buzzed me. "Pinky, there's a lady here to see you." Lu's voice dropped to a whisper. "She claims she was sent from Willow's office."

My God, the love of my life had worked quickly! Perhaps I should ask Willow to train Louis Loomer on how to deal with a customer on the phone. "Lu, make me a airplane reservation from Reno to the airport closest to Camden, New Jersey. Rent me a Mercedes 350C, and make a reservation for me at the best hotel in Camden for seven days. Do you have that?"

Lu said, "But what about the suite I reserved for you at the Hotel Drisco in San Francisco?"

"How many bedrooms in the suite?"

"Two."

"Perfect. Bear and Flo will take the Omni suite until I return."

"Got it."

"Excellent. Now send in the woman from Willow's office."

The door opened and a female, living in the neighborhood of fifty to seventy, walked in.

"Mr. Delmont, my name is Thelma Untermeyer Hathaway. District Attorney Stone told me you are seeking a paralegal for your practice."

Thelma Untermeyer Hathaway's unfettered eye makeup and bright red lips did what they could to her otherwise homely face. Her European physiognomy topped a body I conservatively judged to be thirty pounds overweight. Atop the woman's head sat a yellow straw hat that struggled to maintain a mass of dyed black hair. A long, shabby gray skirt, coral blouse, and a gauche necklace made up of large, polished, turquoise stones completed the initial picture of my potential paralegal.

Was Willow toying with me? The woman was a fright.

I said, "Please come in and sit down. The District Attorney was correct, and you are one of many that I am presently interviewing for that position. Tell me about your training and background as a paralegal."

The woman said, "First, to be sure we're on the same page, I may look old but in this era of non-discrimination, the age of an individual cannot be considered in the case of employment."

I smiled. "Of course not. Now, what is your—"

"Second, I need to tell you who, and what I am. I was married to Giles Hathaway, my childhood sweetheart, for nearly thirty years. One day, Giles grabbed his chest and tumbled to the ground. Before I could bend over, my husband was dead. Let me tell you, Giles' passing was a shock to me in more ways than one."

My afternoon was rapidly disappearing. I still had to go home and pack for my trip to New Jersey. I said, "Mrs. Hathaway, I am sure watching your husband die was a great shock to—"

"In more ways than you can imagine. You see, my husband gave me a monthly allowance to run the household and God help me if I should ever exceed that allowance. Giles controlled everything. Each evening, before dinner, we would sit on our front porch and he would pour us each a stiff drink of cheap Kentucky bourbon. No water. No ice. Just the damned whisky. I hated the stuff, but Giles joked that it would grow hair on my chest, so I downed that vile stuff to keep my husband happy."

"Mrs. Hathaway, I can understan—"

"Hold your horses, I'm getting to the best part. The second evening after my husband's death, as I poured myself a glass of bourbon, I realized that I didn't have to drink his whiskey anymore. I could enjoy a gin and tonic, or a glass of white wine. So I said to myself, 'Thelma Untermeyer Hathaway, it's time for you to take control of your life. I tossed a nearly full bottle of Kentucky whisky into the trash, went to the store and bought myself a case of chardonnay."

My intercom buzzed, saving me from asking her the brand of chardonnay, to determine if the woman had any better sense of wine than she had for fashion. I picked up the receiver. "Yes?"

"Pinky, I have a man standing next to my desk from Rapid Replacement. He claims you hired him for eight weeks. I thought we had agreed on four—"

"I told Loomer eight weeks because you'll need that much time to settle in to motherhood."

"But I can't afford—"

"Lu, I am covering the cost of your extra four weeks. Now explain to the man your duties and I will be out to meet him just as soon as I complete this interview."

I hung the phone up and said, "Ms. Hathaway, That was a very interesting story, but you neglected to give me your paralegal training."

"I'm getting to that, but I felt it was important to explain to you that even though I'm fifty-five, I'm an independent woman who is capable of doing most anything. Now, my education. I attended Truckee Meadows Community College and graduated two months ago with my AAS from the paralegal program. I feel it is important to add that Truckee Meadows Community College offers the only paralegal program in Northern Nevada approved by the American Bar Association. My favorite paralegal instructor called Truckee Meadows the Harvard of the west."

"I said, "Please, Mrs. Hathaway, I—"

"I'll do my best to hurry. I started my internship for the District Attorney's office last month and have received one outstanding review of my work. Mr. Delmont, I fully understand that as a paralegal, I am required to work under the supervision of a lawyer who has been admitted to the bar, but you can count on me to do everything you need, under your guiding hand of course, during your absence."

Frankly, under most circumstances, this woman would not be my first, second, or third choice, but I had a plane to catch, and, after the lunchtime ring fiasco, Willow owed me one. I would have her supervise Thelma Untermeyer Hathaway during my absence.

I said, "Ms. Hathaway, under the circumstances—"

"Please call me Thelma."

"Very well. Thelma, you are hired. While I am absent, District Attorney Stone will stop by occasionally to—"

"To check up on me, I presume. I understand. Will I have a desk?"

"Yes. The one against the wall to the right of Lu's desk."

"Is Lu the pregnant lady that D. A. Stone was telling me about before I came over today?"

"Yes, she is. Lu is in the process of training a man to replace her for eight weeks."

"What's his name?"

"Frankly, Thelma, I do not know."

"Mr. Delmont, are you really going to leave first thing tomorrow morning?"

"Yes, and I will call you Thelma as long as you call me Pinky. Agreed?"

"Pinky, is there a looseleaf binder on my new desk that delineates my duties and responsibilities as your paralegal?"

My God, I did not know what I wanted this woman to do in my absence. "Did Willow have a binder?"

"She did."

"Excellent! Borrow the District Attorney's binder and follow it to the letter."

"Thank you for your trust in me, Pinky. I'm sure Giles would have never given me the opportunity to cover for him."

"What did your deceased husband do for a living?"

"He sold women's shoes at Penney's in the Southgate mall. Giles made sure I understood that selling pumps and high heel shoes to ladies was a very complex profession."

And Thelma Untermeyer Hathaway had fallen for that? Could this woman be Willow's insidious way to get back at me? I thought not. Thelma seemed harmless enough and could actually accomplish much of the mundane work that clutters up my days. I will ask Lu, and Willow, to see if the two could pound a sense of fashion into the woman's head. I could not afford to have a fifty-five-year-old "bag lady" greeting my new clients.

I said, "Thank you, Thelma."

I jumped up and pointed toward my office door. "Now, walk through that door and find your desk. Your first assignment will be to print up two copies of the DA's paralegal binder, one for you, and one for me."

My intercom buzzed. "Yes?"

Lu said, "Mr. Godwin is on your line."

"I will pick him up in a moment." I glanced at Thelma and for some reason she remained at my office door as if she were nailed to the floor. "Thelma, that will be all."

"Not until we settle my salary issue. According to District Attorney Stone, you agreed to pay me thirty-five percent above my previous county salary. Am I correct?"

I glanced at the flashing light on my phone indicating that Charles was on hold. He will have to wait! The amount I had agreed with Willow was in the neighborhood of twenty-five percent. Was this woman attempting to con me? Two could play at that game and she is in over her head. "I believe you are incorrect. The agreed upon amount was five percent."

"I don't think so. Ms. Stone told me thirty percent. No more, no less."

She could not have known that her use of the title, Ms., for Willow, cut me to my very core. I hesitated for a moment to salve my grievous wound, then said, "I am sorry but five percent is my limit."

Thelma said, "Did I hear you say twenty-five percent?"

Now I was pretty sure that her clothing and sad tale about her deceased husband was just that, an act to gain my trust and sympathy. This woman was attempting to rip me off.

After a moment's hesitation, I tightened my jaw and snapped, "Five percent and close the door behind you as you leave."

She pushed on my door then turned back. "Pinky, I know this shouldn't make any difference, but I like you, so I'll accept ten percent. But that's my final offer."

I reached down to my right, picked up my briefcase, looked up, and, as if I had just realized Thelma was still standing in my office, I growled, "Thelma, five percent and not a penny more. Now please remove yourself from my premises."

Thelma wiped away what was most likely a pseudo tear. "Pinky. I lied to you about the thirty-five percent, but Ms. Stone really did tell me you would pay me twenty-five percent more than my county salary."

I sat and did not respond.

Thelma said, "Okay, I'll take the five percent."

I stood and said, "And all future raises or benefits will come from me at my discretion and are non-negotiable."

Thelma nodded.

I said, "Now leave my office and return to your previous place of internship. While there, make two copies of the paralegal responsibilities. When you return, give me one copy, find your desk and go to work."

As Thelma closed my office door, I smiled and congratulated myself for a job well done. I now have one employee who understands who is boss.

I picked up my phone. "Charles, a small change in plans. Bear and Flo will check into the Hotel Drisco in San Francisco tomorrow in my stead and Bear will contact you once they are established. I have a previous commitment that I must complete."

"Pinky, I called to tell you that Rundstrom has agreed to your retainer demands and as we speak, he is wire transferring you one million dollars. Now you tell me that you have a previous commitment? Gregor Rundstrom is a friend of mine and I will not allow you to ruin that relationship."

"Calm down, Charles. Bear and Flo are excellent investigators and . . . " I suddenly recalled the addition of the child from Scotland. "And to make up for my absence I am importing a third investigator from Scotland. Mr. Rundstrom is getting three investigators and when I return, I will join my crack team in San Francisco."

"Slow down. You're bringing in an investigator from Scotland? Why?"

"She was a member of my team that helped

solve a cold case murder in Scotland. She and Flo work very well together. Between Ettamae, Flo, and Bear, they could have Erik Rundstrom cleared of the murder before I arrive."

Charles said, "Where are you going?"

"I am sorry, but where I go, and why, is confidential."

Charles hesitated, as if he was attempting to fit all the pieces of a giant jigsaw puzzle together. "Okay, but tell me something that stops me from feeling I have just bought a bottle of snake oil."

I said, "Charles, you know you can trust me. By the way, the cost of an airline ticket from Glasgow to San Francisco will be my first item on the Gregor Rundstrom expense account."

CHAPTER EIGHT

Bear-Carson City, Nevada

This was one crazy mixed up day.

First we get a call from Fergus in Scotland and he tells us that Ettamae needs to come back to Carson City.

Then, 'cause Ettamae's coming back, me and Flo got into a pissing match, and were about to call off sharing a king size mattress, when Pinky calls and tells us were going to Camden, New Jersey. Pinky's way of telling us about our Camden assignment pissed off Flo so bad that she forgot she was mad at me.

Then Pinky calls back and tells us were going to Frisco instead of Camden and we need to hustle over to his office so he can explain what's going on.

Then, when me and Flo get to Pinky's office, he's not there, but there are two new people sitting near Lu.

One face belonged to a dude with a blue-green Mohawk 'do. The other face was attached to a broad who looked like one of those old hippies I'd seen in pictures.

I said, "Lu, who's the dude with the fancy 'do?"

"His name is Frank."

Frank glanced up and flashed me a sour look.

"Why's he sitting next to you?"

"Frank will be taking my place for two months after I have my baby."

"Cool. Hi, Frank. Flo and me are Pinky's investigators."

Frank grunted and gave me a little nod

Then I checked out the old broad who was sitting at a desk against the wall.

"Lu, who's that over there?"

"Her name is Thelma."

"Why's she here?"

Lu said, "She's a paralegal."

"What the hell's a pair of legals?"

Lu shrugged her shoulders, like she was bugged about something.

While Flo peeked into Pinky's office, she said, "A paralegal is an attorney's assistant trained to perform certain legal tasks but not admitted to the practice of law."

Lu chimed in, "Pinky hired Thelma to keep his office open while he's gone."

I said, "I hope she works out better than that jerk Hennessy, that dippy legal-eagle Pinky hired to hold down the fort while we all wandered around Scotland."

Flo said, "His name was C. Thomas Hennessy, to be exact. Pinky went ballistic and fired him after Hennessy gave Pinky second-billing when he answered the office phone, 'Law Offices of Hennessy and Delmont.'"

Flo walked over and started to schmooze with the hippie broad. While the two talked like long lost sisters, Lu handed me a piece of paper.

"Before he left, Pinky told me to give this to you."

I grabbed the note and read:

> While I am in New Jersey, the two of you will reside in my suite at my favorite hotel in San Francisco, the Hotel Drisco. Lu has reserved the two bedroom suite which should accommodate the two of you and that child from Scotland.
>
> Charles Godwin, an attorney we have worked with before, and my client, Gregor Rundstrom, have both been informed that I will be adding a third investigator, and that the third investigator will arrive from Scotland. That is the sum total of information that Charles and my client need to know concerning the third investigator. If you and Florence value your excessively compensated investigative positions, you will not allow any contact between Charles Godwin and the child. It is my intention to keep the information that she is but a youth in house.
>
> Once you have settled into the Drisco, call

Charles Godwin. Lu has his mobile number. I am sure you will recall Charles. He is the District Attorney we worked with to find the killers who drowned the winemaker in ten thousand gallons of cabernet sauvignon. Bear, in case your memory fails you, that was the case where your mistakes and bumbling placed my life in danger.

But all that is water under the bridge. Charles will provide you with all the information you require to begin your investigation into the suspicious death of the restaurant critic, Simon Rand.

Florence, as you are the brain trust of the duo, I leave you two important duties:

First, do not take the child with you when you are investigating Simon Rand's death. What you do with her is your problem, not mine—leave her in the suite to watch television—drop her off at the zoo—send her to school—just do not let her tag along with you and Bear.

Second, as soon as I join you in San Francisco, you, Bear, and the child, will immediately vacate my Hotel Drisco suite. As you well know, San Francisco can be an expensive location. I would suggest you spend some of your off-hours seeking an affordable location for the three of you once you leave the Drisco Hotel.

To show you my extreme generosity concerning your change of habitat, I will increase your per diem expenses to one hundred for each of you, or a total of three hundred a day.

Also, if you and Bear are fortunate enough to clear my client's son, Erik Rundstrom, from any suspicion concerning Simon Rand's death, each of you will receive an additional one thousand dollars which will be added to your monthly remuneration.

If you have any questions, I can be reached on my mobile number.

I waved Pinky's note at Flo and said, "Babe, the shrimp's offering us each a thousand clams if we can get his Frisco client off before he gets back from Jersey."

Flo walked over. "Let me see the letter."

As she worked her way down the p[age, I could tell from her eyes that she was getting more and more pissed off. "The shrimp thinks he knows more about investigating than we do. What a dork." Flo folded Pinky's note and slipped it between her two best assets. "Lu, Thelma, Frank, we're off to San Francisco. Lu, if Pinky calls in, tell him we're on the case but we're not going to bust our buns until he increases his one thousand dollar bonus offer to ten K. Bear, let's go. A two bedroom suite at The Hotel

Drisco awaits us."

"Babe, I don't know anything about Frisco. Is this place that Pinky's put us in going to be okay?"

She smiled. "Okay? The Hotel Drisco has the reputation as one of the finest, and most romantic, boutique accommodation in Northern California."

CHAPTER NINE

Pinky-Philadelphia, Pennsylvania, not Camden, New Jersey

The bar at the Hilton Philadelphia at Penn's Landing was nearly empty. I was lost in my thoughts when a gruff voice asked, "Ready for another?"

I focused on the sound and looked directly into the large face of the man standing behind the bar. He was tall and structured along the same lines as Bear. I nodded and pondered if excessive physical stature was a prerequisite to being a successful mixologist.

"Here on business?" asked the bartender as he mixed my second gin and tonic.

He pushed my drink toward me. I lifted the glass, enjoyed the combined aroma of quinine and gin berries, and took a sip. "It has been years since I have had a gin and tonic this good."

"Thanks."

I said, "To answer your question, I suppose one could say that I am here on business." My thoughts returned to Florence's admonition concerning Camden's extreme crime rate. "I have a meeting in

Camden tomorrow and, as I have never been to that fair city, I have a small concern. For example, I told my secretary to make me a reservation in the best hotel in Camden and here I sit in the bar of the Philadelphia Hilton, across the Delaware River from my desired destination. Is there something I should know about the city?"

The barkeep grabbed the bottle of Beefeater's gin, topped off my G and T, and said, "Fella, you've got a sharp skirt working for you. Camden's top hotel is a Motel Six."

So Florence's assessment was correct. "I take it that Camden is not a destination that the most discriminating tourist would seek out."

"I'll answer that in a minute." The bartender moved twenty feet to his right, handed the only other bar customer a second bottle of beer, and returned to me. "Fella, I know this is none of my business, but are you taking a cab to your meeting?"

"No. I have rented a Mercedes 350 C, and—"

The barkeep's open palm hit the bar with a smack. "Bum idea. You'd never see a local drive a 350 C into that shit hole of a town."

I was a touch shocked by the man's frankness, but at the same time ,I was intrigued by his assertiveness. I took another sip. "What would you suggest I do?"

He pulled out a towel, vigorously dried his right hand, and then thrust his big paw toward me. "My name is Joey Palumbo."

As he slowly crushed my fingers in the vice he called his hand, I cried, "Stop! That is starting to hurt."

"Sorry. Sometimes I forget and squeeze too hard."

He let go before any permanent damage occurred.

I said, "Honored to meet you, Joey. My name is J. Pinkus Delmont, but you can call me Pinky. Now, what is your suggestion?"

"Pinky, I like that name. I use ta work with a good guy named Ruby at the big sports bar near the Independence Hall. Those were the good old days. Now I'm down to a couple of nights a week on the late shift here, and the other three nights I'm the muscle at the hottest drag bar in Philly."

"You sound pretty busy to me, Joey."

"Hey, I don't need much sleep and my days are free. I could drive you wherever you have to go in Camden."

"My good man, I am considering your offer, but just how much compensation would you expect to receive for driving an ignorant tourist around Camden?"

His expression informed me that his thought process concerning escorting me had not yet reached the simple detail of compensation. "Ah . . . would you go for twenty an hour?"

"Joey, I'll pay you twenty-five an hour plus a bonus of one thousand dollars when you return me, and my Mercedes, unscathed to the airport."

Joey stared at me for a moment, as if he was not sure of the definition of unscathed. Then, as the mental puzzle pieces slowly fit together, he smiled and stuck out his hand to seal the deal. "Pinky, you've got a driver."

I avoided his potentially lethal handshake and smiled back. "Joey, I'll meet you in the lobby tomorrow morning at nine."

CHAPTER TEN

Bear-San Francisco, California

Flo was right on about The Hotel Drisco. It was the classist joint Pinky ever put us up in. We've got two bedrooms, a living room and a kick-ass view of the city.

Flo checked everything out and said, "I want to give you fair warning, when Pinky joins us, there's no way he's going to kick me out of this suite."

"I'm with you, Babe."

Then Flo sat down, called British Airways and found out that Ettamae's flight from Scotland was landing in a couple of hours. She called the dude named Charlie and told him we'd meet him in thirty minutes at a fancy coffee joint she knew about in the Ferry Building.

Fighting my way through the San Francisco traffic between the Drisco and the Ferry Building was like trying to stay alive inside a stampede of wild horses. Once we got to the Ferry Building, it took more time to find a place to park and then I had to listen to Flo bitch about the forty bucks we had to pay to stick my truck into parking slot number fifty-seven.

Flo ran ahead so Charlie wouldn't think we got lost or something but I didn't care 'cause we were only ten minutes late.

By the time I caught up with Flo she was laughing and Charlie's peepers were bugged out while he checked out my babe.

Once he saw me coming, Charlie jumped up and stuck out his hand. "Bear, it's been awhile. Have you recovered from all the trauma that you incurred while solving the Hellman murder?"

"Yup. I'm fine. Now what's the scoop on this poisoned dude, Simon Whatever?"

Charlie laughed. "You get right to it. Okay, the police have their eyes on two persons of interest." The dude pulled out a sheet of paper and gave it to Flo. "Here are two names, but I'm only concerned with one, the man named Erik Rundstrom."

Flo glanced at the paper and said, "So who's the other name, Laura Heath?"

Charlie said, "I don't know. As I said, I am only concerned with Erik Rundstrom."

Flo stuffed the paper in her purse and said, "Why him?"

"First, his father was one of my best friends at UC Berkeley. Second, last month Simon Rand panned Erik's new restaurant. You two need to understand that a bad review from a big-time critic can crush a new restaurant. According to a local critic, Erik's restaurant was very good. Why Rand gave the restaurant a bad review is a mystery. But after Rand's review, the line of customers at the door of Erik's place vanished."

Flo said, "Okay, you've explained why the son of your college buddy could have a motive. What about the opportunity?"

"Erik was one of the chefs who prepared the food at the dinner where Simon Rand died."

I said, "Charlie, as the head lawman in your county you know if this Erik dude had a motive and the opportunity, all that's left is the means. Do the local fuzz know for sure this restaurant critic was poisoned?"

"Not yet, but they'll know once the toxicology tests are in, and they're expected by tomorrow or the day after at the latest."

I checked the clock on the wall and it was almost noon. We had to pick up Ettamae in about two hours and I didn't have a clue where the San Francisco airport was, or how tough it was to get there. I flashed Flo my worried look.

Flo ignored me and said, "Do you have a phone number or an address for Erik? We need to talk with him to get his side of the story."

"Of course." Charlie grabbed a napkin and scribbled down some stuff.

"Babe, we're going to be late for that important appointment."

Flo looked at me.

I pointed at the clock on the wall.

She nodded. "At the moment, I think we have

enough to move on, Charles. We'll talk to Erik and get back to you."

I said, "Charlie, before we go, you seem to know an awful lot about poisoning a dude in Frisco, eighty miles from where you live and work. How do you get the inside skinny? You got some kind of snitch inside the SFPD?"

He looked around, like everybody who downed this frou-frou coffee cared what the hell he said. Then he whispered, "Let' just say that I have my sources."

Flo jumped up, grabbed my hand and pulled me toward the door. "We'll call you."

A couple hours later, this time after driving through a herd of stampeding elephants, Flo started to blubber when she spotted Ettamae walking through the Customs door.

Like Fergus had told us on the phone, the kid was not a kid anymore. She was a sharp-looking teenybopper with hips, boobs, and a fancy-combed crop of red hair and the color didn't come from a bottle.

After Flo stopped hugging the kid, I put my arm around her shoulders and said, "Kid, are you tired from the long trip?"

"Bear, don't call me kid anymore. While I was living with Fiona, she gave me a Gallic name, Kyla. I looked it up and it means lovely. I liked the name because no one ever called me lovely before. If you don't mind, please call me Kyla from now on."

71

She was right on when she told me not to call her a kid anymore, but a new name? I just put it off to being a loony teenage broad. "Okay. Kyla, like I asked before, are you pooped-out from the trip?"

Kyla jumped when some funny music came out of her purse. "Excuse me, that's my phone." She pulled out a sharp lookin' iPhone and said, "Hello . . . Yes, Frank. Bear and Flo met me at the airport. Thanks for the call, Bye."

I said, "Was that Frank Bramble?"

"It was." Kyla dropped the phone back into her purse.

Flo said, "The next time he calls you, let me say hi."

I said, "Cool lookin' phone. Last I checked, they cost a bunch."

"Bear, when you and Flo were in Scotland, you gave Frank an iMac. Now he has a laptop, an iPad, and an iPhone. He's turned into the Macman of Pitlochry. Before I left, Frank gave me this brand new iPhone 6. I figured out how to do most everything during the long flight."

I smiled. Frank Bramble was one cool old dude. "Now, back to my question. Are you pooped after the long flight?"

"A little. Why?"

Flo joined in. "Because we need to talk with a man about a murder before we head back to our hotel."

The Kid's . . . whoops . . . Kyla's face lit up

when she heard Flo say murder and hotel.

Kyla said, "Are you kidding me? You're working on a new murder case? Is that why you picked me up in San Francisco instead of Reno? Who's the guy? Did he shoot the victim with a gun or stab him with a knife? Are we staying in a fancy San Francisco hotel? Tell me everything."

While Kyla was rattling on, we'd been standing by the doors that headed back to the customs place, the spot where those federal, cop-like, dudes paw through your luggage to make sure you're not trying to smuggle some diamonds inside your dirty underwear and I noticed one of those federal cops was giving me the stink-eye.

I said, "Cool it. There's a federal fuzz giving us the once over. We'll tell you all about it when I've found our truck in that giant parking lot."

Kyla glanced at me, then at Flo, and then giggled again like the Ettamae I remembered. "Wow, until this instant I didn't realize how boring my life was in Scotland." She dropped her carry-on and held out her arms. "Come on. It's time for a welcome home hug from my family!"

I knew it. Now we're a family. Shit!

CHAPTER ELEVEN

Pinky-Philadelphia, Pennsylvania

I exited the elevator and entered the lobby at 9:07 am—seven minutes late for my meeting with Joey—the specifically timed delay I purposely place into the initial meetings of all my underlings, just to remind the new employee I am the boss.

Joey stood by the desk wearing a worried expression, as if his standing alone in the lobby was his fault. The man's anxiety visibly eased the moment he spotted me.

Joey rushed toward me. "Pinky, for a second there I thought I'd screwed up the time."

"Not to worry, my good man. Here are my car keys. The vehicle is parked in the garage below. Drive my rental to the front door and let the doorman know you have arrived. " As Joey took the keys I continued, "And as to your compensation, I will pay you the agreed upon twenty-five dollars per hour each day once you return me to this hotel. Is that a satisfactory arrangement for you?"

"That's perfect. I can really use the ready dough. And you'll pay me like that everyday I drive you?"

"You are correct, my boy."

He turned and disappeared into an elevator. Moments later, Joey picked me up and drove toward the bridge that crossed the Delaware River. After crossing the river, Joey drove for a few more moments before he pulled the Mercedes over to the side of the road, along a row of housing that I felt symbolized a financially successful slum lord's neighborhood.

"Okay, Pinky, we're in Camden. What's next?"

"Joey, first I need to locate a specific female. Once you find her address, I need to meet, and talk in private, with the aforementioned personage. The woman I seek goes by the name of Adelaide Carlucci."

The blood from Joey's face drained. His head fell forward and his forehead crashed into the steering wheel as he mumbled, "Jesus, I shudda' known. That's why you gave me twenty-five instead of twenty."

Joey continued to bang his head against the steering wheel, moaning quietly.

I said, "Your extreme reaction to her name informs me that I have missed something important. What is there about the name Carlucci?"

He turned his head and I could see the red bruise on his forehead caused by his self-punishment. "You don't know, do you?" Before I could respond, he said, "The Carlucci family controls everything this side of the river and a few parts of Philly. Big Julie is the Don. He has three kids. Big Julie Junior, known as Junior, Rocco, and his daughter, Adelaide."

As Joey described the Carlucci family in his ominous tone, I began to realize that my situation could be precarious. "Joey, are you trying to say that this Big Julie character could be dangerous?"

"It depends on what you want to talk to his one-and-only daughter about."

"I am sorry, but attorney/client privilege prevents me from divulging that sort of information."

"Huh?"

"What I say to Adelaide will remain between the two of us."

"Not if Big Julie has anything to do with it. Pinky, you don't have a clue who Big Julie is. Watch my lips. The only way for you to talk to Adelaide is through Big Julie."

I glanced out the windows of the car at my immediate surroundings. As Joey had informed me, Camden was a dump. I desperately needed to get out of this shantytown and fly to San Francisco, to my suite at the Hotel Drisco where I woke each morning to a stunning view of the city of San Francisco.

My dismal situation forced me to throw caution to the winds. "Joey, after you return me to my hotel, do what you feel necessary to set up a meeting with Big Julie. Tell him I have traveled thousands of miles as an emissary to discuss a bright and glorious future for his daughter, Adelaide Carlucci."

"Pinky, I'll do what you want, but just in case something goes wrong—you never know what a guy like Big Julie might do—from now on, every day I drive your car, you've got to pay me fifty clams an hour—up front—or you get yourself another sucker!"

I said, "But that is twice the amount we had agreed upon. My good man, what you are suggesting is nothing short of highway robbery."

"Sorry, but once Big Julie got into this deal my price doubled."

"And why do you require that I pay you up front?"

"Pinky, people have been known to go to Big Julie's place and never come back."

"Never? My good man, stop beating around the bush. Are you telling me that Adelaide Carlucci's father, Big Julie, could do me some harm?"

"It's been known to happen."

CHAPTER TWELVE

Bear-San Francisco, California

While I coughed up another forty bucks to get my truck out of the airport parking lot, Flo called Erik Rundstrom, got his address, keyed it into her phone and let the phone babe tell me when to turn left and right until we found Rundstrom's apartment. Actually, finding his place was a piece of cake compared to finding a spot on the street to park my truck.

The apartment was one of those Frisco buildings. Old, but still cool looking. On the way up the stairs to the third floor, I said, "Kyla, me and Flo aren't suppose to bring you along so pretend you're not here, right?"

Kyla looked at me, then glanced at Flo.

Flo nodded and the red-haired teen said, "Right."

So that's the way it's going to be! Now I've got to go through Flo, and Kyla, when I want to suck down a cold one, watch a baseball game on TV, or do all the other crap I like to do.

The stairs stopped at the third floor and there were two doors. Flo found the right one and knocked. It opened and a young good lookin' dude peeked out and said, "I'll bet you're Flo, Bear, and . . . ?"

I pushed my way past him and said, "Her name is Kyla, and as far as you're concerned, she's not here."

The dude said, "I see, I think. Please sit down. Can I get anyone a glass of wine?" His eyes landed on Kyla, "Or water?"

Before Flo could answer, I said, "Erik, we're here to get your side of what went down before that Rand dude bought the farm."

He said, "Sorry, I don't understand."

"Mr. Rundstrom," said Flo after she shot me one of her nastiest looks, "What Bear tried to say was please tell us what happened the night Simon Rand died during the award dinner. It is our understanding that you were involved with preparing some of the food."

"I'd be happy to tell you what I know, but I still don't understand. Rand died of a heart attack." He looked at Flo, then me, and said, "Do you know something I don't?"

The dude didn't look like he was trying to shine us on, so I said, "The police autopsy showed Rand didn't kick the bucket from a heart attack. They think someone poisoned him and they're running some tests to find out what poison was used. Look, Erik, we're on your side, but you've got to come clean about the night Rand keeled over. What were you doing before the dude hit the floor?"

Flo said, "Erik, before you answer, it's been a long day. Could I use your bathroom?"

"Of course. Go through the kitchen and down the hall."

"Thank you. Kyla, do you want to join me?"

"Sure."

After Flo and Kyla disappeared into the kitchen, Erik said, "Frankly, I don't like your tone, or what you're insinuating."

"Dude, I don't give a damn if you like it or not. Clam up and listen to me. The cops have a dead man. Heart attack, no problem. Now they're pretty sure the dead dude was poisoned. Sooner or later they'll find out that Simon Rand killed your new restaurant with his chicken-shit review. All the cops have to do is add a dead Simon Rand with the fact that he did you dirt, and you were cooking the night he hit the deck, and they have a solid suspect for the guy who poisoned Rand. Got it now?"

"Jesus, I never thought, . . . hold on! Why are you on my side? Did my father hire you?"

"Got me. We work for Pinky Delmont. He's a sneaky little fart of a lawyer, but the last I looked, he's never lost a murder case. This time, 'cause we have some inside scoop on the Rand murder, Pinky's trying to get ahead of the game and keep you from being arrested for a murder you didn't do. Pinky's right isn't he? You didn't poison Rand, did you?"

"No, I didn't. Do the police really think I have something to do with Rand's death?"

"Now you've got it! Working in the kitchen gave you the opportunity to slip some bad stuff into his food. And because Rand wrote his nasty review of your restaurant, you could have a motive. All that's left is the means, like they'll find a half-empty can of rat poison in your apartment."

"But I—"

Flo marched in and said, "Kyla, stay here with Erik. Bear, come with me."

I said, "Come on, Babe, me and Erik are—"

Flo flashed me her nastiest glare. "Bear, when I say come with me, I mean come with me, now!"

She grabbed my arm and pulled me into the kitchen. I said, "What the hell are we doing in—"She held one finger to her lips.

I nodded and clammed up.

She said, "Two things seem out of place. First, there's a bra and panties hanging in the bathroom."

"So a broad lives here?"

"It looks like it. But that's not the most important thing." She walked me to the kitchen window and pointed at a bunch of little plants growing in a small redwood box sitting on the window sill. To me, they all looked the same.

I said, "So?"

Flo whispered, "I'm pretty sure the third plant, counting left to right, is Conium maculatum."

I whispered back, "What the hell is that?"

"Hemlock."

I shrugged again. "Is that bad?"

"It looks a little like parsley, right?"

"Babe, they all look like parsley to me."

For a second it looked like Flo wanted to bash me with a rolling pin that was laying on the counter, but then she calmed down. "If I wanted to kill someone, and I was cooking dinner for that person, I could slip some chopped up hemlock leaves into a salad, or a soup, or a entrée, and inside ten minutes, that person's heart rate would slow, followed by paralysis of the central nervous system, and death."

"Jesus, that fast?" I looked back at the pots of green on the window sill. "And our boy is growing that shit?"

"That's what it looks like."

"But didn't that Charlie dude say the cops don't know what kind of poison killed Rand?"

"That's true, but Pinky wanted us to keep this guy out of the hands of the cops."

"Okay, so what would Pinky do?"

Flo said, "If we were in Carson City, Pinky'd tell us to take Erik to his Tahoe Condo and hide him there."

"But we're not in Carson City, so I think Pinky'd tell us to get Erik out of this apartment and hide him somewhere in Frisco before the cops start knocking on his front door, right?"

"I agree. Okay, where do we hide him?"

"Hold on, before we worry about making him vanish, what do we need to do with the poison shit on the kitchen window sill?"

Flo said, "I checked and the planter box is screwed to the sill. I'm afraid that whatever we do would tip off the cops. They would see the screw holes and they would figure out Erik might be hiding something. And they might find some residue of Conium maculatum,"

I thought for a second, "So you're hoping the cops will think Erik was just growing different kinds parsley?"

"Chef's do that sort of thing so I think it's worth a try. Now what are we going to do with Erik?"

I said, "Babe, Frisco ain't my town, let's ask him."

We walked back into the living room and Erik was showing Kyla his collection of cookbooks.

I said, "Erik, Flo and me are pretty sure that the cops are on their way, right this minute, to arrest you for the murder of Rand."

Flo jumped in. "Erik, we're more than pretty sure. In case you don't know this, in this country you can't get out on bond with a first degree murder charge. Unless you want to spend the next year in jail, awaiting trial, throw a few days' worth of clothing and a toothbrush into a carry-on and come with us."

The dude suddenly looked like a trapped rabbit. His eyes darted between Kyla, me, and Flo. Kyla nodded and Erik disappeared into his bedroom. A few minutes later, we ran down the stairs and piled into my truck. While I wandered around the streets of Frisco, Flo asked Erik if he knew a low-key motel where he could spend the next couple of days under the radar.

Erik said, "I do. Bear, head toward the airport. I know a motel near there that'll work. Flo, give me your cell number, and after you drop me off, I'll call you once I get settled."

I said, "No good. The cops will check all your cell phone calls. Buy a cheap one, a burner you can throw away in a couple of days to make your calls."

Flo said, "And Erik, who belongs to the bra and panties hanging in your bathroom?"

"Oh, those belong to Laura. We lived together for awhile, but we had a big argument and she moved out last week. I guess she forgot them."

I said, "By the way, just in case the cops get you, you don't know our names, you've never seen us or talked to us, and we sure as hell didn't drive you to a motel, right?"

"Right! And thanks to all you wonderful people for trusting me. Bear, turn right; the motel is about two blocks away."

Flo said, "Erik, listen to me. We trust you, but I need to know why you are growing hemlock above your kitchen sink?"

He said, "Back in Sweden, my grandmother used tiny amounts of hemlock as a remedy for kidney and bladder problems. I guess I did the same because you never know when you might need a remedy like that."

Sounded like a load of bullshit to me.

"Bear, this is it."

I made a hard right and pulled into the motel parking lot.

Erik got out, and as he walked to the registration door, I couldn't stop wondering if we were doing the right thing. My head told me that this guy was growing a poison in his kitchen. But that was okay 'cause his grandma used the same stuff to help her pee. Go figure!

I thought me and Flo were doing exactly what Pinky told us to do, but if we're doing the right thing, why did I have a squirrelly feeling in the middle of my gut?

CHAPTER THIRTEEN

Pinky-Philadelphia, Pennsylvania

There was a time when I controlled every aspect of my life. Now, I had lost my way through no fault of my own!

All of my acquaintances would agree that I was an extremely intelligent man.

I had graduated at the top of my class at Hastings College of the Law.

I was the sole proprietor of the most successful legal practice in Northern Nevada.

I had reached the financial level where I required a Swiss wealth management team to monitor my extensive investments.

But once I summed up all of my outstanding achievements, one might wonder why I allowed a paid employee—a man whose educational background had groomed him for a career of part-time bartender and gay-club bouncer—a cretin who drove me through the mean streets of Camden—to command my daily activities.

I fully understood that, according to Joey Palumbo, my meeting with Big Julie Carlucci carried the distinct possibility of physical danger.

But I was a man who had faced danger before, and I had more to do with my valuable time than to waste it stagnating in a hotel room waiting for my phone to ring.

By the time the sun was setting, melancholy—a condition that occurs to those who spend their waking hours watching television in their hotel room—had nearly overwhelmed me.

Suddenly my room phone rang and shook me from my ennui. "Hello?"

"It's Joey."

"Who else would it be? Who else knows I am trapped in a Hilton Hotel in Philadelphia? My good man, if I am forced to watch one more rerun of the Oprah Show I could be ready to—"

"Hey, you're talking like your Jockies' are too tight, Pinky. Big Julie's out of town. I left a message for him to let me know when he gets back."

"And just when will that be?" I demanded.

"Dude, it ain't my fault. Big Julie goes where he wants, and comes back when he wants. I called you to see if you wanted me to drive you around Philly, to see the Liberty Bell, or any of that kind of tourist crap."

"And I suppose at our previously agreed upon rate of fifty dollars an hour, paid in advance?"

"Wow, you really are pissed off and here I thought all you left coast dudes are laid back."

I said, "I come from Carson City, Nevada not, as you incorrectly stated, the left coast."

"Geez, I thought you told me Frisco."

I said, "That was an inaccurate assumption on your part. Joey, are you avoiding my question concerning payment for a tour of Philadelphia?"

"Hey, I only charge when I'm driving on dangerous ground. My tourist services are free. Pinky, I take over the bar in thirty minutes. Come downstairs in an hour and I'll mix you up a gin and tonic that'll smooth all your ruffled feathers."

"I have to make a few phone calls and then I will take you up on that offer."

I hung up and immediately called my office.

An unknown male voice answered, "Ahh . . . law office."

"My God, who told you to answer my phone that way?"

"Ahh . . ."

I cried, "What is your name?"

"Ahh . . . Frank."

"Are you the young man that Loomer sent over to replace Lu?"

"Ahh . . . I guess."

"Do you know who I am?"

"Nope."

"My name is J. Pincus Delmont. Your superior in every way imaginable. Now do you know who I am?"

"I think you must be the Pinky Lu's been telling me about?"

I smiled. We were finally making progress.

"That is correct. The man who signs your paycheck. Now, back to your name. Your first name is Frank. Do you have a last name?"

"Yup. It's Wilcox."

"And a middle name?"

"Nope. Just an initial."

"And what is that initial?"

"M."

"Excellent. Now, Frank M. Wilcox, I need to speak with Lu."

"Sorry, Pinky, she's taking a pee."

My God, the man does not know how to answer the phone, and now he discusses a woman's bodily functions to a man he never met. "Frank, tell Lu to call me as soon as she returns to her desk."

"Okay."

The phone went dead.

I shuddered and considered my next move. I should call Bear to see what progress he had made, but after my conversation with the simpleminded Frank, I needed to converse with someone who had a reasonable grasp on reality. I called Charles and he answered on the first ring.

"Charles, is the team making headway?"

"Yes. We met earlier today. Bear and Flo are very likely talking to Erik as we speak. Pinky, my inside contact tells me that we should know the kind of poison that was used to kill Rand by lunch time tomorrow."

"That is good. I will talk with—"

My cell bleeped, indicating another call.

"Charles, I have another call. Call me once you get the toxicology results. Goodbye."

I pushed a button and Lu was on my line.

"Pinky, what do you need?"

"Lu, have you trained Frank on how to answer the office phone?"

"I have, but he's a little slow picking up some of the office procedures."

"Put him on the line. After I have finished with him, he will hand you the phone. Have I made myself clear?"

"Yes, but Pinky, Frank's trying the best he can, but—"

"Lu, hand him the phone."

Frank said, "Yup."

"Frank M. Wilcox, you are fired. I will instruct Lu to give you two weeks' severance pay."

"But—"

"Frank, now hand the phone back to Lu."

Lu said, "Pinky, Frank looks like he's about to burst into tears."

"That is very likely because I just fired him. Cut him a check for the hours he worked plus two weeks' severance pay. Then call Louis Loomer and tell him to send you a replacement who is capable of filling your shoes while you are on maternity leave. Lu, that is my criteria for your replacement, and while I am absent, I am counting on you to winnow out anyone who does not meet my standards."

My cell bleeped again.

"Lu, I have another call. Are we together on this?"

"I'll take care of the Frank situation and call Loomer."

I pushed the button and the voice of Florence Sunderlund scraped against my eardrums.

"Pinky, we've got your man in a good place."

"Florence, what exactly do you mean by a good place?"

"Oh, and we picked up Kyla at the airport. You won't believe how much she's grown. She's at least six inches taller and—"

"Woman, cease your babbling. Kyla? Just who are you talking about?"

"I'm sorry. Kyla's just Ettamae with a new Gaelic name. But back to Erik. First, we didn't feel comfortable leaving him in his apartment so we asked ourselves what would Pinky do? Bear wanted to drive him up to your condo at Tahoe, but I knew that was too far, so we—"

"Do not say another word concerning the present whereabouts of Erik Rundstrom. The less I know, the better. But why did you feel the need to move him?"

"That's the sticky part. On Erik's kitchen windowsill there was a little planter box and inside that box were some fresh herbs. In the middle of the herbs there is a plant that I'd bet everything I own is hemlock."

This was not good. "Florence, why do you think yourself capable of identifying Conium maculatum in it's natural state?"

"I know exactly what I am talking about. In a pre-med class, a class I took before I changed my major, I learned that Conium comes from the hemlock plant and many people use it in a variety of ways within the medical community. It has always been considered to be quite useful and effective as a proven homeopathic remedy."

I said, "And it can also kill a human inside an hour. A few minutes ago I talked with Charles and he told me that the results of the toxicology tests were due soon. Keep our man where he is until then. What sort of a man is Erik?"

"Late twenties. Good looking. Personable. In fact, I think Kyla is smitten."

I tried to recall a mental image of Ettamae, the pre-Kyla, and failed. "Florence, I am positive we will all be back in Carson City in a matter of days. In fact, I hope to be in San Francisco very soon."

She said, "If you're right about joining us soon in San Francisco, get ready for a brawl. Bear, Kyla, and I are not leaving our suite at The Hotel Drisco without a fight."

Before I could respond to her threat, my phone beeped again.

Without saying goodbye, I pushed the button.

"Pinky, Louis Loomer here. Lu just called me and—"

"Loomer, I am fed up with the uneducated and inadequate replacement staff you continue to send over to my office. If you cannot supply me with a satisfactory legal secretary, I will once and forevermore, sever our business relationship. Do you understand me?"

"I do. Pinky, I took a chance on sending you Frank. He's the son of my wife's cousin and I thought that he'd—"

"Now and forevermore. Goodbye."

I shut my phone down, slipped the device into my jacket pocket and checked my watch. Ah, my man was now on duty at the bar. This afternoon turned out to be very productive.

A justifiable firing got my juices flowing.

My client was safely tucked away.

And I absolutely savored the way that wonderfully rhetorical phrase, forevermore, just flowed past my lips.

My good man, you have just earned yourself two of Joey's special gin and tonics!

CHAPTER FOURTEEN

Bear-San Francisco, California

"Bear?"

"Grumphhh."

"Bear, wake up."

"Huh?"

"Just look at that view of San Francisco. You'll never see anything like that in Carson City."

I opened a squinty eye and took a peek. Lots of buildings trees, and other stuff. I rolled over and my head bumped into one of Flo's two assets. "Babe, I like what I'm lookin' at right now."

"Hush. I think San Francisco's a treasure."

"Right." I jumped out of bed. "Got to hit the john."

When I came out of the fancy can, I got that squirrelly feeling in my gut again and it wasn't from something I ate last night. I said, "Babe, you think Pinky will be cool with us sticking Erik in that motel yesterday?"

Flo said, "After you fell asleep watching TV, I called and told him we had his man in a good place. Then I let him know that we picked up Kyla at the airport."

"I'll bet he got all charged up about that. Did you tell him who in the hell Kyla is?"

"I did. Then I explained that I spotted hemlock in Erik's kitchen and he told me to keep Erik where he was until the cops release the toxicology report."

I said, "Okay, Charlie knows our cell number so while we wait for his call, let's nose around to see what we can find out about Erik and his now kaput restaurant."

Flo said, "Good idea. One of my college roommates used to date a guy who's now one of the restaurant critics at the *Chronicle*. Let me look up his number, give him a call, and see if he can open some doors."

An hour later, after a kick-ass breakfast at the Drisco and Flo's phone call to set up the meeting, I drove me, Flo, and Kyla to the apartment of a dude named Plácido Batista.

"And don't forget," Flo said. "No questions about poison."

She knocked and a dude invited us in. "Flo, it's been too many years. Do you ever hear from Trudy?"

"Not really. Once we graduated, she headed east and I stayed on the west coast. Plácido, I'd like you to meet Bear and Kyla. She's our—"

I said, "Pain in the butt, but she's a good kid."

Plácido said, "Flo, is she your—"

"No. We're her guardians."

The dude said, "Kyla, you're lucky to have

found people to take care of you. We live in a tough world. I know, because my parents were both killed in a car crash and I was lucky enough to be raised by my maternal grandmother. Now, Flo mentioned on the phone that you wanted to talk about Erik Rundstrom. I don't know how much I can help, but I'll do what I can."

Before I could open my mouth, Kyla pushed her way into the conversation. "Plácido, I was lucky like you. First my grandpa Ollie, then Flo and Bear, and back in Scotland, Fergus and Fiona. I also had a good friend named Henry Bramble. Henry is an old guy with a wonky eye, but that doesn't stop him from playing opera CDs all the time. Isn't there a famous opera singer with your first name?"

"Yes. His name is Plácido Domingo. He's getting up in years, but he remains the number-one tenor in the world. Now, can I get you something to drink: water, coffee, wine? I have—"

I said, "Okay. Enough pussy-footin' around. What can you tell us about Erik? Was he a really good cook? Why did his restaurant tank? Were you at the big dinner where Simon Rand bought the farm? Did you know that Erik was cooking at that big dinner?"

Plácido shook his head and smiled. "Flo, this friend of yours is relentless."

"That's why they call me Bear," I said. "How about some answers?"

Flo said, "Calm down and let the man talk."

The dude said, "Yes, Bear. Be calm and placid just like my name."

I sighed. "Okay. Let's take 'em one at a time. Was Erik a really good cook?"

"From my viewpoint, he was very good, but not yet great, like a Thomas Keller, or a Gary Danko. But we all need to remember that Erik was around thirty and it takes decades of experience for the world's greatest chefs to round into form."

I glanced at Flo and she gave me a tiny nod, so I said, "If the dude was that good, why did his restaurant go belly-up?"

"I reviewed two dinners at his place and gave each a good review with one caveat. The food was outstanding. The wine list was impeccable and reasonably priced, an impossible combination to find in San Francisco. The service was very good. But there were problems. The restaurant was located in the Mission District, on the edge of the gentrification of the area. Don't get me wrong. If you walked a block north, you felt safe. If you walked a block south, not so safe. There were some risks involved with going to Erik's restaurant. The closest parking was a block north and at night the patrons had to walk along poorly-lit streets sprinkled with a questionable crowd. In a few words, I'm positive that Erik's restaurant would have become a top spot in the city if it had been located in a better area."

Again, Flo nodded, so I said, "Were you at that

fancy dinner where Simon Rand bought the farm?"

Plácido glanced at Kyla, like he didn't want to talk about what happened in front of her.

I said, "Dude, you got a beer stuck in your fridge?"

He said, "I do. Let me—"

"How's about we let Flo and Kyla get my beer."

He nodded. The dude was sharp. "Good idea. Glad you thought of that, Bear."

The minute Flo and Kyla left the room, Plácido said, "Eight of us were sitting at the same table when Rand suddenly stood up so fast that his chair fell backward. He seemed to be choking, or having trouble breathing. Before anyone at the table could move, Rand crashed to the floor. My date that night was a fellow writer. She moved to Rand's side and said quietly, 'It looks like he's having a heart attack.' I pulled out my cell phone and dialed 911, while she loosened his tie and unbuttoned his dress shirt, but all she could do was try to make Rand comfortable. By the time the ambulance arrived, he was dead."

Flo and Kyla came back and Kyla handed me the beer. I took a big swig and said, "Do you know if Erik was cooking at that fancy dinner?"

"I heard that he was one of a half-dozen top chefs who were there that night. Add in the prep crew, I'd guess there were fourteen or fifteen folks who had their hands in food prep. Why do you ask?"

Flo's cell buzzed. "Hello . . . Yes . . . Oh, no.

That's not good. I'll call you back in a few minutes."

Ever since me and Flo got together in LA, I've worked a lot of hours trying to figure out her sometimes happy and sometimes pissed-off looks. Hell, there've been times when my babe stopped me in my tracks with a single nasty glare. But today was different. After she dropped her cell phone into her purse, She flashed me a new, never seen before look, that later she told me was her 'we're in deep shit' look.

Flo herded me and Kyla out the front door as she said, "Plácido, thank you for giving us some of your valuable insights into the restaurant world of San Francisco. I apologize, but an emergency has come up and we must leave."

I took a last swig and handed the empty bottle to the guy. "Thanks for the brew, dude."

Flo hustled us out of the apartment and into my truck.

"Okay, Babe. spill it. What the hell's goin' on?"

"The toxicology report showed Rand died of hemlock poisoning. I've got to call Charles back and tell him what we found in Erik's apartment."

Kyla said, "And are you going to tell Charles that me and you've stashed Erik in a seedy motel?"

Shit, not only could we be in trouble with the cops, but I forgot that Kyla knows everything we've done. "I say we pick up Erik and turn him over to Charlie."

Flo said, "I think that's our only way out of this

99

mess."

I drove south to the motel near the airport, and
while Kyla and I waited, Flo went to the office,
came out and walked up to Erik's door and knocked.
Then she knocked again and harder. Then she
walked back to the office. Flo was pale when she
climbed into the truck. "He's gone. According to the
man behind the desk, a cab picked him up about
two hours after he checked in."

Oh shit. Now we've got a runner!

I got out and walked into the office. "Dude, did
you know the cabbie that picked up our friend?"

"A picture of Benjamin Franklin might help me
recall his name."

I thought of giving him a shot in his schnoz, but
I needed info real fast and a bloody nose would slow
things down. I handed him a C-note, hoping that
Flo would get Pinky to give it back.

"The cabbie's name is Silas, and if he's not
carrying a fare, you'll find him sucking down a beer
at the bar around the corner."

CHAPTER FIFTEEN

Pinky-Philadelphia, Pennsylvania

The following day, the sky remained as gray as my mood while Joey and I visited all the obvious tourists sites in Philadelphia.

The day after that, during an on-and-off drizzle that interrupted the constant, and overwhelming humidity, I wandered aimlessly about one of the less obvious tourists locations. As a trickle of moisture slipped down the back of my neck, my patience ran out. I had spent enough of my valuable time regardless of the threat from Hook. I pulled out my cell from my jacket pocket, ready to place a call to Hook and tell him why I could not afford to waste another minute in Philadelphia, when my cell buzzed.

I answered and heard Bear yell, "From now on, no matter what happens to that Erik dude, just don't take it out on me and Flo. We did everything we were supposed to. It's just that . . ."

I sensed from Bear's tone that he felt like a teen who had been caught lighting up a cigarette behind the barn. His present quandary however, had allowed me to escape from the boredom of my present existence, so I was far from angry. In fact, Bear's point had reawakened my combative self. "Bear, I have no idea what you are babbling about. Slow down and explain to me why I should be angry with you and Florence."

Bear hesitated, then he blurted, "Boss, we're up to our chins in this big mess and I'm not sure—"

"My good man, I have admonished you more than once to stop calling me boss. Now that we have settled that item, explain as best you can using your limited vocabulary just what you define to be a 'big mess'."

"Do you remember that me and Flo sort of hid that Erik dude in a flea-bag motel?"

"Not really, but anything you two do would not surprise me."

Bear said, "Guess what? When we went back to pick him up, he'd vamoosed."

That was my error for sending a boy to do a man's job. "Do you have any idea where he is now?"

"Well, it's like this: Flo told me we should high-tail it back to his apartment pronto. When we got there we knocked, then laid on the doorbell button, but nobody answered. So I picked the lock."

I glanced at my car. Joey was sitting behind the wheel playing some sort of inane game on his iPad. I said to Bear, "I do not understand why you entered his apartment. Did you expect would Erik to return to his—"

"Boss, I'll hand the phone to Flo so you can ask

her. It was her idea to go back to the apartment."

I cried, "Bear, this is a direct order! Do not hand your phone to that woman! Now continue with your narrative."

"My what?"

I sighed. "Your story."

"Okay. I popped the door and Erik, along with the rest of his crap, I mean everything, shoes, socks, that Flo noticed when we were there before, were gone. Oh, Flo just told me to tell you that the toxysomething report said the dead dude died from hemlock."

Oh my God! My worst fears are coming true— this case might actually require me to earn my retainer. "Where are you now?"

"Flo figured that the cops would be heading to Erik's apartment so we hustled out of the place. Right now we're sitting in my truck about a half a block away. Boss, what do we do next?"

Once the police searched Erik's apartment, in addition to finding the abode empty, they would sooner or later discover residue of the hemlock that Erik grew in his kitchen. "Go back to the Drisco and I will call you."

"Speaking of the Drisco, that's a really cool place. Flo told me to tell you—"

"And I told you to hang up and return to the hotel! I will call Charles and get back to you inside of an hour to give you further instructions."

"Gotcha, boss."

I pushed a couple of buttons and Charles answered on the second ring.

"Pinky, I have the results of the—"

"I know, hemlock poisoning. What you are not aware of is that Erik Rundstrom has vanished."

"Why would he do that?"

With each passing day it became more and more obvious to me why I graduated a step ahead of Charles. "Possibly because he left some very incriminating evidence in his kitchen."

I heard Charles suck in a gulp of air. "Pinky, before you say anything more, you are still my attorney of record?"

"That is correct. Now that we have re-established our attorney/client privilege, I will inform you that my investigators discovered that Erik was growing hemlock in a pot on his kitchen windowsill."

Charles sighed.

I continued, "And Erik has vacated his domicile along with all his clothing."

"Oh my God! Did we bet on the wrong horse?"

I said, "Not at all. My team will track down and return Erik Rundstrom to Northern California while you and I construct the Rundstrom defense strategy in San Francisco."

"When can we start?"

I said, "Patience, my good man, patience. As soon as I have completed my task here, I will fly to San Francisco."

"Pinky, where are you?"

"I am sorry, Charles, but the where and why of my present location is part of another attorney/client privilege."

I noticed Joey running toward me and waving a cell phone in his hand.

Charles said, "Pinky, we need—"

The smile on Joey's face told me that he had finally reached my quarry.

"Goodbye, Charles."

Joey handed me his cell phone and whispered, "It's Big Julie."

I took the phone and said, "Good afternoon. My name is J. Pincus Del—"

"Are you the mouthpiece who wanted to talk to me?"

"I am and the sooner the—"

"Talk about what?"

The man has some of the worst phone manners I have ever experienced. I continued, "Mr. Carlucci, as I attempted to say, I represent a gentleman from another state who seeks to obtain your blessing concerning the marriage of your daughter, Adelaide Carlucci, and my client."

"Counselor, give the phone back to Joey."

I said, "But—"

"Just like all the other ambulance chasers. Have you got bad ears 'cause you've been sitting too close to the sirens?"

I said, "No, sir."

I handed the cell back to Joey and watched his expression as he said, "Ah . . . uh, uh . . . uh, uh . . . uh, uh. Got it."

Joey slipped his cell into his pocket and jumped up and down. "You did great, Pinky. We meet in an hour at Big Julie's spread in Cherry Hill. Wow, I never thought that me, Joey Palumbo, would ever walk through the front door of the home of the big man."

I frowned. "Excuse me, but I was under the impression that Adelaide Carlucci lived in Camden."

"Like I told you before, nobody who's anybody lives in Camden. Big Julie's house is in Cherry Hill. You know, the kinda place with the best schools in the state, golf courses with private country clubs, expensive malls, and giant houses. Cherry Hill is where Big Julie's family lives, not Camden."

I said, "Do you have any idea how long the meeting will last?"

"Sometimes Big Julie makes real fast decisions. Like bang, bang, the meeting's over real quick. Other times he moves slower. Sorta like he plants stuff in the ground and you've got to wait around a long time to see if it grows. You never know about a meeting with him. He's been known to go either way."

CHAPTER SIXTEEN

Bear-San Francisco, California

Once me, Flo and Kyla got back to the Drisco, both of the broads sprinted for the john while I got myself a cold brew.

Half way through the bottle, Pinky called.

"Put this call on speaker phone. Now, is Florence there?"

I pushed the button and said, "She's in the can but—"

Flo walked in and said, "I'm here. What's going on?"

Pinky said, "I have new instructions for team Delmont. First, you did the right thing moving Erik to a safe place. Second, you totally failed me when you allowed him to escape. Third—"

I said, "Hey, it's not like we forgot to tie him up. The dude scammed us."

"Bear, do not interrupt me while I am providing you with the latest directions to the team. Third, you are to follow Erik's trail, find him, and then bring him back to San Francisco."

I said, "Pinky, that dude could have gone to South America, or—"

Pinky said, "I am fully aware of how many places a person might travel in this large world. My guess is that Erik will go to the country of his birth, Sweden, but one never knows where a man on the run will end up. Florence, I am putting you in charge of talking with Charles, perhaps a conference call with Charles and Erik's father, to narrow the search. Oh, due to potential legal and ethical ramifications, from this point on, do not use Erik's name when you are talking with Charles on the phone. I have to go now. Keep me informed of your progress. Goodbye."

Kyla walked in carrying a bowl of chips and another filled with nuts to chew on. Like I said, this Drisco joint knows how to take care of their people. Our rooms had all kinds of free stuff—chips, fruit, beer, and wine.

Kyla stood there, face all scrunched up, like she had something important to say.

I said, "Go ahead, Kyla, spit it out."

"Bear, Flo, now that I've left Scotland and am back here with you, going by the Gaelic name seems kinda stupid. My name is Ettamae and I'd appreciate it if you'd call me Ettamae from now on."

Flo put her arm around the kid's shoulder and said, "What you did was not stupid. Your name will be Ettamae from now on." She flashed me her nastiest stink eye and said, "And Bear agrees, right?"

I said, "Got it." Like I really gave a damn if she

called herself Kyla, Ettamae, or the Queen of England. She'll always be the Kid to me.

I took a long swig of beer while Flo poured herself a glass of white wine and called Charlie on my cell.

"Charles, I have you on the speaker phone. With me are Bear and Ettamae. Pinky asked me to call you. First, he suggested we not use any real names over the phone. I suggest we call our client the man in question. If you agree, give us a guess where he might go."

He said, "I don't know exactly, but I just hung up with the man in question's father and he told me that he's pretty sure that you know who is on his way to Stockholm, Sweden."

I said, "Hey, I don't get all this you-know-who bull. What I need to know is why would the dude pick that one place when he could go anywhere in the world?"

Charlie said, "Many Swedes have summer homes located on the hundreds of islands that make up the Stockholm archipelago."

I said, "So your guess is as good, or bad, as any other dude's guess."

"Not totally," said Charlie. "I did some checking with a friend at SAS. Yesterday, the man in question bought a ticket on the late afternoon flight to Copenhagen, Denmark."

Ettamae said, "Why not fly directly to Stockholm?"

I snapped, "Hold it down, Ettamae. You eat those chips. Me and Flo are doing the heavy lifting on this case."

Charlie said, "Bear, I didn't recognize that earlier voice. Who asked that question?"

I glanced at Ettamae and frowned. Flo flashed her butt-out glare, and said, "That was Ettamae," Then she winked at Kyla. "She's the investigator who just flew in from Scotland. Charles, you'll get used to hearing her voice."

"Welcome aboard, Ettamae. To answer your previous question, no airline has a direct nonstop flight from San Francisco to Stockholm."

Ettamae said, "So as we speak, the man in question could be sitting at a coffee house in Copenhagen."

"You've assimilated the facts of this case quickly," said Charlie. "Yes, he could be in Copenhagen, but Stockholm is a day's drive by car, or the man in question could have flown to Stockholm in an hour."

I said, "Or the dude in question could have caught a flight to Istanbul."

He said, "True, but his father is positive that the man in question is on his way to Stockholm."

Flo said, "Charles, we'll fly to Copenhagen, and one way or another, pick up the man in question's trail. Once we find him, Bear and I will convince him that a return to San Francisco is in his best interests. Once we reach SFO, we'll turn the man in question over to you."

Charlie said, "Sounds good to me. Good luck, you three."

Flo dumped the call to Charlie and her eyes lit up like a Christmas tree. "Copenhagen is one of those cities I have on my bucket list."

I pounded down my second beer. "I'm not sure why the dude vamoosed to Copenwagen."

"Bear, the name of the city is Copen*hagen*," said Ettamae.

"Okay, but I still don't know why he'd go to that town with a stupid name."

Flo handed me another beer as Ettamae said, "The week before I left Scotland, we studied Denmark at school as part of a Geography lesson. It's a very interesting country. Flo, I'm sure you're aware that Copenhagen is the capital of Denmark. The country has a population between five and six million. One additional interesting point. Denmark's citizens are the happiest in the world according to a survey prepared by the UN in 2013. I'm overjoyed that we are going to Copenhagen."

I said, "Ettamae, were not flying to Copenwagon to study why they're so damn happy. We're going there to find the dude in questio . . . Shit, Erik Rundstrom, hog-tie him, drag him onto a plane and bring him back to San Francisco."

"She understands all of that," said Flo. "And Copenhagen presents us with an opportunity to start teaching Ettamae how to become one of

Pinky's investigators. Just like you helped me." Running her fingers through my hair, Flo said, "Bear, sit down, put your feet up, and watch a baseball game. I'll call Charles back to see if his friend at SAS can help us make reservations for three business class seats to Copenhagen."

Shit, Ettamae was a short hop from being a teenybopper and I'm suppose to train this babe-in-waiting how to be an investigator for Pinky? But I could see that the two babes had me outnumbered. I sat down, took my shoes off and took a swig of my beer. I grabbed the remote and turned the TV on. Two button pushes later got me an Oakland A's and Chicago White Sox game. It wasn't my Boston Red Sox playing the damn Yankees, but watching a baseball game with a beer in hand beats the hell out of doing nothing.

"Bear," Ettamae called. "Come here and look!"

I jumped off the couch and ran toward her. "What's wrong?"

"Look out the window. This morning we could see the city. Now, in the afternoon, most everything's gone."

"Jesus, that's just the fog pouring into the bay. Didn't they have any fog in Scotland?"

Flo rushed up and said, "Who cares about some fog? I just got off the phone and we have only two and a half hours to catch a plane to Copenhagen."

Ettamae yelled, "Yippee!"

I said, "Yippee my ass. That means we've got to

pack, drive back to SFO, and find a place to stick my truck. How long are we going to be gone?"

"Got me," said Flo. "Sweden's a big place."

Ettamae giggled. "And Copenhagen isn't even in Sweden so I'd think about a long term parking lot."

Jesus, a giggling teenybopper. I growled, "Don't forget, we're on the clock tracking a killer. A dude who poisoned another dude. This ain't a vacation."

Flo said, "She knows that, and she, like it or not, was right about suggesting a long-term parking lot."

As I ran to the bedroom, I yelled, "Okay, let's get this operation in gear. We'll pack and be in my truck in ten minutes." I knew that with only two pair of Levis, six skivvies and socks, and a few T-shirts I'd be there first. "So the last one to climb into the truck has to buy me a beer at the first bar we hit at SFO, and with Flo stuck trying to figure out how to stuff half her closet into a suitcase, Ettamae hasn't got a thing to worry about."

CHAPTER SEVENTEEN

Pinky-Philadelphia, Pennsylvania

Joey's assessment of Camden's physical condition turned out to be one hundred percent correct.

As he steered my Mercedes through the wreckage of what once looked to be a prosperous municipality, Joey said, "I know it's hard to believe, but Camden used to be a nice place to live. It was a town where a factory worker could find a good paying job, buy a house, and raise a family. In the old days there were lots of big companies along the Delaware River—Like RCA, Campbell Soup, and New York Shipbuilding. Hell, New York Shipbuilding alone had 30,000 workers and was the biggest shipyard in the world in the 40's. Pinky, in Camden's heyday, damn near every man in town worked at one of those places, but by the 70's, the factories were closing down and the town started to go south. Some people in Camden are trying to rebuild the town, but the police department and city government keep hosing things up."

The Mercedes accelerated past an official-looking building as Joey continued. "A couple of years ago, in that courthouse building on the right, a bucketful of cops were convicted of taking bribes. Hey, I almost forgot, you probably read about it on the West coast. The cop's payola scam ended up with a hundred and eighty-five criminal cases being dumped and three and a half million bucks paid to nearly a hundred bastards who'd been screwed over by the fuzz. I forget, you're a lawyer. You'd be happy as a clam at high tide to get your crook off that easy."

Joey's callous comment struck me to my ethical core, but considering the source, I made light of his banter. "My good man, judging from the fact that Camden annually ranks as a city with the highest crime rate in the country, I cannot imagine that the jail cells remained empty very long."

"You've got it, Pinky. That's why you're the big time lawyer and I'm just a bartender."

Joey's comment said it all, so I sat back and enjoyed the ride.

As we eventually broke away from the slums of Camden, a municipality that begged for a total redevelopment project, Joey said, "Okay, we've just entered Cherry Hill."

I watched a well-manicured housing development, a prosperous shopping mall, and a beautiful high school named Cherry Hill West pass by my window.

As the educational facility disappeared from my view, Joey said, "Nice school, right? I'll bet you didn't know that from 2005 to 2012, the Camden school system spent more money and got such crappy results that the state of New Jersey took it over."

I said, "Joey, as a highly successful attorney, I abhor apocryphal tales. Frankly, your latest anecdote is a little hard to believe."

"Pinky, I may look stupid, but numbers are my thing. In 2012, after spending more per student on education than any other state, less than one percent, a miserable .0034 to be exact, of the Camden students takin' the SAT scored more than 1550 points. Compare that to the rest of the nation where 43% of the students who took the SAT scored more than 1550."

I said, "Assuming your data are correct, I agree with your assessment and once I have completed my talk with Big Julie, I will do my best to avoid returning to Camden, or any other part of New Jersey."

The Mercedes slowed. "Hey, here we are. Were at Big Julie's driveway." Joey turned right onto a drive that disappeared into a heavily wooded area. About a hundred feet into the forest, the car reached a clearing in the trees where we encountered a six-foot-five, three-hundred-pound man who stood next to a heavy, steel gate.

He moved his imposing girth to the driver's side of the Mercedes, tapped his heavy fist on the glass and said, "What'd youse guys want?"

Joey swallowed hard and said, "We have a meeting with Big Julie."

The monster man pulled out his cell and made a call. After two head nods and a 'gotcha', He said, "Are you Joey Palumbo and a shyster named Delmont?"

We both nodded vigorously.

The hulk pulled out what looked to be a second cell phone, but it wasn't a phone, it was a remote. A few seconds later, the steel gate slowly rolled from left to right. As Joey drove past the entrance, I gave the gate a quick glance and it looked strong enough to withstand a direct hit by an armored vehicle. Joey parked by the front door. I got out and immediately took notice that Big Julie's home looked similar to a Best Western Motel—a two-story L-shaped brick structure with a black, slate-tiled mansard roof. All that seemed to be missing was a large sign that declared free HBO, continental breakfast, and WIFI. It was obvious to me that Big Julie lived big, but it was just as obvious that his sense of good taste was in small supply.

Joey pressed the door bell and a moment later a second very large man, perhaps the twin of the guard at the gate, waved us into a vestibule.

Once there, the two of us were guided through a metal detector and then professionally patted down.

Finally proved weapon-free, the keeper of the house took us through a door and into a large library-like room. The walls were covered with books, none of which looked as if they had felt the warmth of a hand for decades. Sitting at the far end of the room, behind a massive desk, sat the man I assumed to be Big Julie.

The keeper shuffled us closer to the desk.

Seated, Big Julie was not as large as I had expected him to be. Easily under six feet tall, and perhaps topping out at one hundred and sixty pounds, I came to the quick conclusion that his nickname, Big, had to do with power rather than stature.

The man behind the desk continued to read a paper that he held in one hand, a common practice used by people in power to silently establish who is in control. A technique I use often.

I was staring at his silver-gray hair, when suddenly, as if he just realized we had been standing no more than five feet from him for the past minute, the man said, "Hey, whatcha think about backing a new joint in Vegas? Like, how big a risk can there be?"

I was not sure I heard his question correctly. By 'joint' did he mean a new hotel? And why would he ask me? With some trepidation, I said, "Mr. Carlucci, perhaps you have me confused with an accountant. I am here today to talk with you about your daughter's hand in—"

"Shyster, *Ma, che sei grullo?*"

Joey whispered, "Roughly translated that

means just how dumb are you?"

Big Julie hushed Joey with the wave of his hand as he shifted his body around in the oversized black leather chair that had to have set him back at least five grand. "Any smart-ass lawyer in a fancy suit can answer my casino investment question. Are you legit?"

Before I could inform him that I hire Swiss bankers to provide me with the type of investment advice he was seeking, he continued, "Watch my lips. Is a casino on the Vegas strip still a good bet? I know we can't skim as much as we used to, but the odds still favor the house, and with the carloads of suckers that head into that neon slum every day, I want to know, is backing a new Vegas joint a good deal?"

I remained mute, fearing that an incorrect answer might have life-threatening consequences.

Joey, bless him, pulled the cotton out of his mouth and said, "Mr. Carlucci, does your investment opportunity include a hotel?"

Carlucci's cold eyes finally shifted off me and landed on Joey. "Yah, a hotel and casino. Why?"

"I saw a story on 20-20 the other night that Vegas hotels with giant pools, huge sun decks, and a golf course, are making big bucks 'cause they stick the suckers with a heavy resort fee even if they don't swim, lay around and tan, or play that stupid game."

Carlucci gave Joey the slightest nod then

turned his stare on me. "There, that's what I was lookin' for, a man who showed me some balls. A man who's not afraid to answer a simple question."

Carlucci turned his chair so most of his back showed and picked up the same sheet he had been studying when we entered. It was as if our interview had been concluded. I glanced at Joey. He tilted his head toward the door, and said, "Thank you, Mr. Carlucci, for taking a few minutes out of your busy schedule to see us."

Wait a minute! That was that? A week of my valuable time and energy down the drain without any resolution? I think not! Joey's discussion with Big Julie may have come to an end, but not mine!

I took a half step closer to Carlucci's desk and said, "Mr. Carlucci, please bear with me. I have traveled thousands of miles to represent a highly respected magistrate from the great state of Nevada, a man who wants to marry your daughter, Adelaide. I apologize that I was unable to answer your investment question, but I loathe people, and that would include me, who attempt to answer questions beyond their realms of expertise."

Carlucci's dark eyes grew darker as he growled, "Shyster, don't come an inch closer. Not if you want to keep breathing."

I froze, his words hitting me like the wind of death.

He continued, "Lift your eyes and look over the top of my head. Can you spot that little slot in the wall above the picture?"

"I do."

"Behind that slot there's a man who monitors all my meetings and he's been told to deposit a slug just above the nose of anyone who gets any closer. *Capiche?*"

I stepped back. "I understand." I took a big breath and continued, "Now, can we talk about your daughter?"

"Counselor, that took real balls. Like I said before, I like that in a guy. We'll talk, but first . . ." He grabbed his phone, pushed a button, and said, "Adelaide, get your butt into my office." He slammed the phone down, smiled, and said, "Joey, counselor, how about a cold beer while we wait for Adelaide."

Joey said, "Sure."

Not sure how far to push my advantage, I threw caution to the wind and said, "I would rather have a glass of a decent cabernet sauvignon."

Carlucci chuckled. "Like I said before, you've got some big ones. We've got some great Italian reds, but none of that French cabernet crap you asked for."

I glanced at my watch. "A bold Amarone would fit perfectly as an afternoon aperitif."

Carlucci pushed another button on his phone. "Bring me a bottle of my best Amarone with some gorgonzola and dried figs. He laughed, "Thanks, Joey. You brought me a man who knows his Italian wines, and from now on, I'm going to call him my west coast *consigliere*."

I said, "Mr. Carlucci, your selection of Amarone paired with gorgonzola and dried figs informs me that you are a true connoisseur. I can tell that you are a man who has excellent taste."

A moment later the door opened and a man walked in with a tray that contained a bottle of wine, glasses, some cheese, and a bowl of dried figs. Before the man finished opening the bottle, a striking, perfectly formed female, with startling blond hair entered Carlucci's office.

The manservant poured four glasses and handed one to Carlucci, then Adelaide, then me, and finally to Joey, whose stature in Carlucci's eyes had risen, but not quite as high as Carlucci's new *consigliere*.

We all raised our glasses, although I detected that Adelaide's heart did not seem to be totally in the spirit of the moment. Carlucci threw his wine down his throat as if he were a dog inhaling a bowl of fresh meat, and said, "*Per cent'anni!*"

I took a sip and held the bold wine on my tongue for a moment. The Amarone was lush and complex with a Port-like texture along with a faint hint of mocha. I said, "And a hundred years of luck to you, Mr. Carlucci. Now, can we discuss the future of your lovely daughter, Adelaide?"

"*Consigliere*, now that we are *intimo amigo*, you can drop the Mr. Carlucci and call me Big Julie."

Joey pointed at me and said, "And his moniker is Pinky."

Big Julie burst into laughter. "A *consigliere* named Pinky. That won't do. Joey, zip your lip on that Pinky crap." Carlucci flashed me his cold, hard stare "Give me your real name. Come on, spit it out."

I said, "J. Pincus Delmont."

"That's it. *Consigliere* Delmont. Now everybody, and that includes you, Adelaide, sit down. The *consigliere* wants to talk about you."

This was my moment. Just like all of my closing arguments at the conclusion of a murder trial, this was my chance to sway the jury. Win this and this miserable trip east will be flushed away. Screw this up, or piss Big Julie off, and I might have one of those 'fatal accidents' on the way back to my hotel. As Joey had stated so well, those sorts of conclusions to Big Julie's meetings had been known to happen.

I set my glass down and took a step away from the desk.

"Big Julie, all fathers want to see their daughter's settle down with a good man, have babies, and turn them into grandfathers. I am positive you will want to take your grandchildren fishing, inform them of the true odds of playing Texas Hold 'Em, show them how to take a punch in the gut and teach them the intricacies of shooting craps. That happy future is yours if you will give your blessing to the marriage of your daughter and my client."

Big Julie leaned back, stared at his daughter for an extended period of time, then finally said, "Addie, what do you want to do? To me, you're still my little girl. I know you've grown up, and got curves and all, but in my head all I see is my little baby girl. Is this what you want?"

In a voice that sounded a little like Betty Boop on steroids, Adelaide said, "Yes, Papa, I am ready to marry Jonas. I finally found the man of my dreams."

So the judge in question was named Jonas. That meant Jonas Adams was the unnamed judge. I would need to remember that for my future relations with the jurist who rules courtroom four.

Big Julie blinked back tears for a moment, then his eyes cleared and his voice turned as cold as a New Jersey winter. "Tell me counselor, why are you here in place of Addie's dream man?"

I hesitated as my mind raced to find a plausible reason to explain the missing suitor.

Adelaide said, "Yah! Where's my man?"

Instinctively, I began to pace between Joey and Adelaide. "My good woman, to reiterate your enduring term of affection, 'your man' is a respected jurist who is considered to be at the top of his profession in Northern Nevada. Presently, the judge is unable to travel to your side due to his responsibility overseeing the most important trial in the history of Carson City, if not the great state of Nevada."

Adelaide said, "Oh, when we talked on the phone he didn't tell me about any trial. That sounds really important."

I had Adelaide on my side, but Big Julie's expression informed me that he remained unconvinced.

"Shyster, if and when my little girl gets married, the ceremony is goin' to take place here, not in a state that's nothing but sand and rocks."

Adelaide squeaked, "Yah. We're goin' to get hitched by a real priest under the cabana out by the pool." She turned toward the door. "You want a look-see?"

Big Julie ignored Adelaide's open-ended question, and asked, "Tell me, Shyster, where is it that you do that job you call lawyering?"

I did not feel comfortable with the direction this conversation was taking. "Nevada."

"Closer."

"Northern Nevada."

Big Julie slammed his hand on his desk. "I want the town, damn it!"

"Carson City."

Big Julie's lips took on an evil grimace. "All I have to do is snap my fingers and an army of capos will surround your office and burn it to the ground with you in it." His eyes shifted to a stare so cold that I could have sworn the room temperature dropped ten degrees. "So you'll personally guarantee that the judge is clean and will stand next to Addie, in front of a priest, under the cabana on the day of the wedding. *Capiche?*'

He did not offer much of an alternative. Either I made sure that the unnamed judge married Adelaide under the cabana, by the pool, at Big Julie's house, or my days of breathing air were numbered. I said, "Big Julie, I guarantee the judge will be here and ready to marry your daughter at an agreed upon time and day."

"Shyster, until I see the whites of the groom's eyes, you'd better call me Mr. Carlucci. *Capiche?*"

"I understand."

Big Julie turned his massive chair away, picked up what looked to be a second casino investment pitch, and my moment in the sun with the Mafia Don of East New Jersey and South Philly had come to an abrupt end.

My return to the west coast from Philadelphia was an unmitigated disaster. On close inspection, my first-class flight attendant's blonde hair showed some-gray roots. On top of that blemish, the woman was pushing sixty, overweight, and had the IQ of a three-toed sloth. The food she served was disgusting. The drinks tasted watered-down. And the movie was a horrible mess that starred a muscle bound creature named Vin Diesel. I vowed that once I return home to Carson City, I would dictate a letter to the president of United Airlines that stated when a passenger purchased a first class ticket on his airline, that passenger expects more then coach seat mediocrity. All in all, my trip to the west coast was almost more than I could handle.

But once my feet were firmly planted on the ground, I counted my blessings. I had escaped the clutches of Big Julie, and could now spend my time in San Francisco with Charles formulating the winning defense strategy for Erik Rundstrom.

CHAPTER EIGHTEEN

Bear, Copenhagen, Denmark

Jeez, Flo said that Copenwagen was on her bucket list. Me? After spending a day there, I'd dump the whole place into that bucket.

The minute we landed, Flo got all excited and wanted to see all kinds of stuff. I thought we were on our way to find the dude that poisoned that guy in Frisco, but what the hell did I know?

Flo had made our hotel reservation at a joint that was close to Tivoli, a place she said we had to go to before we left Copenwagen. Once we got to our room, I sat down and turned on the TV.

Flo said, "Turn that damn thing off. I'm calling Charles and when he answers, I'm putting him on the speaker."

I shut the TV down just as Charlie said, "Hello?"

"Charles, it's Flo and Bear here. Any further information on Erik's whereabouts?"

"My contact at SAS is scanning the data bases of all the airlines that go in and out of Copenhagen airport. If Erik flies out of Denmark, we'll nail him."

"Charles, that's great. I have an old college bud

who is a big-wig with Hertz and I hope he'll help me with the car rental data bases. While we wait for your call, we're going to see the Little Mermaid, and Tivoli Gardens if we have the time."

"Sounds great. Don't worry, I'll contact you as soon as I have any information." Charlie hung up and Flo hit a couple of buttons. "Terrence, Florence here . . . yes, that Flo . . . yes it has been a long time. Terry, I have a favor to ask . . . yes, we did have some great days back then . . . you'll help me? Great. At the present time I am working as an investigator for an attorney. I'm in Copenhagen . . . yes, Denmark, and what I need is to have you look into the rental vehicle data base, if there is such a thing, to see if a man named Erik Rundstrom has reserved, or rented a . . . Of course, we rented our car from Hertz . . . you can get us a fifty-percent discount? My skinflint boss will love that. Thanks for everything. Get back to me as soon as possible. Bye."

Flo looked at me and smiled. "Now we have some time to visit the Little Mermaid and if we still have time, Tivoli."

We all went downstairs and took a cab to the nearest Hertz place 'cause of the guy Flo knew in college. I wanted to rent a Ford F150 pick-up but they didn't have any, so we rented a car the babe behind the counter called a Ray-No. It's a car made in France. Hell, I didn't know anybody made cars in France. I don't know if the babe told me the car name right because the letters on the rental contract said, R-E-N-A-U-L-T. I think that's what happens when you let a screwy country like France build cars. I mean they don't even speak English there.

But don't get me wrong, the Ray-No wasn't a bad car. Not as much room, or as powerful as my truck 'cause it had this wimpy diesel engine, but with fuel at eight bucks a gallon, and the three of us fit in it, so the Ray-No got us where we wanted to go. I guess the car was okay.

And another thing, the first time I filled the tank of the Ray-No, the dude at the gas station wouldn't take my Franklin. I mean a hundred American clams is a hundred bucks where I come from. The gas station dude told me that they only take Euros or another kinda money he called the Danish Krone. Kyla checked her phone and told us the stupid Krone was only worth about fifteen cents American so I gave the gas dude a credit card and hoped that it still worked on the other side of the world.

After driving around Copenwagen for awhile, we finally found Flo's mermaid statue. We parked and walked to the water's edge, I took a quick gander and turned around to head back to our car.

Flo elbowed me and said, "Stop right there. We just got here."

"I agree with Flo," said Kyla.

Flo took a long look at the mermaid and then

back to me. "I get it now. She's topless but her boobs are too small. Right?"

The mermaid statue was really small. Like if she was standing up, which she wasn't, she wouldn't even come up to my armpit. Okay, Flo was right about one thing, the mermaid was topless, but I still thought she'd be bigger. And she was sitting on a rock out in the water, far away from where I stood, so I could barely tell how big her boobs really were.

"It's not just her boobs. The whole statue's too small."

Kyla said, "Bear, you are a male chauvinist pig."

"Hey, I'm not a pig. Seen enough?"

"No," cried Flo. "Kyla didn't you tell me that you've pulled up the story about the Little Mermaid?"

"Yes, I found it while Bear was driving. Do you want me to read it to you now?"

"NO!" I cried.

But Flo yelled, "YES!" faster, and louder.

Kyla flashed me her best nasty look. Her glare wasn't as good as Flo's, but give her a little time and she'll get better.

Kyla said, "The story of the Little Mermaid is sad. She fell in love with a Danish prince she saw walking near the shore. But like all mermaids, she had no legs, so she went to a witch who gave her legs but took out her tongue in exchange."

I said, "Wow, that was one tough bitch."

"Bear, I said witch, not bitch." The kid continued, "But that's not the saddest part." She eyeballed her phone. "Despite the mermaid's exchange with the witch, she never married the prince, her one true love."

I glanced at Flo, and growled, "Okay, can we go now?"

"In a minute. I want to take a few pictures."

"Me too," giggled Kyla, like she was now Flo's newest best friend.

So there you are. A whole day wasted driving around Copenwagen just to stare at a mermaid statue with tiny boobs.

Anyway, we got back in the car and as I drove away from the stupid mermaid statue, I said, "Okay, Babe, you've teased us enough. Just what the hell is a Tivoli?"

"It's an amusement park, like Disneyland with beer."

"Sounds good so far. Where is it?"

"Head back to our hotel. It's about two blocks from there."

I did, and Flo was right. Tivoli was a little more than a block's walk from our hotel. Driving to see that mermaid was dumb, but walking to Tivoli turned out to be a real good idea.

We paid some of those Krone at the entrance and walked into a place where I was surrounded by beer pubs. It didn't take me long to figure out why the Danish people were so happy. Those Danish dudes make great beer.

Flo said, "You stay right here. Kyla and I are going to walk around the gardens."

I was on my third beer when Flo and Kyla came back.

"Babe, this Tivoli joint's got the mermaid beat by a score higher than I can count. How big is this place?"

Kyla pulled out her phone, hit a button and said, "Tivoli is the fourth largest amusement park in the world and it's been here in Copenhagen since 1843. Before he built Disneyland, Walt Disney came to Tivoli Gardens and he built some parts of Disneyland to emulate Tivoli."

I said, "Okay, you've sold me. As soon as I finish my brew, I'll join you two and we can walk around the joint."

As the last of the suds passed my lips, Flo's phone rang.

"Hello, Charles, hey, slow down. Erik's on a flight from Copenhagen to Stockholm right now . . . with a connecting flight to . . . where? . . . Skellefteå? . . . Is that in Sweden? . . . 500 miles north of Stockholm? Why there? . . . I see. I'll call you back later."

I said, "Okay, what's going on?"

Flo waved for the waiter and asked for the check. "Like Pinky guessed, Erik's heading to his families roots. His grandmother grew up on a farm outside of Skellefteå."

I said, "Jeez, I'm not even going to try that name. So after a couple of plane hops, we've got him?"

"That's what Charles thinks, but I'm worried. If Erik spots us, or finds out we're after him, he'll take off again."

Reading off the screen of her phone again, Kyla said, "In case you're interested, Skellefteå's is a town of 35,000 people that's so far north of Stockholm, few Swedes have ever visited. The town consists of a downtown, a shopping mall, regional medical facilities, a golf course, one of Sweden's most famous ice hockey teams, and a movie theater."

I said, "Hell, we've got more than one movie theater in Carson City, but they got us beat on the hockey team."

Flo said, "Thank you, Kyla, for that background. She's become a real asset."

"Right." I growled. "Hey, I'm starving. Do we have time to get some grub?"

"Sorry, we don't. Charles told me that his inside man made reservations for us on an SAS flight from Copenhagen to Stockholm and then on a another short flight to Skellefteå."

"Come on, Flo. I need some food."

"Our flight to Stockholm leaves in about two hours. See how many bags of peanuts you can con off our flight attendant."

Suddenly a low voice behind me said, "Don't anyone move. You are being watched by three snipers and are locked in their sights. Slowly place your hands on the table. If you make a quick move, I promise that will be the last move you make."

I didn't have a clue what was going on, but just in case the voice wasn't kidding, I said, "Flo, Kid, do like the man said and do it real slow."

I let go of my empty glass, set my hands down flat and spread my fingers out. Flo did the same while Kyla whimpered, "Bear, I'm scared."

"Kid, just do the same as me and Flo and I promise everything will be okay."

Once her hands were flat on the table, I said, "Okay, dude, you can see six hands, so what the hell is going on?"

Three dudes grabbed me, Flo, and Kyla, and stood us up. Then three other dudes frisked us, cuffed our wrists behind us, and pulled us away from the restaurant.

Ettamae was starting to cry and Flo didn't look all that happy. I said, "Like I said before, what the hell is going on?"

Nobody said anything but while they shoved us toward a big, blue van, I spotted the back of the guy pushing Flo. It said, POLITI in big white letters on the back of his black jacket.

I said, "Hey, are you guys cops?"

None of the guys holding us answered and before they shoved us through a door in the back of a tall van, a dude with a big dog sniffed us all over. My guess was the dog was checking for drugs. Once the dog didn't find anything, we were pushed inside the van and someone took our cuffs off.

There was not much light inside the van and it took me a second to make out a dude with gray hair sitting behind a desk at the far end. He said, "Hand over your passports."

One thing I had figured out about flying around the world was you never gave you passport to anyone. "Dude, I'll do that over my dead body!"

The gray haired dude shook his head, grabbed a cell phone and said something that I'd bet was Danish. The door to the van popped open and a guy who was a good six inches taller than me came in and handed the gray haired dude a bright yellow Taser.

The tall guy left and the gray haired dude said, "This device will not kill you, but from what I understand, you will wish you were beyond pain."

He pointed the Taser at Flo and said, "Hand over your passports or your lady friend will endure a shocking experience that she will never forget."

Flo's fingers were shaking so bad she had trouble getting her passport out of her money belt and finally shoved her passport to the guy behind the desk. Me, and Ettamae's passports followed Flo's.

The dude looked at all three, and held them under some kind of fancy light thing. Then he set our three passports down on the desk and said, "You have been detained today for violating the Danish anti-terrorism act. Now, the reason you are in temporary custody of the Danish police comes from your manipulation of various airline and rental car data bases. You have thirty seconds to explain why that was done or you will immediately be placed in prison."

Me and Flo glanced at each other. I shrugged, so she said, "The three of us are a team of investigators who work for an attorney in the United States named J. Pincus Delmont. We have been assigned to track down a man who has been accused of murder. We had nothing to do with any airline database. That was done by a government official in San Francisco. The car rental database, I fear was my fault. I asked an old boyfriend, a man who holds a very high position in a major car rental agency, to look into the data base to find out if the man we are looking for had rented a car and my friend did that for me as a favor."

She stopped for a second and looked at me— like I didn't know she'd had a boyfriend before we teamed up in LA. Then Flo continued, "And believe me, we had no idea that searching those data bases was breaking Danish law."

I said, "Dude, I asked those cops outside a couple of times why we were being cuffed. We're not terrorists. We're Americans. What the hell is going on?"

The gray-haired dude said, "In Denmark, the police force is responsible for airport security. Each year we have to work harder, and smarter, to stay one jump ahead of the terrorist. Your data base invasion ran afoul of one of our latest anti-terrorists algorithms. Now, answer my second question. Madam, assuming you accomplish your initial reason for entering our country and track down your fugitive, if you find him in Denmark, what did you plan on doing with the man?"

I held my breath and hoped Flo wouldn't tell him the truth—that I'd hog-tie the dumb-shit if that's what it took to get him back to San Francisco.

Flo said, "Our job, once we found the gentleman, would be to convince him that returning to San Francisco would be in his best interest."

The gray-haired dude stared at Flo, like he knew she was bull-shitting him, but he couldn't figure out a way to prove it. He said, "And what would happen to him if you failed to convince him of that?"

I jumped in. "Then me, Flo, and Ettamae would scoot right back to San Francisco after spending a great day looking at that cool topless mermaid and downing a couple of great Danish brews at Tivoli."

He looked us over for a couple of seconds, then said, "I apologize that my team had to be so abrupt with you, but when it comes to airport security in Denmark, discretion is the better part of valor. You are free to pick up your passports and leave."

The gray-haired dude grabbed his cell, barked something, and the back door of the van opened. A couple of the cops helped us out.

Before Flo had the chance to get pissed off and chew them out, all the cops piled into the van and drove away, leaving the three of us standing there like the last ten minutes had never happened.

Ettamae whimpered, "Bear, Flo, don't let anyone grab me again like that. Those things they put on my wrists hurt, and—"

I said, "Ettamae, the Danish dudes got the drop on me before I knew they were even there." Then I looked at Flo. "Babe, I don't want something like this happening again in Sweden. How about us making our own reservations from now on. That means no more calls to Charlie, or your old boyfriend."

Flo nodded, "Good idea." Then she put her arm around the kid, and said. "Like Bear said, Ettamae, the bad guys are gone. Now, the three of us have got to hustle if we're going to make our flights to Skellefteå."

I took a quick glance around, to see if I could spot a sniper, or a rooftop where a cop with a rifle might still have us in his sights. The coast looked clear, so I gave Flo a pat on her butt and said, "Okay, let's pack up and get out of here. But don't forget, I'm still starving. They'd better have good grub and beer, and plenty of it, in Skel, . . .Skel, . . . shit, you know, in that burg we're going to end up in that place called Sweden."

CHAPTER NINETEEN

Pinky, San Francisco, California

I had planned to spend a few days of a well deserved break in the great city of San Francisco—to dine in some of the outstanding restaurants—to listen as Michael Tilson Thomas conducted the San Francisco Symphony—to wander through the Japanese Garden in Golden Gate Park on a rare sunny day. Then, after recharging my batteries, so to speak, I would contact Charles to formulate the initial defense strategy for our client, Erik Rundstrom, to be ready when Bear returned with the fugitive.

But the next few hours proved that the immortal words of Robert Burns, 'The best laid plane of mice an' men gang aft agley,' still had merit.

Once my plane had touched down at SFO, I called Charles.

"Pinky, are you back in San Francisco and ready to work on Erik's defense?"

"Sorry. I am not quite finished with my previous assignment."

Charles said, "Can you tell me what you are

141

doing?"

"No, I cannot," I said. "Any news from my team abroad?"

"I talked with Flo in Copenhagen. Last I heard they were about to leave on their way to a place in Sweden called Skellefteå."

I said, "I would love to join them, to move things along quicker, but first things first. Any further news on Erik?"

"None. When will you return to San Francisco?"

"Three to four days," I lied. "I'll call you when I am firmly ensconced in my suite at the Drisco."

"Sounds good to me. By the way, my contact at the SFPD informed me that they were looking at a female chef as a second person of interest. She worked in the kitchen that night with Erik during the fated dinner, and according to my information, she didn't get along with Simon Rand, but now that Erik's fled the country, for no reason, they've put her on the back burner."

"She and a hundred other chefs," I said. "Perhaps you can check her out and together we can come up with a way to move her up to suspect status when I arrive in San Francisco."

Charles hesitated, and then blurted out, "Pinky, are you suggesting I attempt to convince my police contact to move her up to suspect status? Explain what you mean by move her up."

"My good man, the more suspects there are, the easier our job will be."

"So as the elected District Attorney of my county, I will have no ethical concerns following your suggestion?"

"Charles, we both know that I would never do anything unethical."

"I know, Pinky, but I feel much better now that you restated the obvious."

Becoming weary with Charles' holier than thou attitude, I said, "Goodbye, Charles."

After a five minute ride on an automated trolly, and signing a car rental contract, I paced impatiently as I waited in a poorly lighted area for my car to be delivered to the Hertz pick-up zone.

Why poorly lighted? For some reason, all passengers who arrived at SFO with the desire to rent a motor vehicle were subjected to an automated trolly from the main airport terminal to a monolithic, multi-story, dank concrete structure where all rental agencies both store their vehicles and transact their business. I have no idea why SFO, a world-class airport, would do that to their customers. My only guess would be that an uninformed government official who never rode the trolly, or picked up a vehicle in the dimly lighted facility, approved the bizarre and ridiculous set up.

While I continued to wait for my vehicle, Robbie Burns prophetic poem materialized again when I made the error of calling my office.

A male voice, one that sounded somewhat familiar, answered, "Law office. How may I assist you?"

I said, "Who is this?"

"Pinky?"

"Of course this is Pinky, and now that I have answered your question, answer mine. To whom am I speaking?"

"I will but don't get upset. This is Louis Loomer here. How was your trip? Did you have a nice flight? Can I send Frank to pick you up at the Reno airport?"

"Loomer, if you value my continued business, you have . . . Frank? Who is Frank?"

"My nephew. Don't you remember? I sent him to your office last—"

I interrupted, "Never mind. Now, you have thirty seconds to explain to me why you, not Lu, answered my office phone!"

"Pinky, I'm here working with Frank to train him on the intricacies of taking over Lu's position during her absence."

"Put Lu on the phone."

Loomer said, "Ah . . . at the moment, she's unavailable."

At that identical moment, I saw my rental vehicle approach. Attempting to control my temper, I said, "Loomer, my patience with you has reached an end."

"Pinky, please excuse me a moment, I have to answer another call."

Before I could hang up, I felt a tap on my

shoulder.

"Mr. Delmont, your car is ready."

I turned and a Hertz attendant handed me the keys of a beautiful Mercedes 503C. I said, "It is about time. My good man, as a less then happy charter member of Hertz's exclusive Presidents Club, I—"

Loomer's voice floated out of my cell phone speaker. "Pinky, there's a Mr. Dudek on your line and he demands he talk to you at once. Isn't he the man in Carson City with the stainless steel hook in place of his arm?"

"Loomer, as I was going to do a moment ago, I am now going to hang up. Tell Mr. Dudek to call me on my cell phone."

"I'll do that once I explain why my nephew, Frank, is—"

I clicked off and waited for Dudek's call.

I felt another tap on my shoulder.

"Excuse me, Mr. Delmont, your car is ready."

"I heard you the first time when you handed me the keys a few moments ago. I am waiting for a very important call. It is a matter of life and death, and as soon as I complete that call, I will get in my car and drive away."

"I understand, Mr. Delmont, but we need you to move your car out of the pick-up zone at once. Your vehicle is blocking other drivers. I'm sure—"

My cell buzzed and I turned my back to the attendant. "Dudek?"

"Shyster, it seems that Mr. Carlucci expects you and the unnamed judge to appear by his pool, under the cabana, tomorrow afternoon at 2:00 pm, where a wedding ceremony will take place between the unnamed judge and one Adelaide Carlucci. According to Mr. Carlucci, you agreed to be the unnamed judge's best man so you've got to be there, too."

"Dudek, I just arrived at the San Francisco airport. Presently I am standing at the car rental pick-up area and—"

I felt a third annoying tap on my shoulder.

I spun around and said, "Young man, do not touch me again."

The Hertz attendant said, "I'm sorry, Mr. Delmont, but you have to move your car. As you can see, there are other cars waiting to drive through the pick-up zone you are blocking."

Before I could answer the attendant, I heard Dudek scream through my cell, "Shyster, talk to me!"

Ignoring the grid-lock, I said, "Dudek, the only way I can be in New Jersey tomorrow afternoon is to be on the next plane out of SFO heading to Philadelphia."

"Then you'd better do that 'cause I picked up a vibe over the phone from Carlucci that if you want to stay on the right side of the grass, you'd better be at that wedding."

I felt yet another tap on my shoulder. I turned

and stared at the uniforms of two of San Francisco's finest.

I barked into my cell, "Dudek, hold on! I am being confronted by two members of local law enforcement." I smiled at the two cops and said, "Officers, what can I do for you today?"

The younger of the two said, "Move your rental car or we'll place you under arrest for obstructing traffic."

"Gentlemen, I am a lawyer, and as an officer of the court, I question you have the legal justification to arrest me. I note the patch on your arm states SFPD. Letters that I am positive stand for the San Francisco Police Department. I am also sure that this airport is many miles south of the San Francisco city limit. Can you recite to me the ordinance that puts me in jeopardy of incarceration?"

The older one's face, pocked-marked and ruddy from years of excessive exposure to the wind and sun, said, "Sam, I told you that the rich bastards who rent the expensive Mercedes are all a giant pain in the ass. Mr. Lawyer, since 1997 the SFPD has been responsible for the safety and security of San Francisco International Airport, and that includes traffic enforcement and accident investigation. I hope I answered your question concerning our authority 'cause now you know that we have the legal right to arrest you." He pulled out his cuffs and said, "Buddy, you're lucky that my partner has a soft heart. Sam gives you ten seconds to move that fancy car out of the loading zone or you're under arrest."

I tossed the car keys to the startled attendant and said, "Officer, put the cuffs away. Now the loading zone obstruction is a Hertz problem. As the reason for my arrest has been removed, I will conclude our conversation and return to my call."

I turned my back to the cops and said, "Dudek, you get the judge on a plane to Philadelphia. I will reserve him a room at the Hilton Philadelphia at Penn's Landing. Then you can—"

"Shyster, how can you reserve him a room if you don't know the judge's name?"

"Jonas Adams. The judge's name is, Jonas Adams."

"Shit, you're good. Okay, I'll get Judge Adams to Philly and then he's your problem."

I said, "And remind Judge Adams of our agreement. Goodbye."

I clicked off and then placed a call back to my office.

"Law office. How may I help you?"

My God, this time the voice belonged to a different male. I said, "Am I talking to Frank?"

"Yes, this is Frank."

"The last we talked, I told Lu to fire you. At the moment I am pressed for time so I am going to give you the opportunity to redeem yourself."

"Thank you, Mr. Delmont."

"Frank, make two hotel reservations at the Hilton Philadelphia at Penn's Landing. One for me, J. Pincus Delmont, and the second reservation for, and Frank, I will only tell you this name once. You will make the reservation, and then you will erase the name from your memory forever. Do I make myself clear?"

"Just a minute, sir, I need to get a pencil so I can write the name down."

"Frank, listen to me. Do not, I repeat, do not write the name down. Your future employment in my office, and possibly your life on this earth, hangs on your doing this simple task correctly. Are you ready?"

"I am."

"When I give you the name, do not repeat it out loud. Do not let your lips move as you think about the letters. Are you ready?"

"Yes sir."

"The name for the reservation is Jonas Adams."

"Oh, I know him. He's a—"

I screamed, "Frank, forget that name! Go back to what I said earlier and erase it from your mind, forever!"

"But sir, how can I make a reservation if I have erased the name from my memory?"

"My boy, reserve two rooms in my name, J. Pincus Delmont. Are we clear?"

"Sir, that's a cool way you did that. How about an airline reservation? Do you want me to take care of that for you too?"

My call waiting beeped. "Frank, hold on. I have another call."

I pushed a button, and heard, "Boss, it's me."

"Bear, where are you?"

"In this little town in northern Sweden called Skaltiamaria."

I said, "I am extremely busy. Why did you call me?"

"Boss, me and Flo tracked down this Erik dude and we told him why we were here. But we've got a big problem, he doesn't want to come back with us, and he knows we can't force him without some legal exrtathingie."

"I believe you meant an extradition hearing. And what do you and Florence think I can do?"

"Flo thinks you can explain to him that you can get him off, even if he poisoned that critic guy, just like you got me off from that murder-two charge."

"My boy, did I hear you correctly? You and Florence need my help?"

"You got it. Flo says we need more than muscle this time. In fact, she thinks you could talk the clothes off a nun."

"Bear, tell Florence that I thank you both for your confidence in my ability to present the perfect closing argument to a jury. I will takep the first plane to Copenhagen tomorrow evening and thus should be there to assist the members of Team Delmont in a few days."

"Boss, by the way, whatever you do, don't let Charlie's buddy at the airline—"

"Bear, I have another call. See you soon." I pressed a button and returned back to Frank. I said, "My boy, if I recall, you asked me about making an airline reservation for me."

"That's right, sir."

I was delighted with how quickly Frank had learned to address me as Mr. Delmont, or sir. Obviously the lad was bright and capable of learning enough to fill in for Lu during her absence.

I said, "I will not require you to do that for me. I am at the San Francisco airport. I will go to the airline counter and hope they have an available first class seat."

"Sir, my uncle told me that first class seats are really expensive. Is that really true?"

"First class seats are not expensive if your client is paying for them."

"That's a cool idea. Sir, Uncle Louie told me that I'm going to learn a lot from you. Are you coming back soon?"

"I hope so. Frank, I need to speak with Thelma."

"Who?"

"Thelma Untermeyer Hathaway. The last time I saw her she was wearing a skirt, blouse, and a necklace of giant turquoise stones."

"Oh, her. I didn't know her name. What does she do here?"

151

"She is my paralegal."

"Oh . . ." A second later Frank yelled, "Thelma, pick up line one! Mr. Delmont wants to talk to you."

"Pinky?"

"Thelma, legal-wise, what has happened since my departure?"

"Just a call from a client named George Sterling."

Oh God, not George again. I thought I had put that problem to bed months ago. I said, "Did you pull up his file on the computer?"

"I did. He seems to be a long-term client with a drunk driving problem."

"Thelma, you have summed up George perfectly. Why did he call?"

"He wants his driver's license back. According to him, he's attended forty-seven AA meetings in forty-seven days and he feels that proves his readiness to reclaim his driver's license."

At the moment, I did not want to discuss with Thelma the fact that it took me two years to find my one and only pro bono client and that if George Sterling ever became a licensed driver again, I would lose him and have to find another pro bono client who would take no more than thirty minutes of my valuable time every six months. George Sterling was my treasure in the murky, money wasting world of pro bono clients and to keep him, I made an arrangement with Judge Anderson to retain his drivers license in my office safe.

"Thelma, inform George that we have discussed his improving health issues and I will schedule a hearing with Judge Adams concerning handing over his drivers license upon my return."

"Thank you. He will be pleased to hear that. Do you need to talk with Frank again?"

"Not now, I have a plane to catch."

After I hung up, I called Charles. "Charles, I need your assistance with your SAS contact to book me a first class flight from Philadelphia to Copenhagen, continue on to Stockholm, and then on to Skellefteå."

"Have they tracked down Erik?"

"Not sure. As I have to catch a plane, I do not have time to chit-chat. Just set up my flights and text me when my reservations are confirmed. Good bye."

As I returned to the main SFO terminal, I marveled how my best laid plans, with apologies to Robbie Burns, had not gang a glay.

The leader of my investigative team requested my help to return a miscreant to San Francisco.

My unexpected New Jersey mafia adventure would end up working in my favor.

My problem with my pro bono client would be solved by a gentleman's agreement with Judge Adams—to protect George Sterling from harm.

My vacation to Denmark and Sweden would be paid in full by my generous client.

My million dollar retainer would remain intact,

with no strings attached, collecting interest in my Swiss bank.

To sum up my day, from the chaos that grew in strength from the first phone call, everything had turned in my favor.

God, I love the law!

CHAPTER TWENTY

Bear-Downtown Skellefteå, Sweden

I told the boss that we had cornered Erik
Rundstrom, and I know what I'd said was a stretch,
but I didn't lie when I told him we needed his help.
What I forgot to tell him—okay I didn't really
forget—I was kinda wrong when I told Pinky that
we had Erik. Actually, Erik had all of us, me, Flo,
and Ettamae, handcuffed to a water pipe inside the
summer house on his Grandma's farm and I can't
figure out why the dude calls it a summer house!

Shit, all I really wanted to do was to figure out
a way to drag Erik back to Frisco so Pinky could get
him off for poisoning that stupid food critic. Now
we're stuck on a farm outside a town with a stupid
name in Sweden.

But like Flo tells me all the time, I'm getting
way ahead of myself so I'll go back to when we got
to Sweden.

First, we landed in Stockholm, and inside of
two hours, we hopped onto another plane heading
north to that town named Skaltiamaria where we
were pretty sure Erik was hiding out.

At the Skaltiamaria airport we rented another

Ray No, the same kind of French car we had in Copenhagen.

Ettamae checked out a phone directory and found three listing for babes named Rundstrom. Pella Rundstrom, Kristina Rundsrtom, and Annika Rundstrom. She keyed the address for Pella Rundstrom into the Ray No's GPS, and I drove to what we hoped was Erik's Grandma's house.

While we cruised through the streets of the town, Ettamae asked, "Want to get up-to-date on Sweden?"

I said, "Why? Is it any different than Denmark?"

As she punched me on my arm, Flo said, "Of course it is. In fact Sweden is a totally different country. Sweden has a different language. A different political system. A different currency."

"Do they finally call a buck a buck like we do in America?"

"Nope," said Ettamae. "They call their unit of currency a krona."

I said, "Hold on a minute. Wasn't that Danish dollar called a krona?"

Flo said, "That's true. In fact, there are three countries that use the krona as their main unit of currency: Norway, Sweden, and Denmark."

While I tried to figure out the screwy money, Ettamae cried, "Stop! We just passed the address."

I pulled over and parked. Across the street was a ten story apartment building.

156

I said, "If a real grandma lives in that joint I hope they've got elevators like we do in the good old U S of A. Okay, once we get to the door, how 'bout I try, 'Hi, I'm your gas man. Our company records show your meter is not working right and we think you're being overcharged.'"

Ettamae giggled. "Can you say all that in Swedish?"

Damn, she had me there.

Flo said, "How about we first figure out which floor the woman lives on and then knock on her door?"

"And what are you going to say when she answers the door?"

Ettamae said, "I could ask if Frida's home."

I said, "Hold on! Who in the hell is Frida?"

"I just made her up. If the woman is old, like a grandma, that question will get her talking. If she's young, like Flo, that's okay too 'cause we'll know she's not a grandma."

Flo smiled. I didn't know if it was 'cause Ettamae called her young, or if she thought the kid had a good idea.

Flo said, "See there, Ettamae's doing a better job at investigating then we are."

I didn't want to admit it, but Flo was right. I said, "Good plan, Ettamae. Let's go in."

We walked into a lobby, found a directory board that showed Pella Rundstrom lived in 805.

We moved to the elevator and I pushed the

button. Nothing happened. Pushed again and still nothing happened. I took my finger off the button, and said, "I'll bet that the people in this joint have a way to unlock the elevator for visitors. Like the way people back home unlock the front door of their apartment with a buzzer." I walked back to the directory and looked closer. There it was. A small button next to Pella Rundstrom's apartment number 805. I pushed the button and a speaker next to the board spewed out a line of Swedish gobbledygook.

Ettamae leaned close, used her best little girl voice, and said, "Is Frida home?"

More Swedish gobbledygook.

Ettamae kept pushing, "Frida. I need to talk to Frida. Is she home?"

After a couple of counts, the elevator door opened and we were on our way to the eighth floor. When the door opened, standing in the hallway was a really cute Swedish babe with a great bod, the blondest hair I'd ever seen, and eyes blue like that show of glacier ice I'd seen last month on a National Geographic TV special. She was about twenty-five and defiantly not Erik's grandma.

The babe's face told me she was a little pissed off. "Vad vill du?"

Flo said, "Excuse me. We are on vacation from America and don't speak Swedish."

The babe's face softened. "I'm sorry. I asked what do you want?"

"Our daughter," Flo put her arm around Ettamae, "Is looking for her Swedish pen pal named Frida Rundstrom, but she lost her address. All we know is she lives in Skellefteå, so we are visiting all the Rundstroms in the area."

The blue-eyed babe smiled, "I'm sorry. I was on the phone and the damn speaker system in this place is so screwed up that I didn't understand you were speaking English." The babe turned to face Ettamae, and said, "My name is Pella, what's yours?"

The kid grabbed Pella's hand. "Ettamae. I'm sorry we bothered you."

Pella said, "No problem. I'm sorry Frida doesn't live here. Good luck and I hope you find her soon."

As we walked back to our Ray No, Ettamae said, "Well, I'd say my plan worked very well. One down and two to go."

"Okay, who's next."

Flo said, "We have Kristina Rundsrtom, and Annika Rundstrom, but flying from Copenhagen, to Stockholm, to Skellefteå has pooped me out. We need to find a place to sleep."

Ettmae said, "I agree with Flo, but first, let's flip a coin to see who'll be next up on what will be known in the future as the Grandma Rundstrom caper."

Future? Caper? The kid doesn't know that sticking your nose into other peoples' business can get dangerous sometimes.

159

I said, "Okay, I'll find us a motel. We'll get a couple of rooms and then get some grub. I hope Sweden makes as good a beer as Denmark."

Flo said, "At least we know what your number one priority is."

I know Flo was needling me, but I ignored her jab and pulled out a quarter from my pocket. I flipped it in the air, and just before it landed on my big paw, I said, "Heads it's Kristina. Tails, it's Annika."

Both Flo and Ettamae leaned over to see the results.

The coin came up tails, Annika Rundstrom. Up to that point, Ettamae's plan of checking out the Rundstrom names seemed like a good idea, but what we didn't know was that tomorrow we were going to end up with the short end of the stick.

CHAPTER TWENTY-ONE

Pinky-Copenhagen Airport, Denmark

After my flight from San Francisco to Philadelphia to attend the thirty minute exchange of vows between the intellectually challenged Adelaide Carlucci and the ethically challenged Judge Jonas Adams, I climbed aboard a jet that took me to Copenhagen. Once the plane landed I just had enough time to make a quick visit to the Men's room before I had to get into the security line to board my flight to Stockholm.

As I shuffled behind the line of airline passengers, my brain buzzing with exhaustion, I felt a tap on my right shoulder. I turned and stared into the expressionless faces of two uniformed officers dressed in black with the word POLITI stitched on their chest above their heart. The men were over six feet tall and looked as if they both could play linebacker in the NFL, or power forward in the NBA.

Forcing a smile onto my fatigued face, I said, "Is there something I can do for you gentlemen?"

Without a word of response, the two grabbed me under my arms and lifted me, including my

161

carry-on luggage, out of the line and toward a closed door.

As I floated through the air, I stated emphatically, "Unhand me! I am an officer of the court. You have no right to . . . "

The door opened and they pushed me through the opening. Before they sat me down on a metal folding chair, they thoroughly checked me for weapons. That task completed, a third uniformed man, holding a large German Shepard on a short leash, directed the dog to sniff me and my carry-on bag.

Once the sniffing was completed, I looked around the dimly lit room. It took me a moment to make out a gray-haired man sitting behind a desk no more than five feet from where I sat.

With a tone that indicated he was used to obedience, he said, "Stand up, slowly approach my desk and turn over your passport."

I said, "Sir, as I told your gestapo-like minions, I am an officer of the court and as such, I am used to being treated with the respect of my profession. Please show me some deference."

The man's face showed no expression and his voice was flat as he repeated, "Hand me your passport."

I stood as tall as possible and said, "Sir, I have—"

"Hand over your passport or I will direct my minions, as you called them, to immediately take you to prison."

I glanced over my shoulder and the two were still standing there, along with a fully-grown German Shepard. A guttural growl slipped from the dog's throat, as if to say, 'you had better turn over your passport or else'.

Reluctantly, I handed the gray-haired man my passport.

He glanced at it and then scanned the document under some sort of electronic reader. Then the man behind the desk said, with a bored tone, "You have been detained today for violating the Danish anti-terrorism act. The reason you are in temporary custody of the Danish police, comes from your manipulation of various airline data bases. Mr. Delmont, a few days ago we detained three Americans who were involved in a similar sort of airline data base manipulation. They claimed to be investigators who worked for an attorney named Delmont. Is it possible that you are the attorney who sent the three Americans to Denmark?"

I hesitated, not sure how to respond in a way that would put me on the right side of Danish law.

"Mr. Delmont, you must answer my question or by Denmark's anti-terrorism act you will immediately be placed in prison."

I said, "Sir, you have me at a disadvantage. I do not know who you are, or the extent of your authority."

"Mr. Delmont, in Denmark, the police force is

responsible for airport security. Each year we have to work smarter, to stay one jump ahead of the terrorist. Your data base invasion ran afoul of our newest anti-terrorism algorithm."

I said, "Now I understand why I am being detained and I applaud your due diligence in this matter. As we both are sworn to protect our countries' laws, I would appreciate it if you could provide me with your name."

The man seemed somewhat taken aback by my attitude, and request, but after a moment, he said, "My name is Peers Iversen. My rank with the anti-terrorism department of the Danish police is Captain."

"Excellent! Captain Iversen, I am the attorney in question. I did send three investigators to Sweden, and they first stopped in Copenhagen to get a taste of your world famous Danish hospitality."

"Mr. Delmont, I insist you answer my questions."

"I am about to do that. Concerning your accusation that I manipulated an airline's data base, I am innocent. I will tell you that I asked a friend to make my airplane reservations. What he did, or how he did that, I am completely in the dark. I should add that my friend is an elected governmental official in the State of California and I am positive he would never be involved in any activity that would undermine the security of the nation of Denmark." I glanced at my watch. "Captain Iversen, my plane to Stockholm is due to take off in thirty minutes and I hope to be on that plane."

"Mr. Delmont, if you successfully answer my final question, you will be free to continue your journey. Assume for the moment that you are able to track down your fugitive. If that occurred in my country, what would be your plans concerning that person, or persons?"

I considered telling the captain the truth—that I would tell Bear to drug Erik into unconsciousness if that's what it took to get him back to San Francisco—but instead I said, "It would be my job to convince the fugitive that returning to San Francisco would be in his best interest."

Captain Iversen stared at me, as if he had heard that line before. "And what would happen to the fugitive if you failed to convince him of that unlikely scenario?"

"My team and I would return to San Francisco empty-handed."

He stared at me again for a few uncomfortable moments. Then he said, "I apologize that my men had to be so abrupt with you, but when it comes to airport security in this country, we Danes are better off safe than sorry." He handed me my passport. "Mr. Delmont, you are free to go and don't worry, my men will hold that flight until you are on the plane."

"Thank you, Captan Iversen. So far, my visit with you today exceeded all the previous memorable moments of my sojourn to Scandinavia."

CHAPTER TWENTY-TWO

Bear-Six kilometers north of Skellefteå, Sweden

On another bright, sunny afternoon, I scoped out a cute blonde in shorts and a tee-shirt walking down the street while Flo schmoozed with another cute blonde at a tourist office. The tourist babe sent us to a small hotel where Flo got us a room with two bedrooms so Ettamae could have a place of her own. Later, Flo whispered to me that it was important for a girl Ettamae's age to get her privacy. Hell, paying for one or two bedrooms didn't bother me 'cause Pinky, or his client, was picking up the tab!

Anyway, before Ettamae and Flo scarfed down a pizza at a restaurant called Limping Lotta's, Flo was pretty sure that Joe's Pizza Joint in Carson City whipped up the best pizza in the world. But the Swedish pizza showed her that she was dead wrong.

But I didn't order pizza. The waitress, another blonde with ice-blue eyes, told me that I'd love the elk with lingonberry sauce and that babe hit the nail on the head. In fact, if I wasn't sorta tied up with Flo, Sweden would be a great place for a single dude to live. Most every Swedish babe had blonde hair, sky-blue eyes, and big boobs. The food was great. The beer damn good, and cheap. What more could a dude ask for?

After dinner I slept like a baby 'cause I guess Flo wasn't the only one who was pooped out from all the travel.

The next morning, the hotel we stayed at laid out a kickass breakfast spread with all kinds of sliced meat, cheese, fish, breads, and the best coffee I'd tasted since I moved out of my mom and pop's place.

Before we piled into the Ray No, Flo said, "I emailed Pinky and told him we're heading to Annika Rundstrom's and gave him the address."

"Do you think he'll get here today?"

Flo chuckled. "Usually I hope Pinky's on the other side of the world, but I don't know if Erik Rundstrom poisoned that critic, so we can use all the help we can get."

Ettamae said, "Flo, is there a chance that Erik did murder that guy?"

"It's possible."

"Then he could be dangerous," said Ettamae.

I said, "And don't you forget that."

Before I got the Ray No going, Ettamae put the address for Annika Rundstrom into the GPS and while listening to a babe's voice telling me to turn left, or right, a sign flew by that said, KAGE—10KM.

I said, "Flo, my guess is that KAGE is the name of a town, but what the hell is KM?"

Ettamae jumped in. "KM stands for Kilometers. Most every country in the world . . ."

"Shit, all the crap about krona and kilometers was getting me a little steamed. First, I've got to drive this stupid French Ray No car instead of my F150. Can't these foreigners get anything right?"

Flo patted my knee. "Bear, according to that sign, the town of Kage is about six miles from that sign. Okay?"

"Not okay! Signs should show the real miles, nothing else."

Still a little pissed, I sat back and followed the directions from the GPS babe's voice that came from the radio speaker. A few of minutes later I stopped next to a dirt road to look at what we hoped was Grandma Rundstrom's farm.

I backed the car into a bunch of trees to get a little cover and eyeballed the joint. The farm house was off the main road about three hundreds yards down a dirt road. Next to the house sat a couple of barns and another smaller house was tucked back behind the farm house, closer to the forest. South of the main house was a field of wheat.

"Kid, you ready to try the, 'is Frida home', scam again?"

"Sounds good to me," said Ettamae.

Flo said, "Let's go, but remember, Erik could be there."

As me Flo, and Ettamae walked close to the house, the front door popped open and an older, but damn good-looking babe stood in the doorway. She was sixty, maybe seventy, but her skin was smooth. Her hair was mostly blonde with some gray streaks, she had the usual ice-blue eyes, and her boobs were big—at least twice as big as that stupid little mermaid back in Copenwagen.

Flo took a step forward and said, "Good afternoon. Do you speak English?"

"Not well. Grandson, Erik, better. He's, ah . . . Skellefteå with girlfriend."

She opened the door wide. "Come and fika."

I said, "Fika?"

The blonde babe said, "You don't know fika? She scrunched up her face, like she was trying to remember what fika was in English. Suddenly her face un-scrunched. "Coffee?"

Flo said, "Thank you, we'd love some coffee." Then she whispered to me, "Bear, get your eyes off her chest and look at her face. She's a grandmother, for God's sake."

I did what Flo told me to do, but trust me, it was hard to believe that Annika Rundstrom was a grandma. Must be the Swedish water.

"Mrs. Rundstrom, our daughter has a question. Go ahead, Ettamae."

The Swedish grandma said, "Call me Annika."

Ettamae said, "Annika, we are looking for my pen pal friend Frida. I lost her address and all I can remember is Frida came from Skellefteå."

Annika looked up at the ceiling, like the answer

was written there, and then she shook her head. "Sorry. No Frida. Grandson can help."

She herded us into her kitchen, sat us down, and started to grind some coffee beans. I thought about asking Annika for a beer, but Flo, just like she read my mind, flashed me her best 'don't you dare' glare. Someday I've got to ask her how she does that.

While we sat there and waited for our coffee, I noticed Flo punching in some stuff on her phone. "Babe, whatca doing?"

"Emailing Pinky to tell him we've found Erik's grandmother."

"Does he know where to find his email on a phone?"

Flo glanced at me and shook her head. "Pinky is a pain in the butt, but I think he's passed iPhone 101."

After two cups of really great coffee, and a couple of really super cookies, we heard a car pull up outside. The door opened and Erik stepped in. Judging from his eyes he was really surprised to see us sitting in his Grandma's kitchen but he did a good job of hiding that from his grandma.

I jumped up and said, "Hi, my name is Bear. Our daughter, Ettamae, is looking for her pen pal friend named Frida and your grandma said that maybe you could help us."

Erik pulled himself together and said, "I can do that. Is that your Renault parked on the road under the trees?"

"Yup."

"I've been wanting to look at that model. We can talk while I check out your car."

Flo said, "You boys go and look at the car. Annika, it doesn't make any difference if you're in Sweden or America. All boys like to play with their cars."

As me and Erik turned, I saw his grandma nod, like she agreed with Flo.

The second we were outside the house, Erik said, "I know why you're here, but my grandma doesn't know anything about what happened in San Francisco. She's nearly seventy, so I appreciate that you didn't barge in with guns drawn like the FBI."

I said, "Erik, me and Flo are just doing our job. Don't worry, you've got Pinky as your lawyer. He'll get you off no matter what you did, including poisoning that nasty dude in Frisco."

"Bear, I'm innocent. I didn't poison Simon Rand."

"Dude, listen to me. I don't care if you killed him. Pinky wants you back and that's my job."

He stared at me and I could almost hear the gears in his head grinding away. "Okay, I'll return with you to San Francisco first thing tomorrow morning, but I need to say a final goodbye to my girlfriend and she lives in Skellefteå."

I said, "Okay by me, but I'll go with you."

"Bear, my good-bye is the kind that works best

between two consenting adults and will take all night."

"Oh, that kinda good-bye."

Erik said, "I have an idea. You get your Renault and the three of you can spend the night in grandma's summer house."

I know, I know, the dude burned me once so I shouldn't fall so easily the second time, but I thought I had all my bases covered. Who knew Swedes were that sneaky. "Okay, but before you go to say your good-bye you turnover your passport to Flo. She'll give it when we are ready to board the flight back to Frisco."

Erik's face looked like somebody just stepped on his big toe. "My God man, you sound like you don't trust me."

"I don't."

He gave me a sad look, shrugged his shoulders, then said, "I told you I'm innocent of the Rand poisoning, but I guess I can understand why you might feel the way you do. You walk back to your car and park it on the far side of the summer house."

I said, "Hold on, what will you be doing?"

"I'll go to my room in grandma's house, get my passport and give it to Flo, and then I'll walk with Flo and Ettamae to meet you at the summer house."

It sounded okay. Flo could keep an eye on him while I was getting the car and once she has his passport we've got him.

I said, "Okay. See you in a couple of minutes."

"Bear, when we met at my apartment in San Francisco, Ettamae's name was Kyla. What happened?"

"You've got me. Who knows what goes on in the head of a thirteen-year-old teenybopper."

While I walked back to the Ray No, I started to think about my Red Sox and wondered how they were doing. When we left Frisco, they were three games behind the damn Yankees. I'll ask Flo to check out the league standing on her iPhone. I finally got to the Ray No and a minute later I parked it by the far side of the summer house.

I walked up the front steps, opened the door and spotted Flo. She was standing by an old wood stove with Ettamae beside her and they weren't talking!

The hair on the back of my neck jumped a little 'cause those two were just standing there and whenever you stick Flo and Ettamae next to each other, they start chattering like a couple of hens scratching for corn in a barn yard.

I said, "Babe, did Erik give you his passport?"

"No he didn't. Bear, promise me you won't do anything stupid."

"Why would I do something stupid?"

"Because Erik's directly behind you, he's got a rifle, and it's aimed at me."

I turned and Erik was sitting on a bench next to a front window.

Erik said, "Glad you finally joined our little party."

I spotted the business end of a rifle poking out from a newspaper that covered his lap and my gut tightened up faster than a bull's ass at fly time.

Then the dude slid the newspaper off his lap and he lifted the rifle so I could see that his finger was on the trigger and the damned muzzle was pointed at the middle of Flo's heart.

Jesus, how do I get me and Flo into these messes?

I said, "Erik, like I told you before, guilty or not, you've got to go back to Frisco and turn yourself in. Sooner or later, the American cops will get the Swedish cops to send you back to the U. S. Get real! Me and Flo don't know the difference between krona and a corncob. We found your sorry ass in two days and we don't talk Swedish. The Swedish cops will have you on a plane back to California in fifteen minutes."

"Bear, I don't give a damn about the Swedish cops. I have an old school friend, Lars, who's half Sami. He's had, let's call it, a few brushes with the Swedish cops, and he lives in the Sami area along the border between Norway and Sweden. I'm heading north to Lars' place where the Swedish police will never find me. By the way, I hope you won't mind if I borrow your rental Renault for my drive north."

This dude was really starting to piss me off.

First he talks some kind of gobbledygook about a guy named Sami and now he's going to steal my rental car.

Flo said, "Bear, calm down. You promised me you wouldn't do anything stupid."

Hey, I never promised her that! But she was right, so in my head I counted to four before I said, "What or who in the hell's a Sami?"

Flo said, "They're sort of like the American Indians except they live way north of here, in Norway, Sweden, Finland, and Russia along the Arctic circle."

Erik said, "Very good, Flo. Like your Native Americans, the Sami consider themselves an independent nation. Now I have a question for you. Can you name me the Oscar winning actress who's part Sami?"

I growled, "Dude, stop asking dumb questions while you're holding a rifle on my Babe."

Flo said, "Trust me, Erik, rifle or no rifle, don't get Bear mad. Oh, the answer to your question is Renée Zellweger. She won her Oscar for Best Supporting Actress in Cold Mountain."

I said, "Okay dude, that's it! Put the rifle down or I'll personally kick your ass from here to Copenwagen."

CHAPTER TWENTY-THREE

Pinky-Summer house, north of Skellefteå, Sweden

I had always considered Sweden an intelligent, progressive country, but my experience at the Hertz counter inside the Skellefteå airport proved otherwise.

I approached the Hertz counter and said to the comely female who stood behind the barrier, "Hello. My name is J. Pincus Delmont."

"Good afternoon, Mr. Delmont. I have your reservation, but I'm sorry to inform you that we will not be able to supply you with your first choice, the Mercedes SLC 360."

First choice? "My good woman, that vehicle is not my first choice, it is the only vehicle I care to drive."

It was obvious from her expression that she understood simple english, but for a reason that escaped me, a Gold Plus member of Hertz, she went on that they did not have a Mercedes SLC 360 available for me to rent.

"My good woman, the manager of Hertz at the Philadelphia airport guaranteed my reservation. He told me he made my selection from the Hertz

Prestige Vehicle inventory."

"I'm sorry, Mr. Delmont, but he must have checked the Stockholm inventory of prestige vehicles. The Hertz group here in Skellefteå is small, too small to maintain a fleet of prestige vehicles, much less the Mercedes SLC 360. In its place I am pleased to offer you a Volvo S90, the top of the Volvo line!"

I controlled myself from lashing out in anger at the young woman who so amply filled out her Hertz uniform, and decided that this latest affront called for a second letter to the CEO of Hertz. My initial missive detailed the abysmal way I had been treated by the Hertz customer representative at the San Francisco airport. And now, I, a Hertz Gold Plus member in Skellefteå, Sweden, had been given a substitute Volvo S90 in place for my promised Mercedes SLC 360!

Truthfully, the Volvo S90 was an excellent choice. How did I know that? In the absence of something to do while flying from Stockholm to Skellefteå, and anticipating the possibility of Hertz not having my desired Mercedes SLC 360 at an airport that served fifteen to twenty thousand people, I had read an airline magazine article that extolled the virtues of the new Volvo S90. So as I stood at the Hertz counter, I was fully aware that the step down from the Mercedes to the Volvo would be nearly imperceptible to me.

I forced a half-smile, sighed, and said, "My

dear, as I have business to attend to I will accept your offer of the Volvo S90. However, as your company failed to provide me with my desired vehicle, my daily rental fee for the inferior vehicle will be reduced by seventy-five percent."

She leaned forward and snapped, "Twenty-five."

"Fifty percent," I said. "And that's my final offer. The Avis counter sits but a hundred feet down this corridor, and as we say in America, 'a bird in the hand is worth two in the bush.'"

Her pale blue eyes flashed with vexation, but she pulled out the contract from the printer, crossed out the printed daily fee, wrote down the figure that reflected our agreement, initialed the correction, and placed the contract on the counter for my signature.

I signed and a few moments later, I sat behind the wheel of my ersatz Mercedes, a top-of-the-line Volvo S90 at half the daily rental fee!

I keyed the address that Florence had sent me into theVolvo GPS system and fifteen minutes later, turned right onto a dirt road and drove to a house in the middle of a farm.

I got out of the vehicle and knocked on the front door. A lovely woman answered.

I said, "Good afternoon, Madam, My name is J. Pinkus Delmont. I am seeking a man, woman, and a child who . . ."

"They were here but gone now."

I smiled. "Thank you, madam."

She smiled. "Fika?"

"Madam, my name is Pinky."

She frowned, "No fika?"

"No madam, Pinky."

She shook her head, and as she closed the door, I heard her mumble, "Americans."

I returned to my vehicle, drove forward to an area where I could easily turn around and noticed a French Renault parked by the side of a small house a good seventy yards away. I parked next to the Renault, and got out of my Volvo.

The car was empty. I walked to the passenger side, tried the door and it was unlocked.

I opened the door and sat down.

Tucked in the console between the seats was a rental contract made out to Benat Zabarte.

Exiting the Renault, I noticed that the car had been parked out of sight of the farmhouse. It was possible that the woman who told me that Bear and Florence were gone did not realize my team remained on her property.

I locked my Volvo and carefully made my way to the front steps, looking up at each window to check for any sign of occupancy.

I reached the bottom step, stopped and listened. No sounds came from the abode, as if I were the only person within a hundred yards.

Buoyed by the quiet, I bounded up the stairs, twisted the door knob, and pushed the door open.

CHAPTER TWENTY-FOUR

Bear-Summer house, north of Skellefteå, Sweden

Erik said, "Bear, you aren't going to kick my ass anywhere. I'm the one holding the gun, so shut up! I'm going north and before I leave, I need to make sure you can't follow me. Ettamae, in the cabinet behind you there are some chains, and some of the long plastic zip ties. Take out three or four chains and grab a fist full of zip ties."

The kid did what she was told and dragged out three chains. They had big, one inch links, looked heavy, and each one was maybe three to four feet long.

Erik said, "Okay, now lay the chains on the floor next to that water pipe."

Ettamae did what he said and backed away.

Jesus, I wasn't sure what I was going to do next, but I was positive that me, Flo, and Ettamae weren't going to end up spending the night, lying on the floor, chained to that stupid water pipe.

Erik said, "Okay. Flo, run one of those chains around the water pipe."

She did, and then Erik said, "Now take a couple of those plastic ties. Wrap one around each of

Ettamae's wrists, slip the end through and pull it tight."

"Babe," I said. "Don't do that. That plastic tie's going to hurt the kid.

Erik yelled, "Flo, do what I say or I'll be forced to shoot you."

Flo stopped what she was doing and said, "Erik, does your grandma know we're here in her summer house?"

He shook his head. "No, I told her you were going back to America and I parked your car out of her sight. As far as she's concerned, you're all gone."

Flo said, "So we're going to be chained to that water pipe until we die?"

While he thought for a second about how to answer Flo's question, Ettamae wiped her face with her sleeve, and cried, "I'm too young to die."

I slipped a few inches closer to him.

Erik said, "You're not going to die. Grandma will find you and let you go."

I said, "Think about it, Erik. Once you get us chained up, and she thinks we're gone, we're gonna die out here. Are you ready to go from one murder to four?"

Erik said, "Damn it, no matter what you think, I didn't poison Simon Rand. When I'm far enough north, over the border into Norway, I'll call Grandma and tell her you are in the summer house and need help."

By this time, I was about six feet away from

Erik's left side and only needed to get a little closer to jump him. The rifle was pointed at Flo. Ettamae was standing on Flo's left and there was nothing on Flo's right but the wall made out of some kind of wood with a bunch of knots.

I could tell that Flo had figured out that I was trying to get closer to Erik so she stopped fiddling with the plastic tie, and said, "Erik, that rifle looks like it could bring down an elephant."

I don't think Erik wanted to think about anything else but getting in my Ray No and driving north, but when Flo asked about his dumb rifle, it was like some kind of magic spell came over him. Hell, my Babe had that kind of power over most dudes. All men are looking for a reason to stare at Flo's boobs and asking Erik that gun question did the trick.

Eric said, "This rifle was my grandfather's. It's a Tikka Bolt Action 6.5x55mm. He used it to hunt for elk so they'd have meat over the long winter months."

Flo smiled. "That's interesting. One more question while I finish with Ettamae's wrists. When we first met your grandma she said "fika", like we knew what she was talking about. What's fika?"

Now my Babe really had him. Erik's mind was on her assets, not on her boyfriend who was inching closer each second.

"Flo, fika is a Swedish custom where people sit down and have a cup of coffee and a cookie, or a sweet. It's like a coffee break back in the states, but in Sweden, fika happens many times during the day, or whenever anyone says, fika!"

As good as Flo was, my gut told me that we were running out of time and I had to move a bit closer so I could reach the barrel of the rifle before he could pull the trigger.

I said, "Look Erik, like I told you before, we don't give a damn if you did, or didn't poison that dude in Frisco, but pointing that rifle at my Babe could turn out to be a fatal mistake for you. I'll admit you might squeeze off a single shot before I get to you, but that's the only shot you'll get. And one way or another, you're going back to Frisco. But if you shoot Flo, what's left of you will fit in my carry-on luggage for the flight home."

For the first time, it seemed to sink into the dork that he was in deep shit and he looked scared. He glanced at me, then Flo, then all our heads turned around when we heard footsteps on the landing by the front door.

Right or wrong, this was it. I shifted my weight onto the balls of my feet, threw my hands forward like one of those fancy Olympic divers you see jumping off a high board, and reached for that damned rifle.

CHAPTER TWENTY-FIVE

Pinky-Summer house, north of Skellefteå, Sweden

I pushed the door open and was presented with a real life diorama.

Florence and that child were huddled against the wall to my left.

Bear lay on the floor. His large frame was shaking and he howled like a wounded animal.

Underneath Bear's muscular body was his arm that looked to be trapped between a large caliber hunting rifle and the floor.

A few feet away from Bear and the rifle lain a man who looked unconscious. I assumed he was Erik Rundstrom.

My top investigator saw me standing in the doorway. His lips seemingly contorted with pain moved, but no words came out.

Before I took a step, Florence bolted from the wall and tied the unconscious man's hands together with a black plastic zip tie.

Satisfied with her work, she said, "Pinky, we're happy to see you. We had a little situation where Erik threatened to shoot me and you how Bear gets when that sort of thing happens! It looks like we're all fine except for Bear. If I had to guess, I think his arm is broken."

I pointed at the unconscious man. "My good woman, would you please explain to me why you felt the need to bind that man's hands?"

The level of her voice rose to a near scream. "Didn't you hear me? I told you that Erik Rundstrom threatened to shoot me with a rifle that's large enough to take down a thousand pound elk. If that's not good enough for you, then you can take this job and shove it."

I said, "Calm down." Bear's yelping interrupted my train of thought. "Are you telling me that I will have difficulty returning my client back to San Francisco without a fight?"

"Pinky, I would classify that as one of your best understatements."

"My good woman, my job is to figure out how to solve that problem. Your task is to make reservations for the five of us to fly back to San Francisco as soon as possible. Then call Charles and give him our SFO ETA. Finally, call my office and bring them up to date."

Florence's face got bright red and she looked as if she was ready to explode when that child, Ettamae, marched up to me and violated my personal space. She stamped her foot on the wooden floor, shook her finger in my face, and said, "Pinky, Flo will make all that happen after, not before, but after we get Bear to a hospital so a medical professional can check out the damage to his right arm. My God, they're right about you. Even when you do the right thing, like you're a superhero in time to save us, you can't help being a giant, royal, pain in the butt!"

CHAPTER TWENTY-SIX

Bear-Summer house north of the Skellefteå, Sweden

A couple of hours later, after we got to a hospital, Flo told me that I was in la la land for a while. She could be right, but I did remember some stuff that happened, sorta knocked out or not.

I remembered that before Erik figured what I was going to do, I jumped him and knocked the rifle out of his hands before he could pull the trigger.

Then I crashed into him. He dropped like a sack of oats and I remember his head sounded like a bowling ball bouncing off a seven pin when his noggin hit the hardwood floor.

Then I hit the floor and heard a bone snap when my right arm got stuck between that big rifle barrel and the hardwood floor. I'd never broken an arm before, even as a kid, so I didn't know how bad it could hurt. But I think I must have squished a nerve or something 'cause that was the worst pain I'd ever felt in my life.

After my arm broke, I just lay there and voices kinda of floated in and out. Real quick, I figured out that if I moved one finger on my broken arm, I had to scream.

I remember hearing Flo ask me, "Bear, what can I do to make you feel better?"

I know I tried to answer her, but holding back the screams was about all that I could do.

Lying there, I watched Flo pick up the rifle, open the bolt action, and heard her say. "I guess Erik proved he's not a murderer because the rifle wasn't loaded."

Ettamae added. "Maybe he's just really stupid and forgot."

As bad as my arm hurt I wanted to tell them both that bullet in the chamber or not, the dude was ready to pull the trigger and when you pull a trigger you want to shoot someone. But I kept my mouth shut tight to keep me from squealing like a wounded rabbit.

I think I was about to pass out when the door opened and Pinky walked in.

I'd never been happier to see the little shrimp. My arm felt like it was on fire, but I remember trying to say, "Hi, Boss. Glad you dropped in . . . I cold-cocked the bad guy when I jumped him . . . Oh, and I think I broke my arm and it really hurts. You know, I think we could really use a little help here."

CHAPTER TWENTY-SEVEN

Pinky-Lasarett Hospital, Skellefteå, Sweden

Before we left the farm, and while Bear whimpered in pain, Florence exhibited a level of cleverness heretofore unknown to me. The woman tied Erik's hands together with a plastic tie, and then said, "Pinky, you hold Erik while Ettamae puts a plastic tie around my right hand."

For a moment, I was perplexed, but after Etttamae completed her task, Florence's wrist was connected to Erik's hands and the two were locked together.

I said, "Very clever, but how are you going to drive? He could do anything once you get up to speed."

Ettamae said, "I can drive. Fergus taught me in Scotland."

Why not? I am paying for the child's lodging, food, and expenses. Might as well get something in return. I said, "Good. I will take Bear."

I followed the Renault and during the five mile drive, with every bump, or turn, Bear cried out. We reached the emergency center and parked our vehicles next to each other. Before I could exit,

Florence walked a subdued Erik Rundstrom to my car and we all watched Ettamae ran into the emergency center. The child returned in a moment and handed Florence a pair of scissors, so she could cut the tie around her right wrist. Then she handed me the fugitive, saying, "Take one of those plastic zip ties and attach his hands to your steering wheel. That will keep him from running away."

I said, "Florence, your work with the plastic ties was impressive."

"I agree, and don't forget, Ettamae drove the Renault that got us here and she's only . . ."

"My good woman, please do not inform me of her actual age. That way I can honestly describe her as a young woman who has recently joined the investigative staff of Team Delmont."

"Sounds good. Now, Erik's all yours. Don't trust him for a second. I need to get my man in to see a doctor."

Florence helped Bear out of my car and walked him, with Ettamae's assistance, through the open door of the emergency center at Lasarett Hospital.

With Erik attached to the steering wheel, I walked around the Volvo to the passenger seat, sat down, and said, "Erik, you and I are going to fly to San Francisco. Do you have any problems with that?"

"Hell yes! I'm staying here. I don't want to go to San Francisco and you can't make me. Sweden has laws against kidnapping their citizens."

"I understand that Sweden has laws to protect their citizens, but the United States and Sweden also have an extradition agreement. That procedure will take time, but sooner or later, the Swedish government will turn you over to a U. S. Marshall who will return you to San Francisco where you will stand trial for the murder of Simon Rand."

"Nobody seems to care, but I didn't kill him. The bastard murdered my restaurant, but I did't kill him."

"My boy, I believe you, but you still have to go back. Now consider these two alternatives: I, J. Pincus Delmont, as your attorney, will represent you against this spurious murder charge. I am not sure if you are aware of the fact that your father retained me as your attorney of record. He retained me once he discovered that I have never lost a case defending a client charged with murder. Ask Bear for more details when he gets his arm fixed. That is the reason why my operatives followed you to this godforsaken place. From this point on, your job will be to sit back and relax knowing that I will protect you from harm.

"But there is a second alternative you need to consider. I can cut the plastic tie and you will be free until the day comes when you are extradited to San Francisco. Once there, you will be defended by a public defender. To be completely honest, I understand that the San Francisco Public Defender's office is populated with some reasonably good attorneys, but are you willing to risk a conviction, and a sentence of twenty-five years to life, on a reasonably good attorney?

"Erik, you can choose me, an attorney with a perfect thirty-three clients acquitted out of thirty-three murder trials, or a reasonably good public defender. Also, I am a gourmet who loves food prepared in imaginative ways and I understand you are an imaginative chef. You lost your first restaurant due to a poor location. I will back your next endeavor to the tune of $100,000 for ten percent of the operation. That way you can be sure that the location of your next restaurant will bring in customers, not drive them away. My boy, the decision is yours."

"Mr. Delmont, please cut these zip ties. My wrists are getting sore."

"Please, call me Pinky."

"Pinky, cut the damn ties."

"After you tell me your choice."

The lad stared at me. More seconds ticked by as if he was not aware that he was on the cusp of a life-altering decision.

I was confident that with his father's $1,000,000 retainer, I would not run into any financial barriers that stood in the way of his defense. On the other hand, if Erik chose the public defender, I pondered if I should consider returning a small percentage of the $1,000,000 retainer.

A few more seconds passed before he finally

broke his silence.

"Pinky, because my father didn't raise a fool, and because I like the odds of thirty-three acquittals verses zero convictions, and because I didn't kill Simon Rand, and because you'll help me open a new restaurant, I'll take your offer. You are now my attorney. Now, if you don't cut these damn plastic ties, I'll piss all over the driver's seat of your Volvo S90."

I cut the ties using the scissors the child borrowed from the emergency center, and Erik bolted from the car and ran into the emergency center. I followed and found him, as promised, in the men's restroom. Erik was using one of the facilities and at the moment, that seemed to be a good idea.

While we stood side by side, I said, "Just to reiterate, if you run away now, or anytime before we land in San Francisco, your future days will be spent as a fugitive. I am positive you could hide successfully for a period of time, perhaps a year or two, maybe even a decade. But think of those years of living in fear, always looking over your shoulder awaiting the long arm of the law. Erik, it is not a happy picture. And do not forget, even though a decade might have passed, California has no statute of limitations concerning murder, so you will still face a charge of murder in San Francisco. If you run away after you have emptied your bladder, I will contact the U. S. Consulate in Sweden and ask him to begin extradition proceedings against Erik Rundstrom for a first degree murder charge in the County of San Francisco."

He sighed. "Man, you are relentless. I promise I won't run, but please believe me when I tell you again that I didn't poison Simon Rand."

"Erik, I believe you. Now, once I wash my hands, I have a pair of scissors to return."

A few moments later, Erik and I walked into the waiting room.

Florence jumped up from her chair and exclaimed, "Pinky, have you lost your marbles? That guy tried to kill us."

Erik said, "I did not! The rifle wasn't loaded."

I said, "Calm down and sit. Any news on Bear?"

"No," said Florence. "The nurse told me it could take a couple of hours to patch him up."

For the next hour and a half, Florence and the child paced every square foot of the emergency section in the Lasarett Hospital while Erik played some sort of a game on his iPhone. I tried to pass the time by watching a Swedish television variety show, but after a horrible ABBA look-a-like bombed, I decided that my time had to be more valuable.

I pulled out my phone and dialed my office. Frank answered. "Law Office of J. Pincus Delmont. How may I help you?"

The young man had improved his phone manners to an amazing degree. "Frank, where is Lu?"

"Hello, sir. You're lucky you got me. I was about to take a coffee break."

"Coffee break? It is five after six in the evening and . . ." Then I recalled I was in Sweden and there was an eight hour time difference. "Never mind. Put Lu on the line."

"Sorry, sir. Lu's not here. Yesterday afternoon she went to the hospital and had her baby. A little girl. Lu and her baby got home from the hospital this morning. Lu named her child Jiao. She told me that name in Chinese means delicate and beautiful."

A wave of trepidation crept into my soul. With Lu gone, I was totally dependent on this ignorant boy to maintain the course of my corporate ship. "Frank, do I have any important messages?"

"You have three, but if it's okay with you, I have a question for you first."

"Go ahead, my boy."

"Sir, when I was in school my teacher made us read a book. Inside the book there was a picture of a little boy who wore wooden shoes. The boy had his finger stuck in a wall of dirt, something the book called a dike, and he was holding back the ocean. Have you seen that boy?"

Frank's question made me realize that learning how to answer my office phone, address me as sir, and take my messages, required as much mental acuity as a night watchman in a mausoleum. But with Lu gone, and considering I was thousands of miles from Carson City, I was stuck with Frank until she returned.

"Frank, that picture came from a book called _Hans Brinker and the Silver Skates_, and the story about the boy who plugged a leak in a dike with his finger is apocryphal. Do you understand what apocryphal means?"

"No sir. I do not."

"Apocryphal means a story of doubtful authenticity that is widely circulated as being true."

"Ah . . . so are you telling me that you didn't see the boy?"

I considered berating the lad, but it would be the same as pouring water into a pitcher with a hole in its bottom. I will fire him the moment I return to Carson City so I saw no reason to spoil the rest of Frank's day. "My boy, read me the messages."

"The first comes from a man named Charles Godwin. He needs you to call him at once. It's urgent. I have his number."

"I have his number. Hang up now. I will call him and then call you back."

"But Mr Delmont, you have two more . . ."

I clicked off and made my call to Charles.

"Pinky, it's about time you got back to me. We're . . . ."

"Charles, presently I am talking to you from a medical facility in Skellefteå, Sweden. My investigator's right arm has a compound fracture, but I have convince Erik Rundstrom to return with me to San Francisco even though there is the possibility of a jail cell in his future. And, I might add, I have accomplished all this while you sat at home imbibing a glass of Alexander Valley cabernet sauvignon." I took a breath and snapped, "Tell me, my good man, what more could you tell me that required my immediate attention?"

"A San Francisco court just issued a warrant for the arrest of Erik Rundstrom for the murder of Simon Rand."

"Charles, I had anticipated that possibility, but not before we had returned to the bay area. If Erik learns this news, the warrant could rekindle his desire to bolt. As soon as Bear gets patched up, we will return to San Francisco. I will call you the moment we land so we can accompany Erik to the nearest police station where he will turn himself in to be booked. Good-bye."

I placed a call to my office and when Frank answered, I said, "Move on to the second message."

"Hello, again, Mr. Delmont. The second message comes from a Mr. Hook. He needs you to call him at once. It's urgent. Do you want his number?"

My stomach tightened. "No! Next message."

"The last message comes from Judge Jonas Adams. He wants you to call him at once. It's urgent. I have his number, . . ."

An involuntary muscular contraction hit my nether regions and I nearly lost control of my lower digestive tract. As I clicked off the call, I feared I would not make it to the men's rest room, a long fifty feet down the hall.

CHAPTER TWENTY-EIGHT

Bear-Lasarett Hospital, Skellefteå, Sweden

I was sitting in a wheelchair with my head spinning around like I was living in some kind of loopy land.

Flo asked, "How bad was it?"

"I watched a bunch of people, all with blonde hair, cool blue eyes, and dressed in those kinda blue-green clothes you see on hospital TV shows, do all kinds of stuff to my right arm. One dude, I think it was the boss doc, spent a shit-pot full of time poking, pushing, and cutting on my right arm and he said that my arm had some kind of a compound thing. Then they put me to sleep and I woke up when a cute blonde babe wrapped my arm with a green fiberglass cast. Funny thing was that after going through the worst pain I can remember, right now my arm feels okay. I'm a little woozy, but there's no pain in my arm."

Flo shook a little plastic bottle. "The doctor gave me this. Inside are twenty-five pills called OxyContin. He told me that each pill was a super pain killer and we had more than enough to get you back to San Francisco."

Then Flo read the fine print on the plastic
bottle with the pain killers inside, and she said,
"Bear, you're not going to like this, but you can't
drink any alcoholic beverage while taking
OxyContin."

"Not even one cold brew?"

She said, "Not even one."

"Shit! Okay, if I stop taking the pain pills right
now, when can I have a beer?"

Flo flashed me her are-you-kidding-me glare.
"I'll check before we leave, but I think you'll like
these pills because they'll do the job on your pain a
lot better than a bottle of beer."

Then Ettamae had to stick in her two cents.
"Flo's right. OxyContin is a dangerous drug. It's
addictive, and some of the worst side affects include
constipation, sleepiness, nausea, dizziness,
vomiting, headache, dry mouth, and sweating, but if
you really need it for pain, it works great."

I said, "Jesus, that stuff sounds dangerous.
How come you, a little teeny-bopper, know more
about this oxicompton stuff than I do?"

She said, "When I lived in Scotland, we had a
class in school called the dangers of prescription
drugs."

I said, "Okay! Enough about no beer and what
this oxicompton can do to me. Where's the boss?"

"Last I noticed, he was sprinting down the hall
to the little boys' room."

"When he shows up, I've got to tell him I'm

really tired of getting beaten up on these investigations. I've been shot at, nearly drowned, screwed up my leg, and now broke my arm. I think it's time the shrimp started paying me combat pay."

Flo said, "I agree. I don't know what this emergency room visit is going to cost, or that cast on your arm. Back home, all that and thirty OxyContin tablets would set us back about a hundred grand."

"Babe, I don't care what it costs. I deserve combat pay."

Flo and Ettamae both chimed in. "We both agree."

I said, "Thanks, and now I want another one of those pills. My arm's starting to feel like somebody just stuck a hot poker inside the cast."

"Okay, but just one. These pills have got to last us all the way back to San Francisco."

CHAPTER TWENTY-NINE

Pinky-Lasarett Hospital, Skellefteå, Sweden

After considerable time to concentrate on my internal workings in the public facility, I gingerly walked back to the waiting room.

The instant I rounded the corner, I spotted Bear. He was sitting in a wheelchair with his right arm encased in a bright green fiberglass cast. When he saw me, he said, "Boss, I'm tired of getting hurt doing this job. I think you should pay me combat pay."

"I understand, my boy. But tell me, how does your arm feel?"

"Pretty good, considering."

"We are a long way from home, so we will table the combat pay discussion until a more convenient time," I hesitated, "Perhaps when we return to Carson City."

Flo said, "Not so fast. During all of our investigations, my man's the only one getting kicked around. He deserves some form of extra compensation. Bear can call it combat pay. I'll call it twenty thousand dollars for each broken bone. In this case, Bear should receive $40,000 because he broke both his radius and ulna bones, and come to think about it, there should be a bonus for a compound fracture."

I was getting a touch hot under the collar. "Florence, I said we would table this discussion until later so you can cease your feeble attempt to negotiate an early contract. Now that I am feeling better, and Bear looks ready to go, what is holding us up?"

Florence said, "We are waiting for that lady behind the counter to get all the information together so she can figure out our bill."

"Sounds reasonable. Let me know when the bill is ready." I moved to an empty corner of the large room to avoid her snooping. I keyed in a number and Hook answered.

"Shyster, you'd better sit down."

"I am sitting. Hook, what is so wrong that I had to call you during my long anticipated, and greatly deserved, Scandinavian vacation?"

"Can it! Now, tell me! What sort of law do you practice?"

"I believe you know the answer to that question," I stated with an irritated tone creeping into my voice.

"I know you keep guys out of the slam, or keep the needle out of their arm. Am I right?"

"You are."

Hook said, "So you don't know shit about divorce, or all those other kinds of lawyering stuff, right?"

"To be precise, during my matriculation at law school, I studied divorce, trusts, wills, and contracts, what every legal professional terms family and corporate law. Why do you ask?"

"Pinky, that judge we are both acquainted with in Carson City skimmed over a few important nuggets of information concerning his past, and those missing bits have got us all in a canoe, floating down shit creek without a paddle. You could say our Carson City friend is standing with his toes hanging over the edge of a very deep hole on the property of a certain New Jersey citizen."

Suddenly my mouth went so dry that for a moment, I had difficulty responding. "Hook, why do you feel that this is important news at this time?"

"You shoulda burned more of the midnight oil on that divorce section at law school. That New Jersey buddy holds you personally responsible for this mess, and he has invited you, and me, to join the Carson City judge so we can all stand together at that deep hole in the ground."

My blood pressure shot up so fast that I became light-headed. "My good man, stop beating around the bush. Tell me what is going on and use English."

Hook said, "That deal you worked out while you were in New Jersey is kaput! Do you understand that English?"

"I do. Are you aware of what caused the

schism?"

"It turns out that the judge was already married."

I said, "So what? We both know he had divorced his previous wife."

"Yah, but the blonde babe he married in New Jersey is a Catholic, and Catholics believe that getting a divorce only ends the legal part of marriage. Something like a divorce doesn't end a valid sacramental vow." Hook hesitated, and then continued, "Shyster, you can guess the rest of this story. When the judge got married the first time, it was in a church with a minister. So in the eyes of the Catholic church, the judge is still married to his first wife!"

I was about to protest my ignorance concerning this religious matter when a monumental foreboding momentarily paralyzed my vocal cords. I realized that ignorance was not an excuse and I was culpable in this matter.

"Shyster, are you there?"

"Please continue."

"I shouldn't be involved in this mess, but the stupid judge threw me under the bus when he told the New Jersey dude that I was the middle man between you and him. So now here I sit, a totally innocent bystander, and for no good reason I've got a dog in this fight!"

My mind raced for a solution, or at least something I could say to calm Hook's panic.

"Come on, Pinky, say something!" screamed Hook. "You've made a ton of bucks talking your way out of all kinds of shitty situations. Give me something here that'll shows me you can fix this mess!"

I took a deep breath in a futile attempt to control my rising sense of panic. "Hook, I am presently in Sweden and had planned on flying from Copenhagen to San Francisco, but I will change my flight and go directly to Philadelphia. Once I arrive there, I will contact our New Jersey friend, set up a meeting, and I am positive I can resolve our dilemma."

"Jesus, I hope you can 'cause I don't want to end up feeding the fishes off the coast of Atlantic City."

"My good man, that feeling is mutual. Before I leave my present location, and even though we are thousands of miles apart, I will come up with a solution that will resolve our precarious situation, but I need time to think. Good-bye."

I sat back and conjured up a few scenarios that could move me away from the edge of Big Julie's bottomless pit:

The judge could die in a sudden motor vehicle accident!

The judge could . . . .

A young female voice interrupted my reverie. "Pinky, wake up! Are you okay? It's the middle of the day."

"Young lady, go away. My eyes are closed while I am considering various solutions to a monumental dilemma, and I find it difficult to accomplish positive mental activity while you invade my personal space."

The child said, "You called me young lady. Don't you remember my name?"

"With the Sword of Damocles hanging over my head by a single horse hair, I find it difficult to care who or what you are. Now leave me alone. I have to think and it is a matter of life or death."

She continued to prattle on. "But aren't you curious about Bear's condition? Do you think they were able to fix his arm? He had a pretty bad compound fracture and I think . . ."

I jumped up and demanded, "Leave me alone!"

The urchin scuttled away.

Now, where was I? Ah yes, the judge could go to jail for tax evasion!

The judge could catch Ebola.

Or a disease that would render the him impotent.

Or he could come down with tuberculosis.

Or—I have it! The judge is afflicted with Lewy body dementia.

Some years back, as a favor to Willow, I assisted a friend of hers with Lewy body dementia. The friend needed help to set up a trust for his family while he still retained some cognition. While the poor soul sat in my office he suffered hallucinations, lost track of time. Weeks later he missed two appointments because he had forgotten the day of the week. Tragically, less than a year from our first meeting, he died. Lewy body dementia was a horrible way to go and there is no way that Big Julie would want his daughter to remain married to a husband with that grisly disease.

I immediately called Hook.

"Shyster, I've just had time to walk to the can, take a pee, and get back to my couch."

I said, "Our answer is Lewy body dementia!"

"What?"

"Lewy body dementia. It causes a rapid, progressive decline in mental ability. A patient will have visual hallucinations, Parkinson's like symptoms, along with a discernible decline in cognitive ability."

Hook said, "That might work. We can tell Big Julie that the judge didn't find out about his dementia stuff 'til after the wedding. So none of us knew before the wedding that his brain was turning to mush. Shyster, this idea could save our bacon 'cause no father, much less Big Julie, would . . . hold on, we've got a big problem with this scam."

My day had been exceedingly long and I was beginning to fade. I sighed, "What is not right?"

"You got involved in this deal 'cause you're getting something from the judge, right?"

"I don't know what you mean."

"Pinky, I know you, and you don't do nothing for free."

I said, "One could accurately assume there was a quid pro quo involved."

"Shyster, do you think the judge will hold up his end of the bargain if you get him out of this marriage with your dementia crap?"

I must be exhausted to lose sight of the fact that my Lewy body scenario would save our lives, but my life time agreement with Judge Jonas would be null and void.

"Hook, you are correct. We will have to come up with something else."

"Got it. I'm thinking."

"Unlike you, I am not able to think while listening to someone breathe on a phone." I barked, "Goodbye!"

I dropped my phone into my jacket pocket and was staring at the intricate floor tiles when I heard someone approach me.

Florence stamped her foot. "Pinky, why did you do that?"

"Do what?"

She said, "Did you inform Ettamae that the Sword of Damocles was hanging over your head, and then you shoo her away like she was a stray cat or dog?"

"I did. A man has the right to his privacy."

Florence said, "You do understand that the Sword of Damocles idiom means that your life is in imminent peril?"

"I do."

"And do you realize that when I walked up just now you were staring at the floor through closed eyes? And did you know that your lips were moving, and mumbling like you were talking to yourself?"

My lips were moving? Mumbling? I had no idea I was doing that. "My good woman, what I do with my time is no business . . ."

"Damn it, Pinky, listen to me. First, you can't go around telling an impressionable girl the you are about to die. She's at a very vulnerable age, and her grandfather just died."

"Florence, I am fully aware of what I said to the child, but what you do not understand is that the mythical sword is about to fall. An East Coast Mafia Don might kill me. Oh, I almost forgot to include Hook."

"Hook? Carson City Hook?"

"One of the same."

"What the hell does Hook have to do with anything?"

"It is too long a story to recount now. Florence, I am asking you to trust me. I have to come up with a solution to my life-threatening dilemma, or Northern Nevada's most successful attorney will be no more."

Florence said, "A Mafia guy's going to kill you?"

"Perhaps! And do not forget Hook."

Florence stared into my eyes for a moment and

it was as if I could see the gears turning in her head. Then she said, "Pinky, are you sure you're not just making this Mafia story up to get me off your back?"

"My good woman, I am not in the habit of fabricating my premature death at the hands of the mob. Now, if you will excuse me, all I ask is that you, and that child leave me alone. I need time, and solitude, to come up with a solution to my life and death situation."

Florence said, "Alright. Bear should be out soon. Ettamae and I will leave you alone until then, but once my man's back, your walls of silence will have to come down."

I nodded and my concentration returned to tracing the grout lines of the floor tiles.

After a moment or two of contemplation, the obvious solution hit me. I grabbed my phone and called Hook.

"My good man, a few moments ago you informed me that the Carlucci/Jonas nuptials were not valid because the judge and his first wife had been married by a minister."

Hook said, "Where are you going with this?"

"And inside a church where they exchanged sacramental vows. Am I correct up to this point?"

"Right so far."

"What if the minister that performed the first marriage ceremony was not properly ordained, or he had been defrocked before the wedding took place.

Then the sacramental vows the judge and his first wife recited at their wedding would not be binding."

Hook said, "I get it. The minister wasn't a legit padre so the judge's first marriage was only a civil marriage, like going to a Justice of the Peace wedding joint in Reno."

I said, "That is right, but how are we going to make sure that the minister was never ordained?"

Hook said, "Trust me, I'll take care of that little detail. But what I do ain't gonna be cheap."

"Could you give me a ballpark estimate?"

"Shyster, it could go as high as seventy-five, maybe a hundred big ones."

"My good man, de-frocking that minister will save your life too."

"But Pinky, you're the one getting that quid pro quo thing, and I haven't got a clue of how much that's going to fatten your wallet."

My mind was running out of fuel quicker than I could run out of money. Had I been rested, my negotiation skills would have been sharper, but considering the circumstances, I thought I did rather well.

"Hook, twenty-five."

"Sixty-five."

I said, "Thirty-five, and that is my final offer."

He said, "Sixty, and I can't go any lower 'cause most of those bucks are expenses I can't avoid."

I thought for a moment, and then said, "Okay, make it sixty."

Hook said, "Okay, but I'll need the cash right away."

"No problem. I will call my office and give them instructions to give you a cashier's check for sixty thousand dollars."

"Shyster, Bear's right. You're a damn genius when it comes to making up bull-shit stories."

I said, "I will take that as a compliment. Now, if you will be so kind, make reservations in my name for two rooms at the Hilton Philadelphia at Penn's Landing. I will pay for both rooms. I will meet you there inside of twenty-four hours and do not forget to bring the evidence that the minister was not authorized to perform the religious aspects of the first marriage of Judge Jonas. Goodbye."

The moment my call to Hook disconnected, I called my office.

"Frank?"

"Yes, sir."

"A man with a stainless steel hook for a right hand will soon drop by the office to pick up a cashier's check for sixty thousand dollars. That means you have five minutes to get to my bank and have them cut the check."

"Wow! That's a pile of money. Mr. Delmont, what's a cashier's check?"

"Call your uncle and tell him that I said he needs to go to the bank with you."

"Yes sir, I'll do that. How's everything going in . . ."

Suddenly, my promise to Charles to meet him at SFO slipped through my foggy consciousness.

I said, "Good-bye, Frank," and called Charles.

When he answered, Charles said, "My screen tells me that this call is from Pinky Delmont, but that can't be, because he and I just agreed upon a flawless plan of attack less than ten minutes ago."

"My good man, we had, but an unforeseen complication just appeared on the horizon."

"What's happened now? We had everything set and . . ."

"Charles, I must fly to Philadelphia instead of San Francisco due to a conundrum that presents the real possibility of life or death, and that threat includes me. Bear and Florence will accompany Erik and they will turn him over to you at the airport."

"Life or death, and you are included? Level with me, Pinky. What the hell is going on?"

"Charles, all I am asking of you is to trust me. Have I led you astray prior to this moment?"

"If I include all the days we were together at Hastings, more times than I can count on my fingers and toes."

"My good man, I am distressed that you feel that way. I believe that our college days were among the happiest, and most carefree of our lives."

Charles said, "That just goes to prove that everyone is entitled to their own opinion."

"Charles, to reiterate, Florence will contact you

with their ETA. All I ask is that you meet them at SFO and provide moral support for my client as he surrenders to the San Francisco police."

Florence tapped my shoulder. "Pinky, the bill is ready. All we have to do is pay and we can start back home."

Then, still upset at my old school chum's accusation, I closed with an angry, "Good-bye, Charles!"

CHAPTER THIRTY

Pinky, Bear, and Flo-Lasarett Hospital, Skellefteå, Sweden and Copenhagen Airport, Denmark

Jesus! I can't drink beer and I can't drive 'cause I'm high on fake morphine. "Babe, promise you'll keep feeding me those pills and get me back home."

"Gotcha, big guy. We've got a few planes to catch, but we'll be home in no time."

Flo pushed the wheelchair toward the door and a blonde babe behind a counter said, "Excuse me, but you must pay the bill before you can leave. We take Swedish krona, but we will accept Euros, Master Card, Visa, and American Express."

Flo pushed me toward the counter, kinda cringed, and said, "How much is the bill?"

The babe behind the counter stared at a computer screen. "The total comes to 2,019.45 SEK, that's Swedish krona, or 215.09 Euros, or approximately 240 of your American dollars. As I said, if you do not have enough cash, we accept Master Card, Visa, or American Express."

I damn near fell out of the wheelchair when Pinky said, "Florence, I will take care of the bill."

Both me and Flo's eyes bugged out as we saw

217

Pinky actually open his wallet, pull out a credit card, and hand it to the babe.

Flo whispered, "Maybe Visa is giving five times the miles on Swedish medical expenses this month."

"Babe, I'll bet you a Franklin that Pinky takes that credit card charge out of my next paycheck. Find out what the bill comes to in real money. I wouldn't put it past the little shit to add a hundred when he wants me to pay the bill."

As Flo walked over to the counter to get a copy of the bill, a tall blonde, with light blue eyes, and a great rack walked by me. Stuck in the wheel chair, I turned my head real fast to watch her boobs bounce, got dizzy and damn near puked.

Flo tried to show me the copy of the bill. I looked at the paper and my eyes got real fuzzy and the room started to spin.

I said, "Babe, these pills are making me feel really weird. Hell, I hardly looked at that babe who just walk by. I'm going to close my eyes for a while and take a snooze."

After I fell asleep, I could hear a voice once in a while, and some other noises, but it was like I was sitting way down at the bottom of a deep well. Those faint voices and sounds are about all I remember until Flo woke me up when we were almost ready to land in Frisco.

####

Much later, when Bear gave his report to Pinky

concerning our trip to Skellefteå, he asked me, Flo, to fill in the part when he was unconscious and tell what happened during those three flights between Skellefteå and San Francisco. So here is what I recall of those flights.

Once Bear closed his eyes, nothing seemed to wake him. When we left the ER in Skellefteå. except for the not waking up, Bear was okay. The doctor had told me the Oxy could make him super sleepy. Ettamae and I pushed him into the parking lot and to the Renault where Pinky and Erik helped me get Bear out of the wheelchair and strapped into the passenger seat.

Bear always wanted to drive so I was happy he was asleep because I didn't want to listen to him bitch about my driving.

Before I pulled out of the hospital parking lot, Pinky explained to me that he and Erik had struck a deal. Erik would go back to San Francisco without a fight, and Pinky would come up with a way to get him off for poisoning Simon Rand.

On the way to the airport, Pinky and Erik rode in his fancy Volvo while I drove Bear, Ettamae, and myself in the Renault.

We turned in both cars, and except for getting Bear in and out of the plane, the flight from Skellefteå to Stockholm was a piece of cake.

And the flight from Stockholm to Copenhagen was quick, smooth, and uneventful. When we landed, SAS got Bear off the plane, and popped him into a wheelchair. Other than standing in a couple of lines to check papers, nothing much happened in Copenhagen until the last line when, as Bear would say, the shit hit the fan. The five of us were shuffling along, except for Bear who was snoozing in his wheelchair, for the final passport check when four men in black uniforms appeared out of nowhere. They pulled us out of the line and hustled all of us into a room.

At the far end of the room sat the same gray-haired man who had threatened to shoot me with a Taser when the three of us were kidnapped from that beer garden in Tivoli.

The gray-haired man smiled. "Ah, my favorite Americans. We meet again. Today you were not detained because you violated the Danish anti-terrorism act. Today, we noted that you have added a fifth person to your entourage. The man I believe was the reason for your passage through Denmark to Sweden. Before I go further, is the gentleman snoring in the wheelchair in any discomfort?"

I said, "No. My man suffered a compound fracture of his right arm and his Swedish doctor prescribed OxyContin for pain relief."

The gray-haired man nodded. "I understand."

Before I could respond, Pinky said, "Captain Iversen, as we are not being detained due to a violation of the Danish anti-terrorism act, please tell us why we have been seized as we have a plane to catch."

"All in due time, Mr. Delmont. First, I need to talk with the gentleman standing next to you."

Pinky pointed at Erik. "This man?"

The man Pinky called Captain Iversen nodded, and said, "Your name and passport."

Erik looked at me.

I handed his passport to Captain Iversen. He scanned it, read it, and said, "Erik Rundstrom. Is there a reason why this female was holding your passport?"

Erik glanced at Pinky, then me, and said, "Not really."

The captain stared at Erik's face, as if he were looking for the slightest sign that Erik was being held against his will. "Then you will not be upset if I return your passport to the female."

Erik looked at Pinky again. "No problem, Captain. As you can see, I'm wearing a pair of tight jeans. I was concerned that the document could fall out of my back pocket and Flo graciously agreed to carry my passport for me in her purse."

The captain sat back, put his hands behind his head and stared at Erik. After what seemed to be two or three minutes, he said, "Thank you for your patience. My men will take you to the line and for your cooperation in this matter, they will move you to the front of the queue."

Pinky said, "Thank you, Captain Iversen," and I pushed Bear's wheelchair out of the office.

Once we passed the final checkpoint, Pinky

called us together. "Team, I have a change in plans to announce. In thirty minutes, Florence, Bear, Erik, and the child will board the SAS flight bound for San Francisco. Due to the change I mentioned a moment ago, I will board a different flight, this one to Philadelphia. Now, before anyone complains about . . ."

Erik screamed, "What the hell! Flo, I want my passport back! I'm returning to Sweden and heading north to live with the Sami where I'll be safe from liars like Pinky."

Pinky said, "Florence, do not give him his passport. Erik, calm down and listen to me. I have to make a quick stop near Philadelphia to clear up a situation that has put lives in danger. You have cleared the last passport check so you can board your SAS flight to San Francisco. If you do not board that flight, you will lose your opportunity to clear you name. You will become a fugitive. You will spend the rest of your life looking over your shoulder. Trust me and return to San Francisco and I will join you there as soon as possible."

Erik had the look of a cornered animal and took deep breaths for a moment. "Flo, what do you think? Should I trust him?"

I said, "Erik, if we were talking about money, then hell no, I wouldn't trust him. But we're not talking money. If you asked me if I would trust Pinky to defend me against a murder charge, I'd say he's the man to do the job."

Right then, Bear let go with a half belch, half snore and snuggled his head deeper into his pillow. Ettamae giggled and Erik and I both smiled.

I said, "And speaking of money, someone must have coughed up a bucket of cash retainer, plus expenses to defend you, because Pinky doesn't do anything for free."

"I'm sure the money came from my dad."

I said, "It's good to have parents who can help during a crisis like this."

Erik reached for my hand. We shook as he said, "Thanks, Flo, you've been straight with me. Let's get on that damn plane. I've missed freezing my ass off during those San Francisco summers."

On our flight home, the four of us were booked into Business class, row twenty, seats A and B for Bear and myself, and seats J and K for Erik and Ettamae. Between us there were four seats so I could keep an eye on Ettamae, and still get a bit of privacy.

Bear woke up about an hour out of San Francisco and said, "Babe, my arm hurts. I need another pill."

I whispered, "Sorry, but I need you more than you need a pill."

He sat up and looked around. "Really? With all these people around? Okay, I guess we can throw a blanket over us and hope nobody'll notice."

"Bear, I wasn't talking about that kind of a need, but as long as we're talking, if your arm can stand it, maybe later in the hotel."

"Babe, my arm's just fine if we're fooling around. Remember, I told you once that sex is kinda of an afrodeseeack. Once I get in the mood, nothing hurts!"

"Men! Just the thought of sex is an aphrodisiac. Now calm down. I told you maybe later."

"Okay." Bear sat up and looked around. "Hey, I'm as hungry and thirsty as a racehorse after the Kentucky Derby. Do you think it would be okay for me to have a beer?"

I knew I was pushing it, but a beer would get his mind off his arm. I signaled for the flight attendant. "You'll get your beer and anything else they can find for you to eat."

"Before the beer and food come, I've got to hit the can."

For a second I was worried that after all those drugs, and sleeping from Skellefteå to nearly San Francisco, he'd try to get out of his chair and crash to the floor. But I forgot I was talking about Bear. He jumped up, shook his body like he'd just emerged from hibernation, stretched, flashed me a big smile, and whispered, "Save my seat. I'll be right back."

With a sigh of relief, I watched him head down the aisle to the john. My man was back!

224

CHAPTER THIRTY-ONE

Pinky-Philadelphia, Pennsylvania

To my shock, I was unable to book a non-stop flight from Copenhagen directly to Philadelphia so I purchased a first class ticket to Newark, New Jersey. Before the plane took off, I instructed the flight attendant to let me sleep until she served breakfast. I fastened my seat belt, donned a sleep mask, and after six hours of fitful slumber, the plane landed at 12:56 p.m. New Jersey time.

My brain, reanimated by my spasmodic siesta, perked up as I picked up a new Mercedes 350 C at the Hertz agency and found my way onto the New Jersey Turnpike. Ninety minutes later, I arrived at my hotel in Philadelphia, on the verge of total exhaustion, but with the specter of the meeting with Big Julie hanging over me, I knew that I had to steel myself and work through my personal fog of fatigue.

During the drive to Philadelphia, as a mental exercise, and to fend off acute weariness, my brain catalogued the differences between my driving experience with the Volvo S90 in Sweden and the Mercedes 350 C in New Jersey. I concluded that while the Volvo lacked a touch of the polish of the Mercedes, the Swedish vehicle had offered a roomier and more elegant interior. By the time I handed over my keys to the valet at the hotel, I had decided that the Volvo was the equal of, if not better than, the Mercedes, and made a mental note to pick up a new Volvo S90 to drive on trips outside the range of the Tesla's batteries.

When I reached the reception desk, I was pleased to discover that Hook had followed my instructions and had reserved a room in my name and according to the desk clerk, Mr. J. Dudek had already checked in. Before I left the desk, the clerk handed me a note.

As I rode up the elevator, I read:

Pinky,

Remember Me? This is Joey Palumbo, the guy that drove you and your car around Philly.

Anyways, I got word that you were coming back to Philly 'cause Big Julie is totally pissed-off at you, a dude named Dudek, and me, Joey Palumbo. Pinky, and this is really important, when we meet with Big Julie, promise me that you'll tell him that I had nothing to do with anything but driving your car. Anyways, I still don't know what you did to make him mad, but it doesn't take much to piss-off Big Julie. I'll be working the bar tonight at six. Stop by, I'll buy the first round and you can tell me who this Dudek guy is and why we're all stuck in he same shit creek canoe without a paddle.

Joey

P. S. Don't forget you got to tell Big Julie that I wasn't part of whatever dumb thing you and that Dudek guy did.

The note made it crystal clear that Joey Palumbo's connections to Big Julie, or lack of same, were not going to be of any assistance in my life or death situation.

I had reached the point where I needed to formulate a plan of attack, a way out of this mafia maelstrom, but when the bellhop opened the door to my room and I spotted the bed, sleep eclipsed all other needs.

I tipped the bellhop. He closed the door and I checked the time. It was three-thirty in the afternoon. Joey Palumbo would not be behind the bar until six. I pulled out my iPhone, set my alarm for three hours, and the blessings of a deep slumber overwhelmed me before my head reached the pillow.

CHAPTER THIRTY-TWO

Bear-San Francisco, California

My Babe, Ettamae, Erik, and me, got off the plane and hit the customs room where we had to line up and wait while a bunch of dudes in uniforms asked us all kinds of dumb questions. Flo and Ettamae went first while I stuck Erik between me and Flo just in case he wanted to try to jump ship. While I waited for the customs dude to stop asking them questions, I mostly stood there thinking about my arm. It hurt a little, but nowhere near as bad as it had back in Sweden. After Flo and Ettamae got past the customs desk, they waited on the other side for me and Erik 'cause I was pretty sure Flo was watching in case Erik tried to vamoose.

This was my second time to come back to the US, so why was I confused about the US customs thing? It's simple. The China trip went across the Pacific. This trip went across the Atlantic to Europe. When we flew to Denmark, and after we grabbed our bags, we walked toward a big sign on the wall that said, 'Nothing to Declare'. On the other side of the room was a smaller door and I could see a pot full of dudes that looked like cops standing around.

As we got closer to the wall, Flo pulled me over and said, "We go through the 'Nothing to Declare' door."

I said, "How do you know that? Babe, I don't understand what 'Nothing to Declare' means."

Flo gave me her super stink eye and said, "I'll explain later." Then she pushed us all through the 'Nothing to Declare' side.

The same two signs popped up at the Stockholm airport and just like Copenhagen, Flo made sure we went through the 'Nothing to Declare' side.

Later, while we waited at the rental car desk in Sweden, I said, "Okay, Babe, it's later. Explain this 'Nothing to Declare' crap."

Flo said, "In the old days, before the EU, each country had all sorts of restrictions at their borders—like one liter of brandy, or two cartons of cigarettes—but today everything flows freely from country to country."

I said, "What do you mean, the EU's got boarders?"

She sighed, like Flo does when I ask her what she thinks is a really stupid question. "EU stands for the European Union and is made up of twenty-eight member nations. Countries like France, Germany, and twenty-six more nations."

Ettamae piped up. "Bear, even I know what the EU stands for." The Kid got close to Flo and whispered, "Flo, there are times when I wonder why a bright woman like you stays with a dolt like him."

She whispered alright, but I heard what she called me. Before I could figure out what to say to the Kid, and keep it clean, Flo jumped between us. "Because Bear's my man. Don't you remember how he rescued your grandpa from drowning when the Russian River flooded? And how he saved us both from that crazed gunman at the winery? Ettamae, you and I are both standing here today because of his bravery."

Ettamae looked down at her shoes. "I guess I forgot about that."

Flo continued, "Young lady, you're still too young to understand, but sometimes the relationship between consenting adults is difficult to put into words, but I'll give it a try.

"I knew the moment Bear and I first saw each other in Los Angeles that we were meant for each other. Another thing, and this is important. ever since that first day in LA, he has treated me like I'm the most desirable woman in the world.

"And before you ask, I'm completely aware that besides me, my man lives for three things: Boobs— Baseball, and Beer! When Bear's near a TV, he'll search every channel until he finds a baseball game. If he's standing next to a well developed female, he'll stare at her boobs. And if he bumps into a bar, he'll order a cool one.

"In Bear's perfect world, he'd spend the rest of

his life sitting at a bar, watching the Red Sox play baseball on TV, while a topless barmaid would serve him a cold beer."

"Ettamae, as I said, I am fully aware that Bear has a few minor foibles, but inside, he has a heart of gold, and most important, he's my man."

Ettamae started to sniffle. "Flo, I sorta understand a little of what you mean. With Grandpa gone, I'm all alone in the world. Someday I hope somebody comes along and makes me feel safe."

I said, "Kid, as long as me and Flo are around, you ain't alone."

Ettamae gave Flo a hug, and the Kid almost got her hug to me when the rental car babe handed me the keys to our car an we had to leave.

As we walked to our car, I said, "Babe, like I asked a minute ago, why do I care about the EU, and what does the EU have to do with us? We come from the good old USA."

Flo said, "I know where we come from, but we can still walk through the 'Nothing to Declare' door."

"Why?"

Ettamae piped up, "Because we'd be stupid to walk through the other side where those cops ask a lot of dumb questions."

Like I've said before, you never know what's going to pop out of the mouth of a teenager. I said, "Thanks, Ettamae. Now I've got it."

That's how Denmark handled us going from America to their country. And Sweden did the same when we landed from Denmark. So when we landed in Frisco, I was in for a big surprise. After we got off the plane and walked into a big room, I looked around for the 'Nothing to Declare' sign and didn't spot one. All I could see was a bunch of cop-like dudes jostling people into long lines, like we were a flock of rams, ewes, and lambs getting ready for a sheep dip to kill off lice and ticks.

I moved real close to Flo and whispered, "Babe, if we can walk through a 'Nothing to Declare' door in Denmark and Sweden, why don't we have the same kinda thing in our country?"

She shook her head. "Got me. Ask your congressman."

I hate it when she does that to me.

After we all got past a sour faced dude who asked a bunch of stupid questions, like he was pretty sure that everybody who got off the plane was trying to smuggle something into the country, we picked up our suitcases and standing just outside the customs room stood Charlie.

He waved and said, "Bear, what happened to your arm?"

I glanced at Erik. "I sorta fell on it."

Charlie stared at me, like he couldn't figure out how I could do something that dumb., then he said, "Sorry to hear that. You need to be more careful in the future. Now, Erik, I will be your attorney of

232

record until Pinky returns and takes over. Once we leave the airport, I will drive us to the San Francisco police headquarters where you will turn yourself in. I am afraid you will have to remain in jail for at least twenty-four hours, or longer, if I cannot find a judge who will set bail. The fact that you initially fled the country will not work in your favor. However, you just returned to San Francisco," Charlie glanced at my arm, "under your own volition and turned yourself in. That alone should help my argument for bail. I tell you all this so you understand that once you enter the jail system, you are not being abandoned. Both Pinky and I are committed to your defense and your eventual freedom."

Erik said, "I understand, but I do have a favor to ask before you turn me over to the police. I want to find my old girlfriend, Laura, to ask her to give our relationship a second chance, and . . . ."

I said, "A girl friend named Laura? Dude, you didn't mention her before? And what about that girlfriend you wanted to see in Skaltiamaria."

Ettamae said, "Come on, Bear. Even I've heard about the sailor who had a girl in every port."

Erik said, "The girl in Sweden was just a . . . forget her. My real girlfriend's name is Laura Heath. She was the sous chef at my restaurant and about a year ago she moved into my apartment,"

Flo cried, "Erik, hold that thought." Then she pawed through her purse. I don't have a clue how she finds anything in there. But, just to prove me wrong, Flo pulled out a paper, checked it out, and said, "Charles, when we met at that coffee shop a few weeks ago, you handed me a paper with the names of two persons of interest in the Rand murder. One was Erik, and the other was Laura Heath. Why were the police interested in her?"

Charlie said, "I'm not sure, but I'll see what I can find out."

Erik said, "Hold on. Are you telling me that the police thought she could be involved in Rand's death."

Flo said, "That's it exactly. Now, tell us what you know about her."

Erik thought for a second, like he wasn't sure what to say. "Laura and I had a real relationship that lasted for nearly a year."

Flo said, "Then what happened?"

"I'm not sure. Laura was the sous chef at my restaurant. We got along great. I thought I'd found my true soul-mate, but then all of a sudden everything fell apart and she moved out."

Flo said, "Did she leave you before or after Rand was poisoned?"

Erik thought for another second. "A couple of days after."

I could see where Flo was going on this and jumped in. "Erik, was Laura working with you the night Rand was poisoned?"

"Yes, she was in charge of preparing the salad

and . . . ." Suddenly, the look a kid gets when his mom catches him with his hand in the cookie jar got pasted on Erik's face. "My God! I forgot all about that. And Laura hated Rand because his awful review zeroed in on her as one of the reasons my restaurant's food wasn't up to snuff. But she would never kill . . ."

Flo said, "Don't be so sure about that. Over the centuries women have used poison to rid themselves of unfaithful husbands, repugnant boyfriends, or in our present situation, a malicious restaurant critic."

Erik said, "But you don't understand. I know Laura, and she'd never . . ."

I said, "Stop flapping your gums and listen to me. When the police end up with a dead body, and they figure it's homicide, they work really hard to come up with the bad guy who did the dirty deed. But, and this is a really big but, the cops stop looking at other suspects once they've zeroed in on a prime suspect. Erik, when you took off for Sweden, you might as well have called the cops and told them you were their prime suspect! A cop thinks if you weren't the guilty dude, why'd you run away?"

I could tell that I still wasn't getting through Erik's thick skull. "Charlie, tell him I'm giving him the straight scoop."

Charlie said, "Bear's essentially correct. Once the San Francisco police department identified you as their prime suspect in the Simon Rand murder, they would turn their evidence over to the District

Attorney's office, file the Simon Rand murder as solved and shift their resources onto their next homicide case."

I said, "So your girlfriend was hoping you'd take the rap for a murder she did." I shook my head. "That's throwing your boyfriend under the bus, big time. Have you got a clue where she is?"

Erik said, "I heard she moved in with our pastry chef, Claudette. She had an apartment on Mission, in the Mission District, a couple of blocks from my old restaurant. But I still don't think . . . "

Flo put her arm around Erik's shoulder. "Hey, stop thinking and let us do the heavy lifting from this point on. We'll find Laura. You go with Charles, and tomorrow, if you're still in jail, we'll drop by for a little visit."

Eric looked like he was about to cry. I know how he felt 'cause when the Carson City cops threw me into the slam on that trumped up murder charge, I felt like I didn't have a friend in the world 'til I found Pinky. Actually Pinky wasn't a friend, in fact he was a real pain in the ass, but the little shrimp got me off, so like I said, I knew exactly how Erik felt.

Erik gave Flo a hug, then Ettamae, then he started toward me, but when his eyes hit my cast, he backed away.

Erik said, "Bear, sorry about your arm. I guess I panicked. God knows I didn't want to hurt you."

I nodded. "Thanks. Charlie, keep this guy safe

while me and Flo track down this Laura babe."

Charlie said, "I'll do that. By the way, either of you have any idea where Pinky is, or what he's involved with?"

I said, "Nope."

Flo shook her head.

Even Ettamae shrugged her shoulders, like her main job was to keep track of the little fart.

CHAPTER THIRTY-THREE

Pinky-Philadelphia, Pennsylvania

I determined my hotel room was dark through my blinking eyes as a cacophony of noise raced through my murky mind.

As the fog of sleep lifted, I realized that the room filling noise was coming from my iPhone alarm. I sat up and took stock of the time. It was six-thirty-three in the evening, and in my exhausted state, even a free gin and tonic waiting for me at the bar did not generate much excitement.

I keyed in Dudek's room number and he answered on the first ring.

"Shyster, I've been waiting for you to call me ever since I checked in. What the hell took you so long?"

The fact that this cretin expected me to explain the details of my every movement set me off. I hesitated, silently counted to ten, and then said, "Hook, suffice it to say that I am talking with you now. Meet me at the bar in ten minutes. We have much to discuss." Before I slammed down the phone in anger, I snapped, "And do not forget to bring whatever you have that invalidates the judge's first marriage." My level of ire accomplished nothing, but I felt much better as I rode the elevator down to the first floor.

The moment Joey saw me, he gave me a high sign and started to make my gin and tonic. "Pinky, long time no see."

I watched a grinning Joey drizzle tonic over a healthy measure of gin and wondered how he could seem so oblivious to the simple fact that we could both be dead by cocktail time tomorrow. As Joey pushed my drink toward me, I decided that he must live in the present, similar to a dog, protecting him from looking too far into the future.

I said, "Thank you," as Hook slipped onto the barstool next to me. "Joey, this is Hook. Hook, Joey Palumbo."

Joey stuck his right hand over the bar, and when Hook thrust his stainless hook in the direction of the bartender's hand, Joey recoiled and said, "Jesus, be careful with that thing."

Hook growled, "It ain't a thing." He scowled at Joey for a good ten seconds, then said, "Are you working the bar or just taking up space? If you're working, I want an Aberfeldy, neat."

The two were acting as if they were two stags about to fight to the death to determine which one would live to impregnate all the females in the herd.

Joey frowned. "No Aberfeldy but we've got Dewars. I'm sure a smart dude like you knows that Aberfeldy is part of the Dewars blend."

Hook snarled, "Make it Dewars. You'd think a bar in a joint this expensive should carry better Scotch."

Joey stared at the sharp point of Hook's prosthesis for a moment, and then said, "I'll be sure the boss gets your complaint."

The tension was palpable and I could see that neither man was going to back down, so I said, "Gentlemen, gentlemen, calm down. We have important items to discuss. Joey, have you talked with Mr. Carlucci?"

"I did; well actually it was Rocco, the Don's right hand man. I told him that you were in Sweden, or one of those places over there. Rocco told me that Mr. Carlucci didn't give a shit where you were, but you damn well better be standing in Mr. Carlucci's office tomorrow morning at ten."

Hook said, "And what happens if we don't get there on time?"

Joey's jaw dropped, as if he could not fathom a question that ridiculous. "I don't know what you do in that dumb-shit state you come from, but here in Philly, and New Jersey, that'd be the last meeting you ever had, if you get my drift."

Hook downed his whiskey as if his mouth were a vacuum cleaner, pushed his glass forward and tapped it with his hook, informing Joey he wanted a second taste of Dewars. Then he said, "Why so damned early?"

Joey avoided looking at Hook, and said, "Pinky,

who is this guy? And what's he got to do with anything?"

"Hook made me aware of the judge's desire to marry Adelaide Carlucci. I flew to Philadelphia and met you. A few days passed and you drove me to the Carlucci estate. You know the rest."

Joey said, "Not so fast. So Carlucci has a good reason to be pissed off at this Hook character, and God knows you're up to your eyeballs in shit, but all I did was drive you to Mr. Carlucci's home. I don't know what you and Hook did to Mr. Carlucci before you got to Philly, but . . ."

Hook slammed his glass on the bar, and before Joey could move, he slipped the point of his hook under Joey's upper lip. "Joey, in the dumb-shit state I come from, we call guys like you yellow, or chicken, or whatever they call a coward, in Philly. Shut up or I'll rip your lip, and maybe your nose, right off your face and the docs will run out of stitches trying to stick it back on." Then, his hook still under Joey's lip, he turned his head and said, "Pinky, do we really need this pile of shit?"

I said, "Hook, please stop threatening Joey. Yes, we need him. He knows where Carlucci lives and he will drive us there tomorrow morning. Am I correct, Joey?"

As a single drop of blood trickled from his lip, Joey stammered, "Yes. I'll drive you there, and please, Mr. Hook, don't hurt me."

Hook removed the point from Joey's nostril and

said, "Another Dewars and this time don't short me. I expect full measure when I pay for a drink."

"Yes, sir."

I glanced at my own drink and noted I had not even lifted the glass to my lips. I took a small sip and as the cold gin, bubbles, and quinine trickled down my esophagus, I said, "Hook, did you bring the documentation we need to pull this off?"

He pulled a single sheet of paper out from his jacket pocket, handed it to me, and I read:

I, Pastor Earl P. Wilkinson, the undersigned, admit to never having been ordained, thus I never had the spiritual, or legal authority to officiate at weddings.

I confess to being impure of heart and did not partake in ordination, a cleansing process, when I was asked to renew my faith in God and recognize my sins. As I was never ordained, the marriage that I performed between James Jonas and Mary Swain, in Carson City, on February 26th, 1996, was never consecrated by God and is null and void both in the eyes of the church and the state of Nevada.

Signed, Earl P. Wilkinson

This document was signed before me, on August 6, 2016.
Sondra Welman, Notary Public

I said, "Looks good to me. What did you have to do to get Pastor Wilkinson to sign?"

Hook said, "I told you I'd get it done. The how or why is not important."

"Pinky," said, Joey. "Is your G and T okay?"

I looked down and was mildly shocked to see my glass was still nearly full. "It is fine, Joey. I am just very tired. Now, Joey, you need to have the valet bring my car up from the parking garage and meet us at the front door at nine a.m. Hook, we will eat breakfast and let Joey drive us so we will be at the Carlucci home by nine-fifty-five. Any questions?"

Joey raised his hand. "What'd the paper say?"

I said, "That the man who married the judge the first time was not a legitimate minister."

Joey smiled, "I get it now. The first marriage didn't count. But what happens if Carlucci doesn't fall for it?"

"Then, you, a two-bit punk," snapped Hook, "will think about all the cheap Scotch you served me while Carlucci's goons feed us to the fishes." He emptied his glass and growled, "Another."

CHAPTER THIRTY-FOUR

Bear-San Francisco, California

I picked up my truck at the Airport parking lot, dropped almost two hundred bucks for the parking fee, and headed to the Drisco Hotel. If I wasn't making a pile of money working for Pinky, me and Flo could move to Frisco and open up a parking lot. Hell, you can never find a free spot on the street, and it's thirty to forty bucks every time you pay to park, and that's if you can find a parking lot that's not already filled up with cars and trucks.

Ettamae stretched, yawned, put her head back, and was counting sheep before we hit the freeway.

Flo said, "Do you have any idea why Pinky had to fly to Philadelphia?"

"No clue. Babe, I don't even know why you'd ask me that question."

"Because that's where he went when he left us at the Copenhagen airport. I'm going to call Lu. I'll put the phone on speaker so you can hear. She'll know what's going on."

On the second ring a dude answered. "Law Office of J. Pincus Delmont."

I said, "Put Lu on."

"Sorry, she's not here. Can I help?"

Flo said, "Who is this?"

"Frank."

I said, "Okay, Frank. Why's Pinky in Philadelphia?"

"I'm sorry, but who are you?"

"It's me, Bear and Flo. Oh, and Ettamae's here but she's asleep."

"I'm sorry, but who's asleep?"

Flo said, "Frank, since we've not met, I'm positive you don't have a clue who Ettamae is, but trust me, she's asleep. My name is Florence Sonderlund and my partner is Bear Zabarte. We both work as investigators for Pinky. If you need a moment, I'm sure you'll find records of our pay or travel expenses. I'll hold on while you call Lu. I'm sure she'll vouch for us and . . ."

All of a sudden a crazy bastard driving a Prius cut me off and damn near clipped the left fender. I yelled, "Hold on Babe." The stupid Prius shot off the freeway before I could catch up to give him the single finger salute. By now, my arm hurt and I wasn't in the mood to play anymore with Frank. I cried, "Damn it. Cut to the chase. Why's Pinky in Philadelphia?"

"I'm sorry, sir, but I don't know. In fact, I really don't have any idea where Pinky is."

Flo sighed, "Frank, let me try another way. Has anything unusual happened in the office during the past couple of days?"

"Funny you asked. My uncle, Louis, just taught me how to get the bank to cut a cashiers' check."

I said, "Like how much, and made out to who?"

"Seventy-five thousand dollars and the check was made out to a Mister J. Dudek."

Jesus, somehow Hook's tied into this? What the hell does he have to do with anything? I glanced at Flo and she shrugged.

Flo said, "Frank, did Hook say anything when you gave him the check?"

"I find it interesting that a man with his disability turned out to be a pleasant person . . . . now that I think about it, he did mention catching a plane for Philadelphia."

Now we're finally getting somewhere. I said, "Frank, did you make reservations for Pinky in Philly?"

"No. But I did overhear Mr. Dudek make some reservations, but that was yesterday."

What a dip-shit!

Flo turned on her sweet voice. "Frank, when Mr. Dudek made those reservations, what was the name of the hotel?"

Frank said, "I'll check."

Flo fumbled through her purse for a pen while I listened to Frank hum that stupid song where a blonde babe in Argentina sings about not crying for her. Suddenly Frank said, "Here it is. Two rooms at The Hilton Philadelphia, Penn's Landing."

Flo said, "Do you have the telephone number

for that hotel?"

Frank rattled off a string of numbers while I tried to figure out what kind of a scam Hook and Pinky were pulling off in Philly.

Flo said, "Thank you, Frank and good bye."

Once she turned off her phone, Flo aid, "Bear, I've got the number, but before I call Pinky, I need to tell you what he told me at the Copenhagen airport."

"Okay, but make it quick. My arm's killing me. How about you give me another of those killer pills?"

"Sorry. It's only Tylenol from now on."

"Hey!"

Flo smiled in that way she does that always gets to me. "You can't drive your truck if you take Oxy."

"Try Me."

"Bear, don't you remember?" Flo glanced at Ettamae and she was still sawing logs. "On the plane, I told you we could fool around later, after we got to our hotel room."

"Oh boy!"

"But later is not your only problem. Oxy and fooling around in bed don't mix."

"Why not?"

"Oxy knocks you out."

Jesus, this Babe has more ways of telling me we'll do it later than there are airports in the world. "Okay, give me a couple of Tylenol."

247

"We don't have any water and I don't want you to choke. You can take them after we arrive at our hotel room. Now, are you interested in what Pinky told me?"

Not as much as I wanted to get Flo back to our hotel bedroom, but the traffic on the streets of Frisco was against me, so I said, "Okay, what'd he say?"

"He had to go because it was a matter of life or death."

"Shit, he feeds that line to all the babes."

"But this time he has Hook with him, along with seventy-five big ones."

"I forgot about that. Give him a call."

Flo hit a button and we both listened to a bunch of rings before Pinky answered. "Hello?"

"Hi, Boss. How's it hanging?"

"Bear, I am exhausted. My head just hit the pillow and now you call."

"It's not just me, Flo's here too."

He said, "My cup runneth over. Alright, I give up. Why did you call? Don't tell me you lost Erik again!"

Flo said, "That was a low blow. Look, we're trying to figure out if there's anything we can do to help."

Pinky didn't say anything, like he was surprised to find out that me and Flo had his back. I said, "Boss, we know that Hook is with you and he took seventy-five big ones with him. Level with me.

What the hell's going on? Should we catch the next plane to Philly?"

"My boy, thank you for your generous offer. But alas, by the time you would arrive my problem will be all over. Either I pull it off, or I will be dead."

"Flo here. Tell us what's going on, and that's not a request, it's a demand."

Pinky said, "Florence, I have had it up to here with your demands."

I said, "Boss, stop slinging bull and spill."

As we got closer to the Hotel Drisco, the Boss told us about his dumb deal with the judge, his meeting with the mafia don, how he set up the marriage, and then how his house of cards fell down.

I said, "Boss, you can't go into that mafia dude's house unless you have a scam you know will work."

Pinky said, "That's where Hook comes in. Somehow, he convinced the minister who married the judge the first time to say he could not legally perform the marriage."

Flo said, "The seventy-five thousand! Hook needed that cash to get . . . so what you're telling us is that your scam might work?"

"Florence, you are correct. Now, as this could be my last night of voluntary sleep, please, do not disturb me again."

As I pulled up to the Drisco, I said, "Good night, Boss."

Then Flo said, "Pinky, don't die. We'll miss both

you and Hook. Hold on, that's not really true. Pinky, I'd really miss not having you around to argue with. And we sure as hell would miss our fat paychecks. But no one lives forever, so I guess we could sign on with the next guy who takes over your law practice. Don't worry, Bear and I will be fine no matter which way it goes tomorrow. Sleep tight and don't let the bed bugs bite!"

Listening to Flo pour it on, I sorta shuddered. My Babe is great. She's a looker. She's as smart as a whip. But you never want to end up on her bad side. I mean never!

CHAPTER THIRTY-FIVE

PInky-Philadelphia, Pennsylvania, Cherry Hill, New Jersey, and the Atlantic Ocean

During the night I slept fitfully, as if I were unable to comprehend the reality of my premature demise. But the next morning, after a hot shower, two pieces of toast, and a cup of coffee strong enough to strip the enamel off my teeth, I was ready to face my destiny.

At precisely nine a.m., Hook and I climbed into the backseat of my Mercedes and Joey drove us toward the final resolution of the Camden affair.

Joey turned off the main road onto the drive to Big Julie's, and as we approached the behemoth who guarded the main gate, Hook whispered, "Pinky, I don't like this."

I did not respond, and a moment later, Big Julie's gargantuan house came into view. With a second opportunity to view the abode, I decided that, unlike my architecturally designed home, the Don's clumsy structure was heavy-handed and lacked the artistic scope that a talented professional would have brought to a structural project of this magnitude.

Hook said, "Pinky, whatcha looking at?"

I said, "Just reminiscing about my beautiful house back home."

"Jesus, forget that. What's bugging me is how do we get out of here?"

Joey pulled the car up to the front door and said, "Once you passed that gate back there, you leave here if and when Big Julie says you can."

The front door opened, we all walked in, and another of Julie's thugs checked us from head to toe for weapons. The goon's knowledgeable hands stopped at Hook's prosthesis, and he stepped back. "Take off your shirt and jacket."

Hook demanded, "Who's goin' to make me?"

The goon, about six-five and three hundred pounds, pulled out a phone from his pocket. "Carlo, need some help."

A door to my right opened and another giant of a man came through. He stepped behind Hook and in a blink of an eye, grabbed Hook in a full nelson.

The first thug said, "It'll be a lot easier on all of us if you just do what I tell you to do."

Quickly working around the goon that held Hook in the submission hold, the thug removed Hook's jacket and shirt. Then he pulled off Hook's prosthesis, and as he threw it on the floor, he opened a door, and said, "Okay, you're all clean. You can go into the boss's office."

When we entered the room I glanced at Hook and the man was but a shadow of his former self.

Naked from the waist up, his upper body was not imposing, in fact, his physique lacked proper shape and form. But the biggest shock of all was that without that menacing, stainless steel weapon, Hook was nothing more than a man on the brink of old age.

As my eyes adjusted to the lower light in the office, I made out the figure of Big Julie sitting behind his massive desk. As before, he was pretending to be engrossed in an important task, as if we were either not there, or not important enough to interrupt his work.

Suddenly he turned and said, "Ah, Joey, the Nevada Shyster, and . . . who are you?"

Hook said, "Jacob Dudek."

Big Julie leaned forward and said, "What happened to your arm?"

"Lost it when I was blowing a safe."

"What have you done since your unfortunate accident?"

Hook thought for a moment. "I teach a little safe cracking, but mostly I'm retired. Oh, and I'm a school safety crossing guard. In Carson City, we get a lot of crazy tourists. Most of them are drunk, or drive like lunatics, and I make sure the little ones get across Highway Fifty to their school."

Big Julie held up his hand. "Say no more." He reached down and grabbed the phone, and barked, "Carlo, get in here."

The man who had held Hook in a full nelson

walked in the door.

Big Julie said, "Where's this man's shirt?"

"In the hall with Romeo, along with his jacket and that hook for his arm."

Big Julie said, "Bring it all in. This man's concerned with the safety of children and the one thing we need in this world are protected children. Sorry my men overreacted, Mr. Dudek."

Carlo left and in a moment he entered carrying the shirt, jacket, and prosthesis. He handed the items to Hook.

Big Julie said, "While you put your clothes back on, tell me Mr. Dudek, what was your involvement in my daughter's invalid marriage?"

I said, "If I may . . ."

"Put a sock in it, shyster. I asked Mr. Dudek the question."

With his prosthesis and shirt back on, and looking less fragile, Hook said, "Judge Jonas wanted to talk to Pinky about setting up a marriage between your daughter and him. But Carson City's a small town, so the judge asked me to act as a go-between. Until your guy told me the marriage was invalid I didn't know anything went wrong." Hook shrugged, "That's about it."

Hook's attempt to save his skin by throwing me under the bus was not a surprise because I would have done the same thing had our roles were reversed.

Big Julie pondered Hook's situation for a

moment, and then he said, "Sorry to hear you were involved 'cause I liked you. Now, what you three scumbags did was con my virginal daughter into marrying a lying judge who was already married. And now that Adelaide's life is ruined, you three are goin' to pay."

Joey whimpered, "But Big Julie, all I did was drive the shyster to your place. I mean I ain't responsible for nothing."

"Shut up, Joey. Okay, shyster, it's your turn to beg."

I said, "I am not here to beg for my life. In my pocket I have a paper that will resolve your worry concerning your lovely daughter, Adelaide, and this unique situation. May I hand you the paper?"

"Carlo, take it out of the shyster's pocket, hand it to me, and then clear out."

"Yes, boss."

I pointed to my left jacket pocket. Carlo reached in and his giant hand extracted a single piece of paper that would determine the life or death of Joey, Hook, and myself. Carlo handed the paper to Big Julie and left the room.

Big Julie lowered his eyes, read, and sat back. "Very Interesting. This says the minister who married the judge to his first wife was not a minister after all and the judge's first marriage was invalid. Shyster, am I right?"

"I believe you are correct. And I am positive that the Catholic Church will agree with me."

Big Julie sat back and eyed me for a long time. "So you're telling me that my sweet, virginal daughter's marriage to the judge will be valid in the eyes of the Church? Adelaide will finally be happy and give me lots of grandchildren?"

I said, "Yes, and we three are betting our lives on that interpretation."

"Shyster, the one thing I like about you is you've got the balls of an elephant! And you're right about betting your life. I will take this paper to a bishop friend of mine. He will check this out and tell me if you are correct. If it turns out that Adelaide's marriage is copacetic, then you and the rest of your crew will skate free. But if the bishop tells me that this paper is bullshit, then you and your friends will learn just how far you can swim. Capiche?"

He grabbed the phone. "Romeo, it is time to get my friends ready for their swim."

I noticed Joey's knees give way.

My heart skipped a beat as I said, "But you said you would make a determination concerning the paper's validity after you talked with the bishop."

"Mouthpiece, shut up and follow Romeo!"

Romeo pushed the three of us out of the office, down a short hallway, and through an open door. As I entered the room, my visual senses were figuratively and literarily assaulted. The floors and walls of the room were covered with a pure white subway tile. The ceiling of the approximately ten-by-ten foot room had been painted with a matching white. In the center of the floor there was a drain installed. On one wall there was a hose bib and a coil of red rubber hose. Two white plastic benches were attached to the floor the room, and stationed next to the ever present Carlo stood a large laundry basket.

Carlo said, "Take everything off except for your tighty whities. Throw everything else in the basket and follow me."

My bravado faded as my fingers trembled so violently that I had trouble working the buttons of my shirt.

Hook said, "Socks and shoes too?"

Carlo shook his head as if he could not comprehend how ignorant people could be. "Like I told you, everything but your skivvies.

Once our task was complete, I glanced at Hook, Joey, and looked down at myself. I decided that there was no way that grown men could remain dignified while standing around in their under-clothing. Although I, wearing my custom made navy blue silk boxers, made the statement that I remained a man with excellent taste. As we waited for Joey, now sniveling, to finish removing his socks, I tried to recall the last time I stood, nearly naked, in front of other men.

Suddenly, Carlo pointed at a door at the end of the room. "All right, move your sorry asses through that far door."

Once we reached the spot, and before Carlo opened the door, I heard a distinctive whump-whump-whump sound, the racket a helicopter makes as its horizontal blades cut through the air.

I stopped and looked Carlo in the eye. "Big Julie said we were just getting ready for our swim. Why take all our clothes away? And what is the helicopter for?"

Romeo joined Carlo, just in case three nearly naked, normal sized men were planning on making a break.

Carlo said, "Shyster, we've got your clothes 'cause you ain't gonna need 'em anymore."

I struggled to remain upright as my knees wobbled.

Joey cried, "Carlo, you know me. We flunked out of the same high school. You can dump those two where you want, but give this paisano a break."

Carlo replied, "Joey, I do what Big Julie tells me to do. Don't worry. We'll drop you from over a thousand feet. Shit, you won't know what hit you. And if the fall don't get you, the fifty mile swim back to Atlantic City will."

Fighting to maintain my brave front, I yelled over the noise of the helicopter blades. "Carlo, you never answered my question as to why we three are standing here in our underwear."

He said, "Jesus, you've got a big mouth for such a little fart. I see why Big Julie wants to get rid of you. Okay, once we drop you in the ocean, by the time the fish, crabs, and lobsters get done with you, there'll be nothing left but a few clean bones at the bottom of the ocean."

His mental picture made me shudder. Betting that Carlo just might be as stupid as he looked, I launched into what could be my final closing statement to a jury of one. "My good man, before the copter takes off ,I should phone my office and instruct my secretary to inform my clients they need to retain new legal representation. Carlo, I'm sure you can understand my concern. For example, you, or Romeo, could be one of my clients, incarcerated in a jail cell, depending on me to negotiate your freedom."

Carlo clenched his fist, and for a moment I was concerned he would strike me. "The boss told us you were a flannel mouth, and you've gotta know that you ain't making any phone calls. Once the boss gives us the word, you three are going to vanish, just like that Hoffa dude did. Now clam up and move your sorry ass into the copter."

The cabin was plush with seats for four, and room for more if one sat between the seats. Hook and Joey were seated with safety belts buckled. Opposite them sat Romero. Carlo pushed me next to Romeo and sat down beside me, squashing my body between the giant mounds of human flesh.

I said, "Carlo, could I sit on the other side, between Hook and Joey? There is a lot more room over there for me."

"Nope. This is what you get for driving me crazy with that flapping mouth of yours."

After a struggle, I pulled my arms free from the soft, human walls that hemmed me in, snapped my seat belt, and fought the claustrophobic trauma that engulfed me.

A moment later, the helicopter slowly lifted off the ground, filled with three petrified, near naked men, two of Big Julie's four hundred pound thugs, and the pilot. When the aircraft stopped climbing, it turned and headed east, into the late morning sun. From my trapped position between the mounds of human flesh, I saw with my limited vision, farmland, houses, and small towns move by below. And every once in a while, when Carlo shifted his bulk, I could spot the sparkling blue Atlantic Ocean in the distance. My heart rate accelerated and a wave of panic set in as I stared at the final resting place where my cleaned bones would lie for all eternity in a wet grave.

CHAPTER THIRTY-SIX

Bear-San Francisco, California

After we got back to the Drisco, Flo got a plastic bag from one of the hotel maids and wrapped it around my cast so I could take a shower.

My arm hurt, but not so bad, and after Flo made sure Ettamae was asleep, me and Flo did a bunch of fooling around.

The next morning I was still snoozing when Flo's cell phone rang. She answered using her perky voice that sounded like she'd been up for hours. God knows how she does that.

"Good morning. . . . Oh, hi, Charles. Let me put this on the speaker so Bear can join in."

I heard him say, "Good morning. First, I want to congratulate you both on convincing Erik to voluntarily return to San Francisco. He spent the night in jail and first thing today, I am going to see if I can find a judge who will set bail. His voluntary return to the Bay Area will help me in that quest."

By now I was wide awake. 'Charlie, this is Bear. Are you just going to hope nobody tells the judge that Erik took a runner to Sweden?"

"Well . . . if the judge asks me about that, I

261

can't lie, but I can tell him that when Erik flew to Sweden, the police hadn't yet declared him a suspect. As far as the judge is concerned, Erik flew to Sweden to visit his aging grandmother. Can I trust we're all on the same page?"

That Swedish bombshell was an aging grandma? I was about to tell Charlie that the crap he was peddling sounded a lot like the same bull Pinky spreads around, when Flo put her hand over my mouth, and said, "Yes, Charles, we're all on the same page."

Charlie said, "And Bear, even with your broken arm, do you agree with Flo?"

Flo lifted her tee shirt and smiled. With my eyes locked on her bodacious boobs, and a good chance of me getting in some more fooling around before Ettamae woke up, I said, "Yup, me and Flo went to Sweden to tell Erik the police wanted to talk to him about that poisoned dude. The second Erik heard that, we all jumped on a plane and flew back to Frisco."

Flo smiled, lowered her shirt, and whispered, "Sorry, but I just heard Ettamae turn on the TV. Don't worry, we'll get together later."

Charlie said, "That's good. And both of you will tell that same story to a judge if necessary?"

I put my hand over the phone and said, "Babe, Charlie and Pinky both sound to me like a couple of crooks."

She said, "I only know that a lawyer's sworn to

represent his or her client, and they'll do, within the law of course, whatever they need to do. Now take your hand off the mouthpiece and let me talk to Charles."

I did, and Flo said, "Charles, do you have anymore information on Laura Heath, or her roommate, Claudette who has, or did have an apartment on Mission Street in the Mission?"

Claudette? An apartment on Mission Street? In the Mission? My Babe remembered all that? She's got the memory of an elephant. I said, "Yah, Charlie, what about Laura and that Claudette broad?"

"Bear, in the past thirty minutes I received a confidential copy of the police investigation into the Simon Rand homicide. Laura fits the prime suspect role as well as, if not better than, Erik. And I have the address of Claudette's apartment, but will you be ready to work? Will the pain of your broken arm hold you back?"

"Back from what?"

Charlie said, "I didn't want to bring this up, but on the way to the jail, Erik told me he's the cause your fractured arm. Now don't get mad, but will you be able to conduct yourself in an unbiased manner considering what Erik did to your arm?"

I wasn't totally sure where Charlie was going, but I was starting to get pissed off when Flo said, "Charles, Bear's arm is fine. He experienced a compound fracture but that trauma was surgically

263

repaired in Sweden. Granted, he was under the influence of powerful painkillers during the flight back to San Francisco, but believe me, my man's back to normal and he holds no grudge toward Erik. Now give me Claudette's address or call Pinky and tell him you sent us back to Carson City."

"Flo, I never meant to upset you or Bear. I just wanted to clear the air on the overall effect of Bear's injury."

Flo looked at me and nodded. I nodded back, and she said, "Fine, give me Claudette's address and we'll take over the Rand homicide investigation from this point on."

The dude rattled off some numbers while I gritted my teeth. Actually my arm hurt like hell, but I'd never let Flo know that 'cause she wouldn't let me fool around until it was really fixed, and God knows when that could be.

I went into the can and chewed down a fist full of Tylenol.

Flo was gone when I got back to the bed, so I didn't worry about holding back the moans and groans while I put on my jeans, tee shirt, socks, and shoes.

By the time I got to the big room, Flo and Ettamae were chomping down some kind of cereal.

Ettamae, said, "Bear, how's the arm?"

The next person that asks me that question is going to find out real quick. "It's fine. How's your arm?"

"Perfect, but then I didn't have a bone sticking out of mine a couple of days ago."

Flo said, "How about some coffee? I've nuked a couple of your favorite bran muffins. Be careful, inside the muffin some of those raisins can get hotter than hell." Flo stared at me and said, "What's that white powder on your lips?"

"I chewed down a couple of Tylenol."

Flo said, "Then you need to drink a glass of water."

My arm was feeling pretty good now, but I wasn't sure if it was the fifteen to twenty Tylenols, or the bran muffins, or if it was just getting better, but whatever the reason, it felt better.

After we brushed our teeth, me, Flo and Ettamae piled into my truck and we headed to what Frisco calls the Mission district. I read in our hotel room that somewhere near was a super old Spanish mission. I was sorta surprised as I drove down Mission Street that Ettamae wasn't spouting off all kinds of stuff, like how old the buildings were, how many people lived here, that kinda of crap like she did in Denmark and Sweden. I said, "Hey, Kid, you got a problem?"

She didn't answer.

I said, "What's the matter? The cat got your tongue?"

Then she turned on the water works.

Flo said, "Ettamae, what's the matter?"

She didn't answer Flo, and that was a big

surprise. She just snorted, and sniffled while I drove for at least a block down Mission Street. Then, out of the blue she shouted, "What's going to happen to me when this investigation is over?"

Oh shit! I knew we were going to have to face that question sooner or later. I said, "Ettamae, we'll go back home to Carson City, and figure out what happens next."

"Figure out what? You're talking to a thirteen-year-old orphan, and nobody wants to raise a teenage orphan."

Now the tears really let go, like the big cloudbursts in the Northern Nevada that causes flash floods.

Flo wrapped her arm around Ettamae. "Sweetheart, we want you."

Damn, here it comes.

Flo continued, "Bear and I have not been blessed with children. As far as I'm concerned, you're the child I never had. Bear, you agree with me, don't you?"

Before I could open my mouth, I spotted Claudette's address and a parking place near the front door. That on-the-street parking place was a first time for me in Frisco, and I took that as a sign from my Grandma Zabarte that this mess with Ettamae would work out okay.

I said, "Later, Babe. Here's Claudette's place."

I set the brake and jumped out of the cab of the truck before Flo could open her mouth and ran into a real dump of an apartment building. Claudette's apartment was on the second floor, 2C. I sprinted up the stairs, being sure not to trip on the threadbare worn spots on the carpet, and had knocked on the door before Flo and the Kid caught up. The door opened and a really cute babe with a nice shape, medium-sized boobs, and blonde hair, frowned at me. She snapped, "Yes?"

Flo pushed me aside. "Hello, I hope I have the correct address. It's my understanding that you are a pastry chef. Is that correct?"

The blonde with the pageboy haircut nodded. "That's right, but how did . . . "

Flo said, "Claudette, you may think that all pastry chefs work in total obscurity, but I am here to set that record straight. My name is Sondra Wilcox. I am a feature writer from *Sugar and Spice*, the national magazine that highlights the world of pastry—from the homemaker to the three-star Michelin restaurant."

Claudette blinked, "The world of pastry? And who is the teenager?"

"This young lady with me is a high school journalism student who is shadowing me for the day."

Claudette said, "And the man behind you?"

"He's my driver, Herman. Claudette, presently I am working on an article to identify the upcoming pastry chefs in San Francisco. May we come in?"

Up to that point, I would have laid money that

Claudette was about to slam the door, but when Flo hit her with that "to identify the upcoming pastry chefs" bullshit, she fell for the scam, hook, line and sinker.

Claudette said, "Yes, please come in and sit down. May I get you something to drink? A beer, a glass of wine, or some water?"

My arm was aching for a beer, but Flo shot me her don't you dare stare, and I sat down.

Flo said, "No thank you, we've just finished breakfast and are fine concerning liquids." Then she pulled out a pad of paper and a pen from her purse and said, "I have a few questions for you." The next thing I saw was Ettamae rummaging around her purse and almost fell off my chair when she pulled out a pad of paper and a pen. Like I said before, a female's purse is chock full of all kinds of crap, and now I know that crap includes, just in case, a pad of paper and a pen.

Then Flo said, "But first things first. Ever since Herman picked us up this morning, he has complained of tummy troubles that started after he bought a super shrimp burrito off a roach coach at Dolores park. My driver needs to use the little boys' room. Could he impose upon you while I ask you my questions?"

Claudette stared at me for a second.

I made a scrunched-up face, like I thought a dude would make if he was about to let it all go and there was nothing he could do to stop it.

Claudette said, "I guess that would be okay."

I said, "Thank you, Ms. Claudette. I'll be back in a flash, Ms. Wilcox."

Claudette pointed the hallway out. I got up and walked toward two doors as I heard Flo ask, "Now, let us start at the beginning. Have you had any formal pastry training?"

The first door opened to a bathroom. The chipped tiles and worn linoleum floor looked pretty bad, even to a guy like me. There were four pairs of babe's underpants hanging over a torn plastic shower curtain.

I quietly stepped out of the bathroom and slipped open the only other door. The shades were closed and once my eyes got used to the dark, I saw a well-shaped female with long black hair. She was fast asleep, lying on a king-sized bed, her important parts were covered by an old sheet, and her snoring sounded like one of those small Japanese motorcycles.

I quickly closed the bedroom door, walked back into the bathroom, opened up the medicine cabinet and spotted four bottles of prescription drugs. One was labeled for Claudette La Page and the other three were for Laura Heath. Flo's old "my driver has a bad case of the runs" scam worked! That broad sawing logs is the Laura Heath we're looking for. To make the scam sound legit, I flushed the john, and washed my hands.

By the time I got back to the room with Flo, the

Kid, and Claudette, Flo was stuffing the pad of paper back into her purse. She jumped up and said, "There's a good possibility that this article will make you famous in a city known for its top restaurants. Claudette, get ready for job offers from Michelin starred restaurants!"

Claudette stood up, looking a little stunned, and said, "Where can I buy a copy of *Sugar and Spice*?"

Ettamae said, "They're on all the news stands, and you can always go online to read some of Ms. Wilcox's past articles."

Flo said, "Herman, assuming your tummy problems are now resolved, are you ready to drive us to the next address on my list?"

Claudette jumped up and down like she was a little kid on Christmas morning. "Ms. Wilcox, I'd love to know the names of the other pastry chefs on your list."

Flo hesitated for a second, like she was thinking hard about Claudette's question. Then she said, "I'm afraid not. That could be considered unethical. Have a good day."

We walked quietly down the hall, but the second Claudette closed her door, Ettamae giggled. "That was fun."

Flo frowned, "Ettamae, stop laughing. As trained investigators, Bear and I do what we have to do to catch the bad guy. I don't want you to think we pull scams like that for no reason."

Ettamae dropped her head. "I understand."

As I pushed Flo and Ettamae into the truck, I glanced over my shoulder. "Hey, we've got to get our butts out of here. I'm pretty sure that the broad sawing logs in the bedroom was Laura Heath."

Flo said, "And it won't take long for Claudette to figure out there's no such thing as the *Sugar and Spice* magazine."

Ettamae said, "That's okay. All we have to do now is call the cops and tell them their prime suspect is asleep on the second floor."

I said, "Not that easy. The cops think they have their prime suspect sitting in jail. We've got to get hold of Pinky and if we can't find him, call Charlie to figure out what we should do next."

CHAPTER THIRTY-SEVEN

Pinky-Philadelphia, Pennsylvania, Cherry Hill, New Jersey, and the Atlantic Ocean

I gulped short, choppy breaths to hold back my panic as the helicopter remained on a due east course. After a few moments, the coast line vanished from my limited view and all that was left was the blue water of the Atlantic Ocean.

Then, for no reason that I could determine, the helicopter slowed and began to circle. As I realized that the copter had reached Big Julies' desired fifty miles off shore destination, my heart pounded so hard that each beat nearly overwhelmed the noise of the blades spinning above me.

I glanced at Hook. His stoic expression and relaxed body indicated to me that he was not afraid to die. Whereas Joey had whimpered like a baby since the helicopter lifted off the ground at Big Julie's house.

As for myself, as the moment of my impending doom grew closer, I grabbed every thought that might dampen my mounting anxiety. The day I graduated at the top of my class from Hastings . . . My wedding to Willow . . . . For no good reason, an obscure memory popped into my head. I said, "Carlo, what is the maximum speed of this aircraft?"

He looked at me. "What's it to you?"

"Just idle curiosity. Could you ask the pilot?"

"I can only talk to the pilot while I wear a headset with a built-in mike."

I said, "Please! Call it a dying man's last wish."

"Jesus." He donned the headset. "Hey, you up front driving this bucket of bolts. What's the fastest this thing'll go?"

Carlo listened for a moment. "Roughly 140 miles per hour."

I remarked to myself, "Interesting." Then to Carlo, I said, "Would you ask the pilot the name and model of the helicopter?"

"What the hell is it with you? You ain't got time to write a book."

"Please, just ask him."

"You're the big talker." He tossed me the head set. "You ask him."

Trapped between the massive bodies of the two goons, I leaned as far forward as I could and put the set over my ears. "Mr. Pilot, you have me at a disadvantage. My name is J. Pincus Delmont. My friends and colleagues call me Pinky. What is your name?"

A voice answered. "Why do you want to know?"

I did not want to admit to the assembled that I was on the verge of panic. Up to this point in my short life I had lived by my words and wit. This conversation with the pilot might help me to better control the bodily functions of my nether regions until I was pushed out of the helicopter.

I said, "Sir, I fully understand that we meet under unusual circumstances, but I firmly believe that chivalry and courtesy are the only measure of a true gentleman."

He said, "Pinky, only a lawyer talks like that. Okay, my name's Martin but we'll remain on a first name basis. What's your question?"

"Is this a Bell helicopter? And if so, what is the model?"

Martin answered, "Why do you want to know?"

"Sometime ago I took lessons with a helicopter, received my pilots license, and nearly bought a Guimbal Cabri G2."

"Hey, that model was a powerful two seater. Okay, what you're riding in today is a Bell 407GXP."

"And what is the maximum payload?"

Martin said, "A little more than 2,300 pounds. Why?"

I said, "Then we are all lucky that you are an excellent pilot."

He chuckled. "I thought I was the only one that noticed this craft was on the edge of being overloaded when we lifted off."

I said, "Not the only one. In fact, I noticed that for us to climb, you had to . . ."

Carlo ripped the headset off my head, caused a sharp pain to my right ear, and yelled, "Enough of this bull!" He threw the headset onto the floor and glanced at his watch. "Romeo, let's dump 'em now and head back. I've got a hot date tonight and I don't want to be late. Last week that babe turned me every way but loose."

The verbal picture Carlo painted, of a human sea elephant attempting to mate with a normal sized female, nearly made me burst out laughing.

Romeo said, "Okay." He stood up, crossed to the door, flipped open the safety handle, and slid the door open.

A blast of cold ocean air swirled around me, as if I had been dropped into the middle of a tiny tornado.

Joey screamed, and in spite of my attempted bravado, I started to whimper.

I took a deep breath to regain control, and said, "Carlo, I seem to recall that Big Julie said he would call and tell you what to do with us." By now Joey was crying like a new-born and I wasn't far behind. Again, after grabbing a couple of breaths of precious air, I said, "Would your boss be pleased if you and Romeo dropped us before his call?"

Hook yelled, "Pinky, Joey, shut up! Sit up and act like a man or I'll help them throw the both of you out the door."

Ignoring Hook's threat, I continued. "Carlo, what might happen to you if you do not follow Big

Julie's explicit instructions?"

The two goons stared at each other for a moment. Romeo shrugged and closed the door. Carlo said, "Okay, we'll give youse guys fifteen more minutes, but if the boss don't call by then, out you go."

Joey's weeping turned into a full blown lament and to forestall my joining him, I continuously recited Sydney Carlton's last lines from the *Tale of Two Cities*', "It is a far, far better thing that I do, than I have ever done; it is a far, far better rest that I go to than I have ever known."

I abruptly ceased the gibberish when Carlo's phone rang.

After much fumbling, the giant pulled the phone out of his pocket. "Yah . . . Sorry . . . but . . . I can't hear you . . . you're cutting out. We'll head back and as soon as I see enough bars, I'll call you back."

With the promise of a few more moments of life, I stopped reciting Dickens and concentrated on my wedding to Willow, one of the best days of my life.

Carlo continuously checked the bars of service on his phone as the helicopter edged closer to the coastline. After a few moments, the thug's eyes lit up when he spotted the indication of the desired signal strength.

"Hello, Boss? . . . I can hear you now. What do you want us to do with 'em?"

I studied Carlo's face for any sign that I had

276

been given a reprieve, but his smooth, oversized mellon rebuffed my attempt to read his thoughts.

Finally he sighed, as if he were disappointed. "Okay, we'll bring 'em back."

As my auditory system processed those four magic words, we'll bring 'em back, I wanted to jump for joy, but sandwiched between two mounds of blubber, the only thing I could do was relax and let flow the tears of relief.

My reverie was cut short when my olfactory nerves picked up the abhorrent aroma of urine, so malodorous that the stench overpowered the musky body odor that emanated from my corpulent bookends.

Martin yelled, "Jesus, something smells bad back there! Did one of those guys piss all over the floor again?"

I heard a window open, followed by a puff of fresh air that was immediately engulfed by the miasma of human urine.

I glanced down and was overjoyed to see that my navy blue shorts appeared unscathed. My gaze darted to the right seat opposite me. Hook remained lost in thought and as far as I could see, his boxers were dry. That left Joey. He sat on the left seat and his tighty whities were now wet and a pool of yellow liquid lapped at his feet.

Romeo looked at Joey and shook his big head. "Damn."

Carlo put on the headset. "Martin, head back to

the house."

Through Carlo's headset I heard the pilot. "Why? We're not done yet."

"'Cause the boss says so."

I heard a click and Martin's voice boomed over a loud speaker system, "Okay, we'll go back, but you and Romeo are stuck with that mess back there this time."

Carlo looked at Romeo. He shook his head. Carlo said, "Nope. The copter's your job."

Martin said, "Hey, this is not the first time this has happened and I had to clean it up after the last incident! You and Romeo clean up the mess or Big Julie's going to have to find himself a new copter pilot!"

Romeo grabbed the headset from Carlo and growled, "Martin, you know that one word from me to Big Julie could change you from a dropper to a dropee. Capisce?"

Martin was silent for a moment. "Got it. I'll get that half-wit back at the hanger to clean the mess up. But between you and me, you guys have got to come up with a better way."

Romeo said, "You got any suggestions?"

Martin said, "Sorry, not my job. I fly the chopper. You're in charge of the cargo."

Martin revved the engine, the helicopter turned and headed back into the sun.

As the aircraft turned us back toward Big Julie's house, I nearly broke down as I realized I was going to live!

During the forty-five minute flight to the helipad, Joey continued to whimper like a baby while Hook remained locked in his stoic demeanor.

Once the helicopter landed, Carlo and Romeo herded the three of us out of the aircraft and back to the all-white room.

While Carlo hosed Joey down, Hook and I sat on the benches and put on our clothes, socks, and shoes. There was no rejoicing, in fact we three were strangely quiet. But as my angst dissipated, my anger grew! Yes, I was alive, but I had lost face—although none of those who flew with me could, or would, ever be considered by me as a peer.

Now fully clothed, Romeo escorted us down the hall, past Big Julie's office door and out the front door to my Mercedes.

As Joey walked past me, I detected that he remained odoriferous.

I said, "Romeo, take Joey back and hose him down again. The man still reeks of urine."

Romeo said, "But if I do that, he'll get the front seat of your nice car all wet."

"Not my problem. It is a rental."

When Romeo turned to take Joey back into the house, Hook opened the back door of the car and started to enter.

I said, "Not so fast. I have a few calls to make and I will be using my vehicle as a portable office."

Hook snarled and waved his hook in my

direction.

"Mr. Dudek, moments ago you and I were stripped down to our undergarments. Prior to that time, when we were together, all I could see was your menacing hook. But now I know you for what you are, an old man hiding behind his weapon. When we return to Philadelphia, I will pay for one night's lodging, and your airfare back to Carson City. Concerning our future relationship, stay away from me, and my office, or I will be forced to call the police and ask them to arrest you as a common stalker. Now, close the door and move away from my car."

As he pulled away, Hook said, "Don't worry, Pinky. I won't tell any of your friends that you were about to puke, or piss in your drawers, before the pilot turned the copter around."

I glared at the man. "Shut up, and move away from my car." But we both knew, now and forever more, that he had been the stronger when faced with imminent death.

I opened the eear door, sat down, and closed the door. After a moment of quiet solitude, I could feel the self-confident J. Pincus Delmont return. I pulled out my mobile phone and made a call.

A female voice answered, "Chambers of Judge Ross."

I said, "I apologize. I wanted to talk with . . . Judge Ross? I am not familiar with that name."

"Pinky? Is that you, Pinky?"

I said, "Yes it is. Is this Marie? Judge Jonas' clerk?'"

"The same."

"Marie, as I previously stated, I would like to speak with Judge Jonas."

"Then I wish you good luck."

I said, "Why is that?"

"Judge Jonas has vanished. Yesterday, a deputy saw him get on a plane in Reno with two rough looking men and since that sighting, not a word. The court brought in Judge Ross to handle Judge Jonas' case load, and until Judge Jonas returns, it looks like Ross will take over. Would you care to speak with Judge Ross?"

I sat back. Jonas had vanished! Considering the quick temper of Big Julie, Jonas could have been Carlo and Romero's companion on a short trip to a long fall just hours before my helicopter flight. I shuddered. "No thank you, Marie."

"Pinky, before you go, you're scheduled to appear before Judge Ross in two days. You have a preliminary hearing concerning your client, Edward Ruzek."

Without any warning, I coughed up an uncontrollable, violent hack. "Marie, I just left my doctor's office. As you may have noticed, I have a terrible cough. My doctor is worried that what I have could be contagious. I tried to wear a mask in court but it interfered with my closing argument. I fear if I appear in court, without a mask, the spray from my coughs could shut down the system of justice in Carson City."

She sighed. "Do you have any idea how long it will take you to recover from this mysterious coughing disease?"

"Perhaps a week, but two weeks should clear everything up. Thank you, Marie."

"You're welcome. And if you see Judge Jonas, let him know I've lit a candle for him at church."

"I am sure he would have appreciated your kind gesture."

She snapped, "What do you mean, he would have appreciated? Pinky, you're talking like he's . . ."

I coughed, "Good bye, Marie."

I sat back and considered how kismet seemed to have won this contest. As I accrued nothing of value from my quid pro quo with Judge Jonas, it only seemed fitting that Big Julie would be stuck with his almost virginal daughter! The only saving grace of this whole affair was that, other than Hook, no one knew anything about my involvement in this fiasco. And Hook knew better than to say anything, to anyone, about the caper. My favorite ex-wife, Willow, would never know. Nor would Lu, or Bear, or that nasty female who would never forget, Florence.

I looked up and Joey was now standing by the front door, dripping from head to toe and as the full sun highlighted his waist, he gave visual evidence of his commando underwear status.

I waved my driver in.

Then the back door opened, and Hook peeked in.

I gave him a tiny nod. He entered and buckled up.

Once the Mercedes started to move, I began to feel like my old self. I pushed a button and my window lowered. I said to Romeo who was standing less than ten feet away, "Tell me, who is your cell phone carrier?"

"Ah . . . Verizon. Why?"

"You need to write them a note to complain about the large gap in their cell phone network."

Romeo's head and neck were one, as if made from a solid block of oak, so I was pleased that the Mercedes was moving forward when I saw from Romeo's expression that he finally figured out what I had said.

"Shyster, you've got diarrhea of the mouth. If you're not out of my sight in two seconds, I'm gonna pull you out of that car and rip your head off your shoulders."

I yelled, "For God's sake, Joey, hit the gas pedal."

A moment later, between the house and main gate, I reminded myself to drop Verizon a note to commend them for their poor service.

After Joey exchanged a few unintelligible mumbles with the main gate guard, the three of us rode in silence while Joey drove back to the hotel.

Hook and I exited the vehicle, walked through the lobby, and took separate elevators to our rooms.

Once inside my suite, I locked the door and removed my jacket. That was when I noticed that I had not buttoned a single button on my shirt. Even now, when I attempted to grab a button, my right hand shook so violently that I was not able to close my fingers.

I walked to the minibar, removed three small bottles of brandy, filled up a glass and downed the liquid. The cheap brandy burned my throat, but it had the desired effect of calming my trembling fingers.

I now understood that my ride on the helicopter had come with a cost. What I did not know at the time was if the damage to my self-esteem would be permanent.

I picked up the phone and dialed the concierge's desk.

I said, "This is J. Pincus Delmont in suite 700. Due to a totally disagreeable business meeting, I require a change to my travel plans tomorrow morning."

"Mr. Delmont, I am truly sorry for your unpleasant day. You sound exhausted. What can I do for you?"

"I will require a business class seat on an early flight to San Francisco. And I need a wakeup call so I can easily make that flight by taking a cab from the hotel to the airport. I also have a rental Mercedes parked in your hotel garage and I need that vehicle returned to the Hertz office at the airport."

He said, "Mr. Delmont, I see we have your credit card on file. Do I have your verbal approval to charge your requests to that card?"

"You do. Will you need a written confirmation to that fact?"

"Not required, Mr. Delmont. We record all calls to the concierge desk for situations like this. Good night sir. I trust you will have a good rest."

I hung up the phone, removed all my clothing and was shocked to discover a small spot of moisture on the frontside of my navy blue silk shorts.

After a long, and futile attempt to scrub away my shame and humiliation in a hot shower, I returned to the mini-bar, took out the last two bottles of Brandy, downed them both, lay on the bed, and eventually drifted off into a tormented sleep.

CHAPTER THIRTY-EIGHT

Bear-San Francisco, California

Me, Flo, and Ettamae jumped into my truck. I pulled away from the curb and drove about a block, pulled a U-turn, and moved into an empty parking spot about a half a block from the front door of Laura's apartment.

Ettamae said, "Bear, you can't park here. Get out and take a look. You're blocking a driveway into that house."

Without moving my eyes off the front door of the apartment, I said, "I don't care. If somebody needs to get in or out, I'll move. So don't get on my . . . hey, there goes Claudette. Flo, I'll bet she's heading into the little market across the street to see if they've got a copy of *Sugar and Spice*. You know, that stupid magazine you made up."

Flo said, "That worries me. If she doesn't find a copy, she'll run back into her apartment and check out Google. When that search shows there's no such thing as a *Sugar and Spice* magazine . . . whoops, there goes Claudette going back to her apartment. What happens now?"

Ettamae said, "She'll tell Laura something

weird's going on and we'll see both of them running out of the apartment in a couple of minutes."

I said, "You wanna bet on the time?"

She giggled. "Sure."

I said, "Okay. Anything under four minutes you win a coke. Anything over four minutes, I win a beer, and you've got to pay for my beer out of your own money."

Ettamae thought for a second. "Not fair. You can buy a coke for around a buck or two. A beer will cost me four bucks or more."

Flo said, "She's got you there. Ettamae, tell him to make it three cokes to one beer or the bet's off."

Ettamae nodded. "I agree with Flo. Bear, it's three cokes to one beer or the bet's off."

There they go again. This two against one crap is getting to be a pain. I said, "Okay, it'll be three cokes to . . .shit, here they come."

Laura and Claudette walked out of the apartment building, climbed into an old gray VW bug, and headed north on Misson.

Ettamae cried, "I win! That was less than four minutes. When do I get my three cokes?"

I said, "Later."

I fired up the truck, popped another U-turn, and we followed the bug north on Mission to Fifth street where the bug pulled over and Laura got out.

Flo said, "What do we do now?"

I pulled over, parked the truck along the curb, and said, "Everybody out. We can't lose her."

As we ran across Mission, Ettamae called, "Bear, you just parked the truck in a blue zone, a disabled space reserved for vehicles with a disabled license, or a disabled placard that must be prominently displayed on a dashboard, or hung from the rearview mirror."

Jesus, she's getting to be as much of a pain-in-the-ass as Flo. I yelled, "Don't have time to move the truck now."

About a hundred feet ahead of Flo and the Kid, I pushed my way past a couple of panhandlers just in time to catch up with Laura, who'd stuck herself into the middle of a pack of people crossing Market Street.

On the sidewalk the crowd joined a second bunch who were all lined up watching a cable car get turned around at the end of Powell. The people around me sounded like they were speaking Swedish, Danish, and Chinese all at the same time. The cable car looked cool and if I didn't have to follow a murderer, I'd jump on it and take a ride. No doubt about it, Frisco was a great town for tourists.

Staying close to Laura, I glanced across Market, caught Flo's eye, and pointed at a cab that was sitting near her.

She gave me the thumbs-up sign and pulled out her cell phone. I flashed the old knife across the throat move. She shrugged her shoulders and stared at me.

I pointed at the cab again, but just then I had

to move fast 'cause Laura had pushed her way through the crowd and was hustling up Powell. I followed her as best I could and hoped that Flo got my drift.

At that point, except for all the damn tourists, tailing Laura was going to be easy 'cause she didn't know me from Adam, but I knew her, so I could get as close as I wanted to.

Just as I was feeling comfortable, Laura darted in front of a couple of slow moving cars on Powell and jumped onto a cable car that had to slow down to keep from plowing into three dorks pulling their suitcases across Powell. I pushed my way down the crowded sidewalk, just missed getting hit by a car, and hopped onto Laura's cable car. I was still getting my feet under me when the cable car jumped forward almost pulling my good arm out if its socket.

Finally settled in, I was standing about five people away from Laura, holding onto the leather strap with my good arm while we headed up Powell Street. For a second I had some time to watch the dude who ran the cable car. At least I think he was running it. He'd ring this bell, Ding-gada-ding-gada-ding, let go a big brake-like handle, pull up on something else, and then ring the bell again. To tell the truth, I don't have a clue what the dude did, or how a cable car works, but it was fun to watch him. In fact, the only thing I learned about cable cars was how to hold on and not fall off.

The next thing I knew, we were going through a place called Chinatown where I saw damn near as many Chinese as I did when we were chasing that broad in Beijing.

That was when my phone started ringing.

You know how there are days when nothing works right? This looked like one of those days.

I knew I couldn't close the fingers on the arm with the cast good enough to hold onto my phone, and I was afraid to let go of the leather strap with my good hand 'cause I might fall off the damn cable car. Like I said, some days everything turns to shit.

The phone kept on ringing.

Then, the cable car slowed down suddenly, and I bumped into an Asian teeny-bopper standing to my right.

Maybe she could help me with the phone?

I smiled. "Excuse me, but would you put your hand into my pocket and . . ."

She whipped out a bright red can from her purse, stuck it in my face, and snarled, "Buster, I may look small, but you're playing with fire. If you make a wrong move, I'll fill your eyes so full of pepper spray that you'll wish you were dead."

I waved my arm in her face. "Look, kid, my arm's in a cast. I can't answer my cell phone and even you can hear it's ringing."

She said, "Yah, I can hear it. Okay, but don't pull anything 'cause I'm still ready to give you a face full of pepper spray."

The kid slipped her hand into my jacket pocket, took out the phone, and lifted it to her ear. "Yes? . . . I guess that's who I'm standing next to . . . you've got to admit Bear's a very strange name . . . sure, I'll hold the phone up so he can talk."

Once the phone got next to my ear I said, "Babe?"

"Bear, the minute I let you out of my sight you get into the damndest situations."

I said, "Babe, it's not my fault. My right hand doesn't work so well, so I had to ask—"

Flo said, "I know all that, now listen. We are in a blue and white cab about a half-a-block behind you. I talked with Charles and told him that we're following Laura Heath. He told me you need to keep Laura in sight because he thinks the San Francisco District Attorney will want to bring her in for questioning. Just hang in there. We've got your back."

"Got it. Bye."

I glanced down at the teeny-bopper. "Thanks kid. You can put the phone back in my pocket."

"Okay."

"Kid?"

"My name is Dolores."

"Ain't that the same name as that old mission in Frisco?"

"It is. Bear, the people here don't like it when tourists call our beautiful city by that name."

"What name?"

"You're gonna make me say it, aren't you?. Frisco!"

"Sorry, won't do that again. Dolores, I just noticed that you aren't holding onto a strap, or anything!"

"That's 'cause I'm Asian and too short to reach the strap."

"So why don't you just fall off the cable car when it makes those turns or stops real fast?"

"Just born with good balance, I guess."

"Kid . . ."

"It's Dolores."

"Right. Dolores, I want to pay you a couple of bucks for helping me out with the phone, but I'm afraid to let go of the strap."

"That's okay. Where's your wallet?"

"In my back pocket."

"Don't worry, I'll get it." Before I could blink she had my wallet in her hand, and said, "How much are you willing to go?"

Jesus, did I just do a dumb thing? The kid could jump off the cable car with my wallet and be a block away before I could convince that dude driving this thing to stop.

Dolores said, "Look, it's a simple question. How much money do you want me to take out?"

"Sorry, I kinda spaced out there. How about a five?"

"How about a ten?"

By this time all I wanted to do was get my

wallet back. "Sounds good to me. Pull out a Jackson, and then put my wallet back into my pocket."

"One Jackson it is. And Bear, just so you don't think all teenage females are dangerous, my can of pepper spray is a fake. I'm too young and nobody'll sell me the real stuff, so I carry this bright red can of Safeway Canola Oil spray. So far it's worked. Whoops, almost missed my stop. Bye."

The cable car barely slowed down and Dolores jumped off. There was a kid that Flo would like to meet. I glanced ahead and Laura was still there.

Most everybody riding the cable car got off at the end of the track, down near the bay. Laura hopped off, walked across the street, and into a joint called the Buena Vista Cafe.

I followed her in. By now it was around eleven and the bar was more than half full. I sat down about three stools from Laura.

The bartender said, "Mornin' Laura! The usual?"

She nodded.

I watched him pour hot water into a clear glass then dump the water out. He added coffee plus a healthy slug of Irish whiskey. Just before he served it, he topped the drink off with spoonful of whipped cream that floated on top.

He wandered over to me. "What's your poison?"

"The same as the lady."

As he mixed my Irish Coffee, I said, "I tended bar in Nevada for years. I could never get the cream on our Irish Coffees to float like that. You guys have a special secret?"

Laura musta heard my question 'cause she turned toward me and smiled. "I read that they age their cream for forty-eight hours. Isn't that right, Jack?"

The barkeep said, "That's what the boss tells me."

The dude served me my Irish Coffee. I took a sip and smiled. "That's the best Irish Coffee I've ever had."

The bartender said, "That's why we make 2000 every day."

He nodded and moved back to Laura. "Still cracking crabs for the tourists at the same joint?"

She nodded. "Yes, and I'm getting tired of doing that crappy job. I'm a trained chef, and have worked in some of the best . . ." She glanced at the clock behind the barkeep. "Whoops, I've got to get my ass in gear or I'll be late."

"See ya." The bartender and I watched Laura leave the Buena Vista.

I said, "She's cute."

"She is, but she's not your type, if you get what I mean."

I thought back to Claudette's apartment—got it now. Her and Claudette! I wonder if Erik had a clue? I said, "Hey, my motto is if you're lucky enough to find the right one for you, then you'd better grab hold and not let 'em go."

I pulled out my wallet and Jesus, that little crook on the cable car grabbed two twenties instead of the ten she was suppose to take. Now I'm down to a measly fifteen bucks. I laid a five on the counter, hoping that the barkeep would give me a fellow bartender's discount.

He glanced down and said, "Dude, I know you said you came from Nevada, but here in the big city of San Francisco, a five barely covers my tip."

I had to get out of the Buena Vista or Laura would get too far away. I added my last ten and ran out the door as the bartender yelled, "Thanks, big spender!"

I spotted Laura walking toward Fisherman's Wharf on Beach Street. I just picked up my walking pace when my damn phone rang again.

"Flo?"

"Who else are you expecting to call?"

"Come on, Babe, cut me a little slack. I just got fleeced out of forty bucks."

"How could that . . . never mind, I'll figure out a way to convince Pinky to cover it. Where are you?"

"Following Laura. She's a block ahead of me and we're both on Beach Street walking toward Fisherman's Wharf."

"Pinky just called. He's landed at SFO and he's going to get hold of Charles. After Pinky got off my line, Charles called. The police agree about bringing Laura in for questioning. I think Pinky and Charles are going to get together with the cops, so when you are ready, all we have to do is call Charles, tell him where Laura is, and he'll ride in with the cavalry."

Laura was about a half-a-block ahead of me. I said, "How'd Pinky sound?"

"Why?"

"I don't know. Just the way he talked during his last call made me think he was really worried about something."

Flo said, "You can ask him soon. He'll be with Charles when the police grab Laura."

"Babe, I just had an Irish Coffee with Laura and you know, she didn't seem like someone who'd poison a dude. She was really nice."

"An Irish Coffee? You told me you were just following her."

"I was, but she told me how the boss at the Buena Vista figured out how to float the cream on top."

Flo didn't say anything for a second. "Bear, there are times when I think you can't be trusted out of my sight. And don't tell me again she's really nice. To you, anything with boobs is nice. Hold on, I can see you walking down the sidewalk ahead of us. We'll finish this discussion later!"

The cab pulled up, I jumped in.

Flo acted like I wasn't there. "Driver, stay back and follow that woman wearing the black pants with the stylish gray jacket."

The cabbie said, "Lady, I've been driving a cab in San Francisco for ten years and I never once had a customer tell me to follow anyone. Now, in one day, I hit the jackpot."

I said, "What the hell does a jackpot have to do with anything?"

Ettamae said, "Flo told the driver to follow the cable car, and just now she told him to follow Laura, hence the cabbies reference to hitting a jackpot."

I said, "Hence? What kind of a word is that?

"It means as a consequence of. For example, there are too many cars in San Francisco, hence there are too few parking places."

Flo said, "Excellent! I can see that your English classes in Scotland were top-notch."

Ettamae said, "Flo, this cab driver is great. Do you think you could get this quality of service from Uber?"

The cabbie said, "Not in a million years. Little girl, you stick with real cabs in the future."

Ettamae said, "I'm not a little girl, but give him a good tip anyway."

I glanced out the front window just in time to see Laura turn into a narrow alley between two of those restaurants that sell crab cocktails to the tourists when they walk by.

"Hey, we're about to lose Laura." I jumped out as the cab stopped.

While Flo paid the cabbie, I walked down the alley. It ended with a ten foot drop to skuzzy looking water. To my right there was a door.

I ran back to Flo and the Kid. "Flo, call Charlie.

Give him the address of this joint. I'll go through the back door, see if I can corral Laura, and hold her until the cops get here. After I go inside, Flo, you cover the alley, just in case that broad run out the back way."

I glanced at Ettamae. She was about the same size, and age, as that little crook who took my forty bucks. "Ettamae, you got your cell phone?"

She rummaged around her big purse. "Of course I do."

"Okay. You hang by the front door, like you're waiting for your aunt and uncle to pick you up. If Laura gets past me, Flo, and she cruises out the front door, you've got her. Just let Laura go by, and drop back at least a half a block. While you're walking, call me, or Flo, or Charlie, or Pinky, and tell us where Laura's heading."

Flo said, "Ettamae, whatever happens, don't do anything stupid. Like Bear told you, if Laura comes out the front door, just let her walk by. Then you can try to follow her."

Ettamae giggled. "Bear, isn't this where you tell us to synchronize our watches like they did in all those corny old movies?"

I grabbed her shoulders, turned her until she was looking straight at me. "Kid, this ain't a movie or a game. Laura murdered a dude and killers work like this—after they do in the first one, the second one's a lot easier. If Laura figures out that you are following her, she'll kill you."

Ettamae gulped. "You can count on me."

I glanced at Flo. She nodded, so I said, "Okay. Everybody get where you're suppose to be. I'm going in!"

CHAPTER THIRTY-NINE

Pinky-San Francisco, California

After a sleepless flight from the City of Brotherly Love, I arrived at SFO worn out. But despite my inordinate state of weariness, the moment I entered my cab, I summoned up the energy to call Charles.

"Pinky, am I pleased to hear your voice. Much has happened during your absence. Your team of investigators has successfully shifted the focus away from Erik and onto Laura Heath, the other person of interest identified by the police concerning the Rand murder. Presently, Bear is following Laura and he will call me as soon as he has her corralled, to use his continually challenging vernacular. Now that you have returned to the bay area, are you at liberty to tell me what you were doing that was so important?"

"Charles, I am not now, nor will I ever be able to discuss why I was taken away from my San Francisco obligations. Now, I need to check into my hotel and perhaps take a short nap to resolve my desperate need for sleep. After a brief respite, my physical problems will take a second seat to closing out the Rand murder and meeting my legal obligation with Erik Rundstrom's father to protect his son at all costs. Please call me if and when Bear calls for help. I will be ready and able to fight on to the conclusion."

"Good. I'll do that."

At the completion of my taxi ride from SFO, I reached the Hotel Drisco and checked in. As usual, the staff at the desk treated me as a king. The bellhop accompanied me to my suite and prior to opening the door, he said, "Mr Delmont, we apologize. We were not expecting you this early and the maid service has not yet cleaned your suite."

I nodded and entered. A cursory glance around the living area informed me that my well deserved nap was going to be longer than a few moments away.

Shock and disappointment were the two words that properly described my feelings. Empty aluminum beer cans and white popcorn kernels littered the carpet around the plush chair that sat in front of the television.

I shuddered and walked into the master bedroom and gazed at a mound of soiled clothing on the floor by the bed. The bathroom sported used towels and a large bra was draped over the shower door.

With trepidation, I scanned the second, smaller bedroom. Again, shirts and jeans, along with five empty soft drink cans littered the carpet by the bed. The adjoining bathroom's counter was cluttered with lipstick, eyeliner and deodorant while three pairs of small, lace panties were hung over the towel rack.

After my tour of the suite, I turned to the bellhop, and said, "My good man, the condition of my suite is absolutely unacceptable. Go downstairs, find the manager, and bring him to me at once!"

"Sir."

"Yes."

"Once the maid completes her job, your suite will look fine."

"Looking fine does not meet my standards. Now do what I asked, find your manager and bring him to me."

While I waited, I walked to the window and gazed out at the panoramic view of the city known as Bagdad by the Bay.

A short knock announced the manager. The door opened and an officious young man, slightly shorter than myself, entered and frowned as he absorbed the disgraceful condition of my suite. Once he completed his tour, he said, "Mr. Delmont, before I say anything about the condition of your suite, the Hotel Drisco is pleased to welcome you back to our establishment. That said, the state of your suite is deplorable. Do you have any idea how this could happened?"

"I do. While I was forced to attend to important business on the east coast, I made a grievous error and allowed my investigative team to occupy my suite. Obviously, I have returned and their belongings, and this mess cannot remain. Do you have an available room, the smaller the better, that can accommodate my investigative team— three adults?"

"We do. I could move them into the smallest of our ground level rooms. Once we add a cot, the room will just accommodate three adults."

"Excellent. Send up a team to my suite. I will supervise them while they pack up all the clothing, shoes, and the bathroom hodgepodge. Once your crew has completed their packing task, they will move the lot to the ground level room you have selected."

"Mr. Delmont, before we do what you ask, I would feel safer if I contacted our legal staff concerning the legality of our staff removing the personal belongings of your employees."

"Are you aware that I am an attorney?"

"I didn't know that, sir."

"And you are aware that I have a standing reservation for two weeks during the fall of each year and have availed myself of the Drisco's hospitality for more than a decade?"

"No, Mr. Delmont. I was not."

"And that the proprietors from the Inn at the Presidio have been hounding me to spend my annual, two-week fall respite at their establishment?"

"No, sir. I did not know that."

"Then get to work and activate your team."

"Yes, sir."

As the manager turned, but before he marched out of my suite, I said, "One final item. Is it possible to deny access to my suite for my investigative staff?"

The manager turned back toward me and nodded. "As you are aware, we here at Hotel Drisco do not use the ubiquitous electronic key-card system. We proudly retain the traditional room key attached to a heavy fob method. But, for you, a valued guest, I will contact a locksmith at once. I am positive the lock to your suite can be changed in less than an hour. A bellhop will deliver your new key fob upon completion of the locksmith's task."

The manager and I supervised a team of maids and bellhops as they packed up all the clothing, both soiled and clean, and tossed all of the bathroom clutter into a cardboard box as the locksmith completed his job. Two minutes later, a bellhop gave my new key.

With a clean and secured suite, I sat down in the plush chair, relaxed, and immediately fell asleep.

A loud noise radiated from my cell phone jarring me awake.

I snapped, "Yes?"

"Pinky, don't kill the messenger. This is Charles. You told me to call you when we were

304

ready to arrest Laura Heath."

I glanced at my watch. Only thirty minutes had passed. I said, "I see you called me as promised."

"Flo called. They have Laura Heath cornered at one of the Fisherman's Wharf restaurants."

My mind snapped to attention when my ears pick up the word cornered. "Charles, what did she mean by cornered? Have they captured the woman?"

"Hey, like I said before. Don't get mad at me. I'm only passing on Flo's message. I can stop by and pick you up, or not. It's up to you."

I stood up. "I might as well tag along. Will the police meet us there?"

"Yes, along with a representative from the District Attorney's office."

This could turn into a financial opportunity for me. As I will be there when Laura Heath is arrested, I could offer to represent her, through Charles of course, on what could turn out to be an erroneous charge of murder. As Joey Palumbo so aptly pointed out to me— that sort of thing has been known to happen

I said, "Charles, how long will it take you to arrive at the Drisco?"

"With any luck, I'll be there in five minutes."

"Excellent. I will wait for you outside the hotel entrance."

CHAPTER FORTY

Bear-San Francisco, California

Before I walked in the back door, I grabbed a couple of empty cardboard boxes labeled crabs that were stacked close to the rear entrance and opened the door. I hoisted the light cardboard onto my shoulder, pretending they were filled with fresh crabs, and waltzed in.

The kitchen was big, like twenty by twenty feet. To my left was a short dude washing dishes. To my right stood two guys chopping up all kinds of stuff like carrots, celery, onions, and peppers.

Straight ahead stood three cooks who were manning stoves. All three cooks were faced the other way.

Everybody was working real hard and nobody lifted his head, or seemed to care that I was walking into their kitchen. That was cool, but Laura wasn't in the kitchen.

I walked to a big door in the back, opened it, and peeked in.

Inside was lots of fish, beef, and all kinds of other food, but again, no sign of Laura.

I set the boxes down on a shelf next to a wire

basket full of mussels and clams and cruised past the line cooks working the stoves.

I cruised past the line cooks and pushed on the door and popped out into the restaurant where waiters were hustling around and people were eating. A quick glance around told me that Laura wasn't there.

Then I heard a door open behind me. I turned and spotted a sign that read, Women.

I walked up to the door just as a short babe with gray hair moved by me and started to open the door.

I said, "Excuse me. My wife wasn't feeling so good and she went inside there a few minutes ago. Would you check all the stalls and see if there's a broad who answers to the name of Laura?"

She gave me the once over, like I was kind of wacko.

"What is your wife's last name?"

"The same as mine."

She kinda sighed and sounded just like my old Elko High algebra teacher did when she gave up trying to get me to figure out what the hell X was equal to. My old teacher tried hard, but I never did figure out those X and Y things.

"Do you have a last name?"

"Yup."

"And it is?"

"Zabarte."

"So I am looking for a female named Laura

Zabarte?"

"Yup."

The gray-haired babe walked in and came out inside of a minute.

"Mr. Zabarte, I do not know what sort of a game you are trying to play but except for me, the ladies restroom was completely empty."

"Sorry, no games. Just trying to find my wife."

"Mr. Zabarte, have you ever considered that she came to her senses and does not want to be found?"

I nodded. "Guess that's possible. Thanks for all your help. Got to go."

I walked toward the entrance of the joint, and that's when I finally spotted Laura. At least Laura's back. Outside the front door of the restaurant was a line of stainless counters with refrigerators and pots and pans underneath. Laura was one of two people who made crab and shrimp cocktails, and served clam chowder inside one of those loaves of sourdough French bread for the tourists who walked by.

I marched out the front door and got into the middle of a bus load of tourists who were milling around. They looked like a flock of seagulls trying to spot their next meal.

I got behind a big, fat dude win a giant red sweatshirt with Iowa State on the front as he worked his way down the line waiting for Laura to fix him some crab, or shrimp, or chowder. While we moved along, I tried to figure out what I was going to say to Laura when it was my turn to order. Finally, the fat dude somehow figured out how to hold onto three crab cocktails with his chubby fingers and moved ahead. Now it was my turn to order.

Without looking up, Laura said, "What can I get for you?"

"Hi, Laura. Me and you got a date with the DA."

Her head lifted and she didn't move, like her brain couldn't quite figure out what I'd said. Then she smiled, "Oh, I know you. You are that guy from the Buena Vista who wanted to know about the cream. I'm sorry, but I didn't catch your order. The Dungeness crab cocktails are fresh, but I'd hold off on the shrimp 'cause they've been around the block once or twice, if you know what I mean."

"Laura?"

"How do you know my name? Do I know you?"

"Sorry, but take off your apron. Me and you've got a date with the DA."

She stepped back, grabbed a cast iron skillet and smashed the damn thing on my arm and broke my fiberglass cast. A gut busting shot of pain ripped up my arm. I had to fight to keep from passing out.

Staggering from the pain, and before I could move, Laura dropped the pan and grabbed a meat cleaver. She snarled, "I'm only going to say this once, move your ass out of my way, or I'll cut you in half with this damn cleaver."

She jumped to the right and popped through an opening in the line of countertops.

I fought to clear my head and pushed my through the line of tourists.

Laura stopped, turned toward me and lifted the meat clever over her head.

That's when we started to circle each other like a couple of boxers in the ring.

Through clenched teeth, I said, "Laura, the jig is up. The cops know it wasn't Erik that poisoned that dude. The DA knows it. Shit, even I know it. Drop the cleaver and let's make this easy."

"Easy my ass," said Laura, and she took a swipe at me with the cleaver. It only caught the air, but I could hear the blade whistle as it flew past my ear.

The fat dude from Iowa standing next to me, squealed like a hawk with a broken wing, dropped his crab cocktails, and waddled away as fast as his stubby legs could move.

I glanced over and noticed an old broom stick leaning against the counter. I figured that even though she's got a cleaver, if I could somehow get hold of that broom stick, I'd be in an sorta even fight.

I jumped, grabbed the skinny broom stick and ducked just as Laura took another swipe at me. That time I guessed right by ducking down cause the blade went over my head, but we both knew that if I didn't get her first, sooner or later I'd guess wrong and she'd get me.

Like I said, we'd started to circle and the mob of Fisherman's Wharf tourists backed away to give us lots of room, like they were watching a bull fight in Frisco.

Laura'd make a lunge with the meat cleaver. I'd counter with the hardwood broom stick.

I knew damn well that one hit with her cleaver could cut off my arm, or head, but she knew that if I got lucky and hit her wrist first with rap from a stick of hardwood, she'd probably drop the clever.

I wasn't sure what was going to happen next when I heard Ettamae yell, "Laura, over here. It's me, Claudette!"

The Kid's cry came from my right and Laura's eyes shifted off me for a second to see if she could spot her roommate. That was all the time I needed. I took a hard swing and hit her arm just above her wrist. The cracking sound of a breaking bone in Laura's arm came a second before the crash of the metal cleaver blade hitting concrete.

Laura screamed, dropped like a rock and rolled around like one of those pill bugs.

I knew how bad she felt, and was almost sorry that I had hit her so hard, but when it came down to it, I'd rather she had a broken wrist then me getting my ear lopped off like that famous painter Flo likes so much!

I stepped back and dropped the broom stick.

All of a sudden, the crowd of tourists started to clap, like they thought me and Laura's fight was a daily part of the regular Fisherman's Wharf entertainment package.

I heard a police siren then three cars pulled up. Out of the first one jumped Pinky, Charlie, and another dude in a suit. The other two black and whites were just full of cops.

They all ran toward me and Laura. One of the cops leaned over Laura, who was now just crying, and read her the Miranda rights. About the time the cop got to the part where she could talk to an attorney, Pinky got close up and personal.

I watched him lean down and say,"Laura Heath, my name is J. Pincus Delmont. I am an attorney who specializes in defending persons accused of murder, the ultimate crime. Ms. Heath, before you speak to anyone, I am here to protect your legal rights. Do you happen to have a dollar on you?"

She blinked through her tears. "Yes . . . I keep my tips in . . . my . . . apron."

Very gently, Pinky stuck his hand in and pulled out a buck. "Ms. Heath, with your undamaged hand, please hand this dollar to Charles, the man at my side."

She looked a little out of it, but she still did what Pinky told her to do.

Pinky said, "Now say, loud enough so a witness can hear you, 'Charles, I retain you as my attorney.'"

Again she did what he wanted.

Pinky smiled, "Ms. Heath, from this moment on, do not talk to anyone but Charles or myself, and that includes the man in the blue uniform standing next to you. In a moment, the police with help you up, but do not worry. I will accompany you where ever you go, to the police station, or the hospital, and I will protect your legal rights. Trust me, Ms. Heath, I fully understand your ordeal."

As two cops helped her up, Pinky said, "My dear, are you in pain?"

"Yes. I think my arm is broken."

"Did that happen when you fell?"

Laura glared at me and with her good hand she pointed a finger at me. "No. That bastard hit my arm with a broom handle."

I said, "Don't forget, babe, that's the same time you were trying to kill me with that meat cleaver."

By now some of the tourists had crowded closer. One dude behind me yelled, "He's right. She damn near killed him with that big knife!"

Then a woman pushed her way into the front of the crown and pointed at me. "I don't trust that man. He tried to sneak into the Women's restroom in the restaurant!"

Shit, she was the same babe with gray hair that I had conned into checking out the Women's can.

That did it. I'd had it up to my armpits with all

these Frisco tourists. I yelled, "Ettamae?"

The Kid pushed her way to my side. "Yes?"

"Good job distracting Laura. Now, go find Flo. We're heading back to the Drisco."

While she ran down the alley, I watched the cops and Pinky walk Laura to a squad car. Pinky almost tripped over the cleaver and he didn't seem to care that Laura had almost took my head off, but that's okay. It won't take long for Pinky to find out that his new client hasn't got a pot to piss in. Hell, she couldn't be making much more than minimum wage, if that, dishing up crab cocktails. She's probably just scraping by on her salary and tips.

And don't tell Flo this, but she was right and I was wrong again. Laura was about as nice as two starving coyotes fighting over a pork chop.

Ettamae and Flo finally got to me. Flo said, "Not much happened back there. I did hear some applause. Was a street artist performing out front? Did Laura turn herself in?"

I shuddered as I remembered hearing that cleaver whizz by my ear. "Right, she just held her hands up and said, 'Bear, you've got me. I poisoned that bastard of a critic. Take me to jail.'"

Ettamae said, "Bear, that's not what actually happened and you know it."

"Kid, do you want to take a cab back to our truck, or ride the cable car?"

She jumped up and down. "The cable car for sure." The Kid started to run back toward the cable car station.

Flo said, "Just because you got rid of Ettamae, doesn't mean I don't want to know happened. "

"I had to dodge a few bullets."

"I didn't hear any gunshots."

"Okay, so they weren't bullets. How about I dodged something pretty dangerous that came damned close."

"What kind of something?"

"Babe, you don't want to know. But that Laura did break my cast with a frying pan and my arm still hurts like hell."

"Do we need to drop by an emergency room and have someone check it out?"

"Na. I can chew on a fist full of Tylenol. Babe, all I want to do now is get back to that Drisco joint. I can't wait to sit down in that soft chair, put my feet up, pop a beer and watch a baseball game on TV."

Flo said, "Okay with me. In fact, we should spend a couple of days wandering around the city. There's a lot to see and Ettamae's never been to San Francisco before."

I said, "Sounds good to me."

But none of that wandering around Frisco happened!

Why?

'Cause an hour later, Flo blew her top when she found out that Pinky'd moved us from our cool two-bedroom suite to what the bell hop called the ground level guest room.

The room had no view, unless you think looking at sidewalks and parked cars is a view. All three of us were stuck together in one room. There wasn't any beer in the mini fridge. I mean the damn fridge was empty and the chair in front of the TV was hard as a rock. But the worst of all, Flo wouldn't let me do nothing with Ettamae sleeping on a cot right next to our bed. So we checked out of the Drisco the next morning and for the next four to five hours, while I drove the truck back to Carson City, Flo was as quiet as a mouse. In fact, she didn't say a word the whole trip! I didn't know what she was thinking all that time, but I shoulda known that she was scheming on a way to get back at our chicken-shit boss.

CHAPTER FORTY-ONE

Bear-Carson City, Nevada

It took a little more than a week before Pinky called and told us we had to come to his office—like right now!

As I set the phone down, Ettamae walked through the front door with a big frown plastered above her nose.

"What's up, Kid?"

"I know how old I am, but the kids at school act like little kids. Do you know what I mean?"

"I think so. Hey, you've got to realize that you've been through a lot of life since we met at your grandpa's place on the Russian River."

"I know. Bear, I really miss Grandpa, Scotland, Fergus and Fiona, and Frank Bramble."

"I know, but you're still too young to work with me and Flo every day. You've got to go to school."

"You're right. Tell me, where did you go to school?"

"In Elko."

"Did you think school was worth it?"

I was trying to think of a line of bull to feed her when Flo barged in and saved my ass.

I said, "Pinky just called and he wants us to meet him in his office, pronto!"

Flo flashed her evil smile, the one that sorta scares me. "That's perfect timing."

"Why's that, Babe?"

"As soon as we returned home and got Ettamae enrolled in school, I've been working on a project."

"I noticed you've been gone most days. Whatcha been doing or don't you want me to know?"

"Bear, do you remember that a month ago Pinky was ready to send us to San Francisco. Then he changed his mind and wanted us to go to Camden, New Jersey, and then, before we could pack, back to San Francisco?"

I glanced down at the newspaper and saw that the Red Sox game was starting in a few minutes. I didn't have a clue where Flo was going with all this crap, but I sure hoped she'd be done before the game started, so I said, "Yup."

Flo said, "Ettamae, go do your homework in the kitchen. I need to discuss something with Bear, in private."

Ettamae stood up as tall as she could. "Flo, I am into puberty, nearly an adult, and have just completed an investigation that took me from Scotland, to San Francisco, to Scandinavia, and back to San Francisco. During that investigation I was nearly shot by an accused murderer, flushed out a suspect, and watched Simon Rand's actual murderer almost chop Bear's head off. Please, do not feel that you need to be circumspect when you and Bear discuss past, present, or future investigations in front of me."

I said, "Babe, I didn't think girls her age knew anything about circumspection."

Flo shook her head. "Two things are very wrong here! Bear, you are confusing circumcision and circumspection. They do not mean the same thing. Next, Ettamae, did I hear you say that Laura nearly chopped Bear's head off?"

"I did, and she was using a very sharp meat cleaver. Oh, I remember now, you didn't see him fight with Laura because you were covering the back of the restaurant while I was covering the front. The fight was wild. Bear had a broom stick and Laura had a meat cleaver. The two waltzed around in circles for awhile before—"

Flo said, "Please do not say anymore. Bear, you and I will discuss your lack of candor concerning the meat cleaver later."

I snuck a peek at my watch and it was only five minutes before the game started. "Babe, if you think I was lying you're wrong. I told you what Laura did was pretty dangerous. Now, can we get back to your project?"

Flo stared at Ettamae, then me, like she could look inside our heads to make sure we were giving her the straight skinny. "I guess so. We all know how Pinky works, sort of between the lines of ethics, morality, and legality. I was looking for something he did over the past month that we could use as leverage against him."

"Why?"

"Because as a strong, female human being I refuse to accept the way he treated us at the Hotel Drisco."

Ettamae said, "As a strong, close to being an adult female, I agree with you. What Pinky did was bad, even for him."

Flo said, "So to build my case, first I talked to Frank."

I said, "Who?"

"Frank! That guy Pinky hired to take Lu's place during her maternity leave. He told me that Pinky flew to Philadelphia while we were in San Francisco."

"Babe, we already knew that, and I've got a big game starting in one minute. Cut to the chase."

"You and those damned Red Sox. Okay, the Philadelphia trip was part of that mysterious Camden trip we never went on. While you were picking up a compound fracture in your arm in Sweden, Pinky was playing footsie with the Mafia Don of New Jersey and East Philadelphia."

"We know all about that." I grabbed the remote, turned the ball game on, and hit the mute button. With Flo, I get away with lots of crap, but Grandma Zabarte did not raise a stupid grandson. While my eyes watched the silent baseball game, I said, "Did something else happen?"

"I talked to to Hook and he told me that Pinky, and a guy named Joey were all about to be dropped into the Atlantic ocean when the Don changed his mind and let them go."

"Babe, I get it. And then the little shit comes back to San Francisco and bops us out of that cool suite."

Flo smiled. "Right. Before we go, I need to call Lu. Then we'll be ready to head to Pinky's office."

While Flo talked to Lu, I sat down and watched Big Popi hit a home run in the bottom of the first inning. My Red Sox are really going to miss that guy next year.

Flo said, "Turn off the damn game and let's go."

Ettamae said, "Bye."

Flo said, "Ettamae, you have to come with us. You're part of the deal."

The Kid popped out the door and said, "Deal? Oh boy, I always wanted to be part of a deal. This is getting exciting."

We all jumped into my truck and when I pulled into Pinky's parking lot, Lu's car was already there. We watched Lu take her baby out of her car and we all walked in together.

Frank was sitting at Lu's desk staring at the ceiling, and that broad who dressed like an old Navajo hippy was still playing solitaire on her computer at a desk along the far wall.

As we headed to Pinky's office, Frank jumped up and tried to block the door. "Excuse me. I should announce you first."

"In your dreams." I shoved him out of our way and pushed the door open. "Hi, Boss. How's it hanging?"

"My good man, I have no idea why you keep asking me that. Now, I have summoned Team Delmont here today to . . . why did you bring that teenager and Lu?"

Flo sat down on the edge of Pinky's desk and folded her arms underneath her terrific ta ta's. "Pinky, I'm happy you asked that question. I can answer you now, or we can discuss that item after we negotiate a few benefit upgrades."

"Negotiate? Benefit upgrades? We have nothing to negotiate. In fact, I refuse to say another word until you remove your . . . ah . . . posterior from the rich, hand rubbed surface of my imported Mahogany desk."

Flo flashed Pinky a dirty look and slipped her beautiful butt off the bosses desk. "Pinky, we know all about the deal that fell through with the Mafia Don, and how he sent you on a helicopter flight over the Atlantic Ocean where you nearly pissed all over your navy blue silk shorts."

Ettamae giggled and Lu even cracked a tiny smile.

My Babe ignored the giggle and kept going. "We know all about your quid pro quo deal with

Judge Jonas." Flo sighed, "All the mafia stuff is just embarrassing to you, but when Frank took off one day for lunch, he left his desk unlocked and I took the opportunity to look over your expense log and discovered that you've charged four first class airline tickets to Philadelphia, fancy hotel suites, car rentals, and food and drinks to Erik's father's account. To the Nevada Bar, your quid pro quo deal with Judge Jonas, and that little expense discrepancy is a guaranteed ethical no-no, if not an offense that could get you disbarred. Do you want me to continue, or are you ready to discuss Bear's combat pay benefit along with a couple of other items."

Pinky's eyes jumped around in their sockets, like he was a cornered rabbit staring into both barrels of my Pop's shotgun. The cords in the little shrimp's neck were tighter then a bull's ass at fly time. Finally, he sat back, took a big breath, and said, "Florence, I will stipulate that there may have been times during a Delmont investigation when Bear endured a few minor scratches and scrapes."

Flo smiled and in her sweetest voice said, "Pinky, I'm positive that Willow would just love to hear what the mafia actually did to Judge Jonas and why he'll never be seen again."

Once my Babe said Willow's name, Pinky's face got all scrunched up. After a couple of seconds, he relaxed and said, "Florence, what do you have in mind for this 'combat pay' benefit?"

"Five thousand each time he is struck by someone. Ten thousand for each broken bone. Twenty-five thousand for each bullet wound."

"But those calamitous events could, and do occur to Bear, during a normal weekend in Carson City."

"You're right. I will agree to the stipulation that any injuries to Bear must occur during a Delmont investigation while working under the direction of J. Pincus Delmont."

"My good woman, I agree. Now, can we—"

I said, "Boss, what about Flo? Somebody could hurt her too."

Pinky said, "I will agree to include Florence's name in the combat pay benefit codicil, although so far, you are the only member of Team Delmont who has been injured during an official investigation. Now, moving on to—"

Flo said, "Not so fast, buster, we've just started. Next, Frank, that eighteen-year-old pathetic excuse for a secretary sitting outside your office has to go. Just because you found a sycophant who kowtows to you does not mean he's capable of doing a proper job."

"Florence, as long as I continue to breath, I will retain absolute control over who works in my—"

"Boss, clam up and listen."

Ettamae said, "Yah. Flo's got a really cool great idea."

Pinky glared at Ettamae and snapped through clenched teeth, "What is your proposal, Florence?"

"You can keep Frank, but not as your legal secretary. Pay him to cut your lawn, paint your house, or wash your car, I don't care what you do with the guy but don't ever let him into this office again."

"And whom do you propose would fill the secretarial position?"

Flo said, "Pinky, before I move on, I have to acknowledge the social progress you have made concerning Lu's maternity leave benefit."

The boss sat up and puffed a little. "Thank you, Florence. I pride myself on being a forward thinker concerning employee relations."

"I wouldn't go that far, but in this one situation you did the right thing. Now, here's your opportunity to move up to the top of the class. I have discussed this with Lu, and she has agreed to return at once, as long as you pay Ettamae to take care of Lu's child while Lu covers your legal secretarial duties."

"Florence, are you out of your—"

"And you will match the salary you pay Ettamae, dollar for dollar, into a college fund, your contribution to be administered by Lu."

"Let me understand this. I pay Ettamae to be a nanny for Lu's baby, and while I do that, I also contribute an identical amount of the salary I pay to Ettamae into a college fund so Ettamae can afford college."

Flo nodded.

Pinky said, "And how much is the salary I will be required to pay Ettamae?"

I said, "Boss, I did some checking on this and fifteen bucks an hour should do the job for a nanny."

Pinky leaned forward, "But it is not only fifteen dollars an hour. With the college fund, I am paying thirty dollars an hour for a nanny and that is outrageous."

Flo went on. "Calm down and listen. I have a few more items to cover. Since we've arrived back home, Ettamae has attended junior high school and her school experiences have been less than positive. Lu has agreed to act as Ettamae's home school teacher."

"Florence, are you asking me to turn my office into a school for a teenager?"

"No! I'm telling you."

Ettamae said, "Pinky, wake up and smell the coffee. You'd be getting Lu back months early. I'll take care of Jiao, her beautiful, sweet baby, and Lu will make sure I learn everything I'm suppose to so I can go to college and become a pediatrician."

I said, "Kid, you never told me you wanted to be a doc."

She flashed me one of those looks she learned from Flo. "You never asked, and not just a doctor, a pediatrician."

Flo said, "Pinky, one final item. That woman,

the one who goes by the name of Thelma? I don't think you know it, but all she does is play solitaire all day. She needs to join the ranks of those who do not work for J. Pincus Delmont."

"She plays solitaire all day?"

"Yes! Now, Lu and I have looked over your office space and the area Thelma presently occupies would make a perfect nursery with enough space to provide a partitioned study area for Ettamae."

"Florence, can you guarantee me that I will never require a paralegal to assist me in my law practice."

Flo smiled. "Pinky, face it. You're a one-man show!"

Pinky stared at Flo. "But when I hired that woman I agreed with Willow that I would keep her on as my paralegal."

"No problem. Call up Willow and tell her that your circumstances have changed and that your needs for a paralegal have vanished. And while you're talking to your favorite ex-wife, ask her out to lunch. Everybody in town thinks it's about time you two get back together again."

Pinky's eyes lit up, at least during the part when Flo talked about taking Willow out to lunch. "Florence, you could be right. Concerning this homeschool situation, I will take Judge Robertson out to dinner. He was on the statewide committee that helped write the Nevada State law that set up homeschooling in the Silver State and he can

327

provide me with valuable insight on the process."

Flo pushed her hand in Pinky's direction. "So we agree that Frank and Thelma are out. Lu's back and you will pay fifteen dollars an hour to Ettamae for her services as a nanny for Lu's baby and match her salary for her college fund. You will provide the partition so Ettamae can study her lessons in peace. Finally, Lu will monitor Ettamae's home school progress and her college fund. Pinky, if I didn't know you better, I'd nominate you for Carson City's employer of the year."

"Florence, cease and desist. Now, if you are all done with your piracy, we need to discuss your next assignment."

I sat up. "Okay, boss. What's next?"

"You and Florence are to return to San Francisco to dig up more on the untimely death of Simon Rand."

Flo said, "But we just did that."

"I know what you did, but your work concerned the previous prime suspect, Erik Rundstrom. I have discussed Laura Heath's delicate situation with a gentleman who goes by the name of Harrison Heath."

Flo said, "I know that name . . .give me a minute . . . that's it. He's a big time TV producer. In fact, he's just been nominated for an Emmy for that great series I watch on HBO, *The Sand On The Beach*. Don't tell me this guy is related to Laura Heath."

"He's the woman's father, and he has offered me a substantial finder's fee to recommend a California attorney who will defend his daughter during her time of need."

I said, "A finder's fee? So you're not going to defend Laura Heath?"

"No. I have neglected my practice here in Carson City, and—"

Flo said, "And you can't be sure of winning her case, so you're going to dump her?"

"Florence, I take umbrage at your insinuation. You need to know that—"

Ettamae jumped up. "I'm really excited with this new home school thing, but I've changed my mind about college."

Flo said, "Ettamae, you're going to college and that's the end of this discussion."

"Flo, I didn't mean that I'm not going to college. I just have to change my major from doctor to lawyer."

Pinky said, "Smart move. If there is anything I can do to help, just let me know."

Ettamae looked at me, then Flo and gave us both a big, wide grin. "I'm sorry, Pinky, I know this will come across as fickle, but I'm switching from pre-med to pre-law because I want to become a lawyer who defends those clients who can't afford an expensive attorney. I don't want to end up like you who only takes on clients who can pay big retainers, or who can add to the numbers on your winning record. That means I'll have to work hard to be as good an attorney as you are while maintaining the high ethical and moral standards you lack. If I need any advice on maintaining high ethical and moral standards, I'll seek out someone I can trust to do the right thing, like District Attorney, Willow Stone.

"As I work my way through my college education and discover I'm missing out on some of the important stuff, like the intricacies of drinking lots of beer, and tasteful cussing, I'll go to my good-old buddy, Bear, for advice.

And if I'm seeking the straight skinny on how to grow into a strong, viable woman, the exact type of female I plan to become one day, I'll seek counsel from my best friend, Flo, because she's my heroine."

After a few seconds, Pinky blurted out, "Changing the subject, I summoned Team Delmont here today—"

My cell made one of those burps that said I've got a text message. I glanced at the screen, couldn't understand a word, grabbed Flo's arm and dragged her out of the shrimp's office.

Flo pulled my hand off her arm and said, "What's gotten into you?"

"Check out this message."

She looked at the screen. "Interesting. It's written in German!"

"What's it say?"

"Let me see. My German's not good anymore . .

. . geld, that's means money . . . schnell, that means fast or quick . . . and Pinky . . . a word that defies translation."

I said, "Who's it from?"

"Do I look like Houdini?"

"Babe, we ought to show this to Pinky."

Flo sighed, "I don't think so. I was hoping to take some time off to kick back and look for a larger apartment."

Jesus! Walking through apartments was about as bad as being hogtied and dropped into a den of rattler's.

"But this sounds like it's right up Pinky's alley."

"We both know that once Pinky smells money, he'll send us off on a new investigation. We can show him the message later."

"But if he figures out that we've screwed him out of a big bucket of bucks, he'll get his Mafia buddy to drop us into the Atlantic Ocean."

Flo said, "This time you could be right. Hand me your phone. I'll tell Pinky what the message says." She flashed me a smile. "Did you know that the German's make the best beer in the world?"

"Hells bells, what are we waiting for?"

Author's Notes

Yes, there really is a small statue of a mermaid in the Copenhagen harbor. And Tivoli, the amusement park, is like Disneyland with beer!

But the most interesting part of writing this book was traveling to Skellefteå, Sweden.

The town is small by California standards with 32,000 residents, sits about 500 miles north of Stockholm, and is so far off the beaten path that the majority of the Swedish population have never been there.

So how did Bear, Flo, and Ettamae end up in such an isolated location?

That's easy. Our two Swedish daughters invited us to spend a few nights on the farm where Susanne grew up. Truthfully Eva, and Susanne are not our daughters by birth, but they have been beloved members of our family for decades.

The reader might ask what makes up a farm in northern Sweden? As Bear noted, there is some grain grown, cows in the pastures, and chickens and pigs, but the major crop in the Skellefteå area is trees.

Now it takes a long time to grow a tree and in northern Sweden, about eighty years for a planted forest to mature. Think about that for a moment. Let's say you are twenty-five and just purchased a farm ten kilometers north of Skellefteå, You plant ten acres of trees, sit back and wait for the money to roll in when your trees are harvested. Twenty-five plus eighty means that you will be a cool one hundred and five when you receive the money from your first cash crop!

Obviously, that's not the way Susanne's family worked their farm. Each year, they would harvest, and then replant trees in a section of land as the picture of Eva shows her holding a newly planted tree.

And I found it interesting to note that the type of tree planted was pine. Where I live, pine trees are considered a soft wood. But in northern Sweden, pines are considered hard wood due to their cold winters and the eighty years it takes to grow the tree to maturity.

Now, for a couple of other quirky observations on Sweden. In Sweden the term fika is usually heard in the morning, or afternoon, as a sort of coffee-break, but fika means much more that a regimented, fifteen minute break from work. The Swedish seem to understand, better than the American's, that life is short, so when two friends meet on the sidewalk, they will smile, say "Fika?", and find a coffee stand where they will sip, nibble, and talk, regardless of other pressing demands.

In my hometown, we have a bakery downtown with a bench sitting outside the building and every morning you can walk by and see men and women sipping their coffee and discussing the affairs of the world, sort of an American fika. But, in my hometown, most everyone sitting on that bench is retired. In Sweden, if you are looking, you will see fika clutches everywhere at all times of the day with all ages. I say more power to the custom of fika and hope that someday fika reaches our shores.

Prior to going north to Skellefteå, we spent a week in Stockholm, a city of islands that is both beautiful and vibrant.

The picture on the next page shows how someone on the street below our apartment parked

their bike on the street across the intersection.
Why? Got me. But it did slow down the traffic.

But it was our encounter with pizza salad that
sticks in my mind. After a long day of walking
around, we went into a pizza place and ordered a
pizza. While I waited, I noticed people walking by
my table carrying a bowl of what looked like a
salad. I got up and followed a patron toward the
back of the building where I spotted a large bowl of
chopped cabbage that had been tossed with a light
vinaigrette dressing. Half way through our salad,
our pizza arrived.

Never once did I consider the possibility that all
pizza restaurants in Sweden provided a cabbage
salad, but I began to wonder after finding pizza
salad in a pizza restaurant in Skellefteå. I asked

Eva if a gratis pizza salad was the standard in Sweden. She nodded, as if she had never considered anything else.

The final punch line to the pizza salad story happened some time later, when the four of us, Eva, Susanne, my wife, and I were in Lillehammer, Norway. Naturally we found ourselves in a pizza restaurant and when Susanne asked the waitress where the salad was, the waitress said, "You're from Sweden, right?"

Eve said, "Yes, we are."

The waitress shook her head. "You Swedes!" Then she walked away from our table.

As you may have picked-up at the conclusion of this book, the next Pinky and Bear mystery, titled *The Heretic's Hymnal,* takes place in another part of Europe and should be available in the summer of 2017.

One final thought. I just released my first non-fiction book, *Polio and Me,* and here is a brief synopsis.

The year was 1943. A five year old boy wakes up. He cannot stand or hold an apple in his hand. The boy is rushed to his family doctor, diagnosed with polio, and taken from his mother's arms to the contagion ward at the county hospital.

Despite decades of futile research, polio epidemics continued to paralyze and kill hundreds of thousands of adults and children well into the 1950's.

Polio and Me provides a view of the past, present, and future—the saga of one boy's pain, fear, and loneliness—the long struggle to find a vaccine and effective treatments—the world-wide goal to eradicate the polio virus, and in some twenty-first century cancer research trials, the polio vaccine eliminated cancerous tumors.

Polio and Me is a powerful read, and as the five year old boy who had polio, I highly recommend this book.

A closing note on *Polio and Me*, I am contributing 50% of all my book royalties, and 25% of all Kindle royalties to the Orthopaedic Institute for Children, the same organization that gave me the opportunity to walk just like everyone else!

If you have a question email me at: ken@kendalton.com

www.ingramcontent.com/pod-product-compliance
Lightning Source LLC
Chambersburg PA
CBHW050919250626
47155CB00001B/304